GRACE IN STRANGE DISGUISE

BOOK 1

CHRISTINE DILLON

www.storytellerchristine.com

Grace in Strange Disguise

This book is a work of fiction. Names, characters, any resemblance to persons, living or dead, or events is purely coincidental. The characters and incidents are the product of the author's imagination and used fictitiously. Locales and public names are sometimes used for atmospheric purposes.

Cover Design: Lankshear Design.

ISBN: 978-0-6481296-0-8

With grateful thanks to my Saviour and King.
Many years ago, your word gave me life, and started me
on a new journey. Now you've led me (sorry for the kicking and
screaming) to write fiction. Thank you for providing your strength at
every stage.
This is my 'first fruits' offering. Use this book for your glory.

NOTES TO READERS

• Our worldview is like a pair of glasses through which we view, and more importantly, interpret the world. Worldview is formed by our past experiences, the things we're taught by parents, schools and life in general. It is also strongly influenced by our culture and the time in which we live.

• The job of a novelist is to show you the worldview of the characters in the book whether it be humanist, Hindu, communist or, in this book, Christian. If you're not a Christian the views expressed by the characters might appear strange BUT it's a great opportunity. Why? Because Esther's story allows you to stand outside and see things from a perspective totally different to your own. It also allows you to see how Esther's worldview changes. Is her new view consistent and does it make sense of the challenges in her life?

• Please note that this novel is based in 1995. Mobile phones were not commonly used back then. Hence, the use of phones and pagers (in hospitals), rather than mobile phones. Also, letters and notes, rather than email or messaging.

• Since this is an Australian novel, the spelling and grammar mostly follows Australian conventions.

PROLOGUE

"Y ou have cancer."

Acid surged in Esther's throat. *No, no, no, no, no.* Impossible. William Macdonald's daughter couldn't have cancer. Esther wrapped her arms around her stomach. The nausea reminded her of that horrible day she'd taken her first rollercoaster ride as an eight-year-old. The car had chugged slowly, slowly, slowly to the crest of the ride, then plunged down, down, down. She'd been unable to escape, unable to do anything but hang on, knuckles white, and try not to throw up.

The doctor was still talking, but Esther's brain was stuck on those three short words. Thirteen fateful letters. Meaningless on their own, but strung together. Cannonballs. Cannonballs, punching ragged holes in her life.

She was only twenty-eight. How could she have cancer? This wasn't what she'd been promised. Or, what she'd been raised to expect. Hadn't her father always preached that those who have faith would be protected from the problems that plague other people?

She'd taken the tests the doctor had ordered ten days ago, but only because that was expected of her. She hadn't anticipated anything would be wrong. Not this wrong. And if there was something wrong, surely God would cure her. Wasn't that his job?

You have cancer.

Three stark words.

No more fantasies of health. No more hiding. No more false hope.

Cancer.

There was no escape. No way out. Just like on the rollercoaster. The only option was to hang on for the ride, and hope she'd survive.

CHAPTER 1

EIGHT MONTHS EARLIER
November, 1994
Sydney, Australia

*E*sther had been running late all morning. No time to dawdle or daydream, and no time before the weekly staff meeting to do anything but park her car in front of the cluster of sprawling white cottages housing the physiotherapy department. A stark contrast to the modern mirror-glass buildings surrounding the hospital.

Esther locked her car and rushed towards her workplace, hoping she hadn't dropped her diary nor forgotten her lunch.

She stopped at the door. Rearranged her blouse. Dabbed the sweat on her upper lip.

The building was quiet. Too quiet. No familiar clatter of therapists preparing for the day, no opening and closing of drawers, no cubicle curtains whizzing wide, no voices exchanging morning greetings.

Had she messed up and arrived early? She checked her watch. No, the time and date were correct. She gently touched the door. It swung open with a slight squeak. Silence.

Strange. More than strange.

Esther took five steps into the room, shoes tapping on the polished wooden boards. Perhaps she should tiptoe. Or stop breathing.

"Surprise!"

Shoes stomped, toy trumpets tooted, party streamers popped. A cacophony of cheering, clapping and congratulations. At the far end of the room was a banner, blazoned gold on blue. Close to the banner stood a stranger with an impressive camera. Why the celebration? It wasn't her birthday.

Her boss, Sue, came towards her, arm outstretched in welcome. "You should see your face."

"Sue, what's going on?" Esther's cheeks flushed. After a lifetime of being on show, she never liked being the centre of attention.

"I nominated you, 'Hospital Employee of the Year'. And you won. First time ever, for a physiotherapist."

Now Esther understood. Not only was she the first non-doctor to win in, what was it—ten years? But the prize also came with a $100,000 cheque for the winner's department. Sue was probably already planning how she'd spend the money.

Sue clapped her hands for attention. "Sorry to rush this. We'll have our usual staff meeting in a moment."

Esther's knees shook but she must smile. This was a big deal for Sue.

"Esther has been at this hospital since she graduated. Her clients love her and so do we."

Other therapists nodded.

"She's a team player. She pitches in whenever and wherever

we're short-staffed. Always quick to encourage others. Always ready to do the less glamorous jobs to keep this department functioning smoothly."

Esther wanted to shuffle her feet at the stream of compliments, but she controlled herself. She avoided looking at her colleagues so she wouldn't blush under everyone's scrutiny.

"In addition, she has initiated practical research that has made this department proud. Her example inspires others."

Sue was focusing on the physiotherapy side of things, but Esther suspected running the annual hospital fete was the clincher. No one else had wanted the unpaid task that consumed so much time. This year's fete had raised more money than ever before. The cynic in her guessed the hospital hoped this award would make her feel obligated to organise the event for years to come. Would five years work off her debt?

"We're privileged to have Mr Ron Scott, the hospital director, here to present the cheque," Sue said. "And lucky Esther wins a weekend for two at the historic Hydro Majestic Hotel in the Blue Mountains."

Esther walked forward to the applause of her workmates, shook hands with Ron Scott and accepted the oversized presentation-style cheque. She couldn't stifle a feeling of triumph as they posed together for photographs. What would Dad say? He'd opposed her choice to be a physiotherapist. He'd championed a 'real' medical career, but Esther hadn't wanted all the pressure. She'd wanted time to volunteer at church, and volunteering required regular work hours. Maybe this award would placate him for her first act of rebellion, something he still seemed to resent.

"Speech, speech," called her workmates.

They wouldn't want her to waffle. "First, thanks to Sue for having the audacity to submit a physiotherapist's name for this award." Esther was popular at work but it was still encouraging to see her workmates smile and nod. "And thanks to all of you. I love working here with such competent and enthusiastic colleagues. This award belongs to all of us. Thanks for allowing me to be part of your team."

Her colleagues clapped and Sue flashed her a grateful look. The hospital director shook her hand one more time, then left, and Sue brought the meeting to order.

There weren't many announcements, so the meeting was soon over and everyone could get going with their appointments. Esther turned to leave.

"Esther." It was Sue. "Can you walk with me back to my office? There's something I need to run past you."

A flicker of anxiety caught in Esther's throat, the same anxiety she used to feel whenever she'd been summoned to the school principal's office. Not that she'd ever had a reason to fear, but the fear had always been there. Was it a fear of failure? Of rejection? Or simply the fear of not pleasing somebody? Surely there was no need to be nervous.

The two women entered the sun-filled office, and Sue waved Esther towards a seat.

"This'll only take a moment. I'm delighted you won. I only have one problem—"

That flicker of anxiety returned, along with faint nausea. Had she done something wrong?

"—You won't let me promote you."

Esther's shoulders relaxed, and she let out a shaky breath. She should have noticed the twinkle in Sue's eye. This was a conversation they'd had several times before. A promotion would mean more administrative work and less of the direct client contact she loved.

"But I think I've come up with a solution that allows you to keep your client contact. I've talked to the board, and they suggested I offer you a Grade Two post, on the condition that you do extra mentoring of junior employees. You already do this, so you won't be any busier. What do you say? Will you accept a Grade Two position with matching salary?"

"On those terms, how can I refuse?"

The window behind Sue showed an incredible day outside, glorious and golden. And now this. An award, a paid holiday, and a promotion. Esther wanted to caper around like a small child, bouncing and anxious to tell her father and her boyfriend, Nick, about her day. They would both see these things as sure signs of God's abundant blessings.

CHAPTER 2

The alarm jerked Esther awake on Saturday morning. She groaned, rolled over and hit the alarm's stop button.

Five a.m.

Her body longed for more sleep, but today was a day worth getting up for. She and Nick seldom had a whole Saturday together, and today they did. They were going to the Blue Mountains. She swung out of bed, and donned the top-of-the-line hiking gear she'd draped over her chair the night before.

She grabbed a quick breakfast of gourmet muesli with banana and yoghurt. Lunch had been prepared last night—roast chicken, home-made bread, avocado salad, crackers, a selection of cheeses and fruit, plus plenty of snacks. She placed the lunch in her day pack along with plenty of water and the numerous necessities for a day's hike, then headed out to wait for Nick in the hushed, dewy predawn.

Esther rubbed her chilled arms and jogged on the spot, her stomach fluttering. There was something special about being up before anyone else. Mature plane trees lined both sides of the street, creating a tunnel of shifting shadow. Their mottled ivory trunks gleamed in the street lights. Through their spindly branches, the last stars dusted the sky like diamond icing sugar.

Behind the imposing gates and fences were the mansion-like houses of the wealthy. Houses where ride-on mowers and part-time gardeners weren't unusual. Houses known by name and not merely by numbers. Some of Esther's friends thought her weird, to still live at home. But paying expenses to her parents beat paying rent, and allowed her to save money for her own home.

Nick arrived on time—unusual for him. He unfolded himself from the car and came around to kiss her cheek. "Hope you haven't been waiting too long." He opened her car door, and gave Esther time to get settled. These old-fashioned manners were one of the things Esther loved about Nick.

With such an early start, they'd reach the starting point for their hike within a couple of hours. As they drove, the sky turned a pearly grey, and the stars disappeared along with the streetlights. Behind the car, the golden glow of the sunrise painted colour back into the waiting grey world. They soon turned onto the highway which would take them to the foot of the mountains.

"Finally—decent weather," he said. "Can't believe rain ruined every Saturday last month."

"The news report promised a perfect day. The announcer even mentioned perfect for camping." Like the weekend they'd first met.

"You're not going to bring that up again?" Nick glanced across at her with a grin.

"You mean the way you tripped over my guy rope and collapsed my tent on top of me with both our youth groups watching?" Esther gave a wicked smile. "They certainly got a lesson on how to gain a lady's attention."

Nick wriggled his eyebrows, a party trick that always made Esther giggle. "Smooth move, eh?"

Esther snorted. "The speed with which you ferreted out my name and phone number impressed me more."

"And here we are, two years later."

"Yep. Once Dad spotted you, he seemed more enamoured with you than I was. I can't believe he hired you a month afterwards."

"Maybe he has good taste." Nick wriggled his eyebrows again. "You can't blame me for being flattered. It's not every day a nobody is poached by the second-biggest church in Sydney."

"Not second for long. Dad sees you as vital to his strategy to become the biggest church in Sydney." Esther stretched out the next words as though she was an advertiser. "The colossal church in the city, his magnificent megachurch."

Nick chuckled. "If anyone will do it, he will."

Esther had known her father would like Nick, but she hadn't been prepared for how much. Her father constantly talked about how Nick hadn't let his father's death, when Nick was seventeen, prevent him from going places. Why did Dad keep pushing Nick at her? Didn't he know matchmakers were well and truly out of fashion? The one good thing was that at last she had a boyfriend that her father approved of. More than approved. Her father was a huge influence in Nick's life. Nick practically lived at their place.

Esther reached across and placed her hand on Nick's shoulder. They had plenty in common. Hiking and horse riding. Cycling and camping. Swimming and swing dancing. Active at church—probably too active. A model couple.

Sometimes she wished they could just be Nick and Esther. Physiotherapist and youth worker, or even a store manager. Like he'd been before. Normal.

"Penny for your thoughts," Nick said.

"Do you ever wish you'd stayed at your old church, where you were the youth worker in your spare time?"

Nick scratched the side of his nose. "It might have been simpler in those days, but it was also more of a struggle. At Victory, if I want something, resources appear. There are leaders and volunteers for anything I want to do." He glanced across at her. "Victory is a youth worker's dream."

Esther looked out of the window. The houses had been replaced by bushland. "I can see that, but there must be downsides."

"What do you mean?"

"Don't you ever struggle with always being on show? Or with—I don't know—the busyness. The demands on your time." Nick drummed his fingers on the wheel, his habit when he wanted to change the topic.

"Hasn't bothered me so far." He shrugged. "I mean, I wanted to do this, and I'm studying theology, which is awesome. It's meaningful, you know?" He stopped as though musing on the last thought. "World-changing. At least, more than before, when I was just working to support my mother and brothers."

Esther didn't rejoice in Nick's hardships but if he hadn't been supporting his family, he'd probably have married years ago.

Nick patted the dashboard of the car. "At least I no longer drive an old bomb. This car was the first perk of the job."

Now the road twisted and turned. Around every corner, Esther caught sight of islands of rock, floating on surging seas of mist. Or metamorphosing into blurred, bulbous beasts.

They sped past the main towns and finally approached their destination. The last small town stirred with Saturday life. Nick turned right. The corner café had just opened, and a woman in a crisp white apron positioned the menu board on the footpath. Two minutes later, their car passed an elderly man shuffling back to his house in a dressing gown and ugg boots, with a paper under his arm. Smoke puffed lazily from chimneys and drifted in the chilly air.

Leaving the houses behind, they drove down the final stretch of road into the national park. The trees hung over the road, and screeching parrots darted across the gap. Nick swung the car into the deserted car park. Esther stretched her cramped limbs and added an extra layer of clothing. Together they walked over to one of the most famous lookouts in the Blue Mountains. The valley bowl was filled to the brim with mist, the valley floor invisible.

Esther shivered and drew her coat tighter. She and Nick found a place on the edge of the viewing platform and sat together, in companionable silence, sipping hot tea from the first of two thermoses Esther had prepared. They awaited the coming transformation.

As the sun strengthened, the mist started to rise. A cool breeze sprang up, blowing wisps of mist hither and thither, beading their clothes with moisture. Transient rents in the white fluffiness hinted at the valley, far below. The mist lifted and dissipated faster and faster, leaving only isolated pockets lingering in damp hollows. Now the tree-filled valleys were revealed, encircling the soaring cliffs with a grey-green collar. The sandstone glowed pale yellow.

They continued to soak in the silence, broken only by the moisture dripping from the trees and the melodic burbling of hidden birds.

Twenty minutes later, Nick stood and stretched. "We'd better get going. If we wait any longer, it will be too hot coming back up."

Esther groaned. "I always wish this walk could be done in reverse. It seems wrong to have the easy part first, then have to work hard coming up later."

"Come on, lazy." Nick pulled her to her feet. "We're fit enough, so it won't be a problem."

As they made their way down the irregular timber and stone steps, they stopped often to visually track the whirring wings of birds or peer at plants. Clumps of cream flannel flowers with their olive-green tips were scattered along the path, so soft that Esther kept reaching out to stroke them. Their boots squelched in wet patches or crunched along the dryer sandy stretches.

The sandstone warmed from yellow to orange.

Halfway down the cliff, Nick cupped his hands around his

mouth. "Cooo-eeee." The echoes bounced back. Cooo-eeee …
cooo-eeee.

Esther joined in, and the echoes mingled and merged, harmon-
ising alto and bass.

"That will let anyone up ahead know we're coming," Nick said.
A brief drink and they continued down, step by uneven step,
descending the cliff face, right to the base, where they found a spot
to eat lunch.

Nick was quieter than usual as they ate, but the magnificent
scenery distracted Esther from probing the cause of his preoccupa-
tion. The waterfall cascaded in a narrow ribbon, plunging from the
full height of the escarpment into its pool. Moss and feathery ferns
clung to the cliff's cracks and crevices. The wind whipped behind
the waterfall, so Esther climbed onto a high flat rock where the fine
spray blew around in a cool lacy curtain. She'd wanted to do it
since the first time they'd visited. Today, knowing they were alone,
she finally dared. No one was here to think her insane. She flung
her arms out and twirled, laughing with an exuberance she seldom
showed—or even felt.

"You're-a-crazy-lady-but-I-love-you-will-you- marry-me?"

Nick's shouted voice broke into her private moment. His words
ran together as though he had blurted them out in one continuous
waterfall-like spurt.

Esther stopped mid-spin and turned to face Nick. He was
looking at her with an expression of anguished uncertainty. Had
she heard him right?

"What did you say?"

Nick's face relaxed a little. "You heard me. You just want me to
ask again. Okay, Esther Macdonald." He dropped to one knee and
clasped his hands together in pleading mode. "Please, please
—marry me."

"That's what I thought I heard, but I wasn't sure." Dizzying champagne bubbles of delight fizzed in her head. "Yes. One hundred times, yes."

"Woo-hoo." Nick pumped his clenched fists into the air in a victory cry. Before Esther could laugh at his antics he was leaping down from his rock. From her higher rock, Esther peered over the edge, hoping he wouldn't break anything in his haste. He stumbled once or twice before she heard him scrambling up. His eager face appeared, and she pulled him up onto the top of the rock. He was panting so much it was ten seconds before he kissed her.

Long minutes passed, until the waterfall's spray was no longer cooling but cold. Esther shivered. She didn't want the moment to end, but she eventually pulled away and climbed down the rock to gather their lunch things. Nick placed all the heavier items in his backpack and they began to dawdle back up the path.

The steps didn't seem as steep today. She'd always laughed at what she'd called trite romantic clichés, and yet here she was, floating on a cloud of euphoria, feeling her feet were a metre above the ground, breathless with heart palpitations every time Nick touched her. It was ridiculous, but it was true. Esther was soon spinning dreams and weaving visions of a fantastical, fairy tale future.

CHAPTER 3

*E*sther bounced out of bed the next morning and bounded into the shower, singing. She dressed for church with more care than usual. Her father always insisted she and her mother, Blanche, look impeccable. As a teenager, she'd often longed to slouch around in slippers or coddle herself in comfy clothes, but hadn't dared.

There was the usual Sunday bustle at Victory Church. Billboards outside informed visitors there were four services on Sundays and a full programme during the week. A multi-level car park catered for the crowds, and teams of welcomers funnelled people past tasteful flower arrangements and through wide double doors to the auditorium.

Victory smelled of fresh paint, plush carpet, and expensive deodorisers. Nothing but the finest for William Macdonald, for Victory.

Displayed along the side walls were her mother's pride and joy, enormous banners quilted to look like stained glass, in exquisite emerald, ruby, sapphire, and gold. Her father had been dubious about the idea of 'handmade banners', but the string of champi-

15

onship prizes from Sydney's Royal Easter Show guaranteed them pride of place.

Esther moved to a foldaway seat in the second-to-last row. She usually sat with her mother in the front row, but this morning her father had asked her to sit towards the back. What was he up to? Hopefully not announcing her engagement. She wanted to keep that private a little longer, as she'd told Dad last night when they'd given him the news.

Being engaged was something she'd been dreaming about since her teenage years. She'd had plenty of young men interested in getting to know her better, but something had always prevented things moving forward. Her heavy church involvement, or that most guys didn't dare date the pastor's daughter. The three who had dared, hadn't met her father's exacting standards. Two hadn't been a big loss, but she regretted the third. What a relief that Nick received the gold stamp of approval.

She leaned back to appreciate the atmosphere, choreographed to sweep people along in swirling symphonies of sound and to emotionally emphasise parts of the programme. The music quietened, and one of the elders moved to the middle of the stage.

"Let us welcome the Reverend Doctor William Macdonald to share God's word with us."

Her father strode across the stage, his hair steel grey perfection and his Italian suit, flawless. He placed his weighty Bible on the podium, looked up at his audience, and smiled. How did he establish an instant connection with every person present? Whatever his secret, he had people ready to do whatever he asked in seconds. Fund-raising was a cinch at Victory.

He paused for the perfect length of time. "Let us pray. King of the Universe. Thank you for your blessings on this, your church. Help us to be fit to hear your message to us. In your mighty Son's name, amen."

Her father had honed and polished his communication skills

through to doctorate level. Every day he sweated, polishing his skills, layer by layer. Burnishing every word of every book. Refining every sentence of every radio programme. Sharpening every syllable of every sound bite.

"I asked the Lord which story should be next in our sermon series. He told me to share the story of the bleeding woman."

So her father would be preaching on one of his favourite themes. Faith.

He was a brilliant storyteller, and Esther was caught up in the woman's desperation, her shame, her fear. She even heard the quaver in the woman's voice as she reached towards Jesus.

Esther had long ago given up opening the Bible to keep up with the passages her father quoted—he flitted forward and back, back and forward. Instead, she let the words roll over her as though she was being tumbled in the surf.

Her father's voice suited public speaking, slow and sonorous. People trusted him. His sermon style was simple—pound the Bible, proceed to pertinent application, and paint a vision of lives transformed. There had been those who'd objected to his teaching over the years, but they didn't last long. In private, her father referred to them as 'the unbelievers'. Esther had never known them well enough to judge. How could she know everyone in a church Victory's size?

"Faith resulting in healing. That's what we want to see here. Amen?"

"Amen." The audience echoed in well-practiced unison.

What were they saying 'Amen' to? She must concentrate. Although, come to think of it, her mind often strayed during Dad's sermons. Looking around, she could see she wasn't alone. Maybe others also struggled under the torrent of words.

"All these people were commended and healed because of their faith. What about you? Are you receiving little? Or much? Is your faith an itty-bitty faith, or an elephantine-tyrannosaurine faith? Big faith leads to big results."

Her father stopped and looked around his audience. "So what are you doing to strengthen your faith?" Esther recognised the question as the beginning of one of his classic series of statements. People shifted in their seats as though emerging from hibernation. "We need to dig up rootlets of doubt. Dig up fear. Dig up what others say to make you doubt. Ignore them. Concentrate on faith. We will be a people who are firm in faith."

Did she doubt? Did she fear? She didn't think she was much of a doubter, but fear and anxiety were a part of her life. Why? Her father was still talking, so there wasn't time to puzzle over it.

"Firm in faith when everyone else doubts. Firm in faith when others laugh. Firm in faith, even if we're the only one standing firm." Her father looked up, and everyone in the auditorium leaned forward in their seats, ready to spring into action.

"Stand and repeat this commitment with me."

The auditorium was filled with rustling and shuffling as everyone stood.

"Firm in faith. Got it? All together now." He conducted his audience, swinging his arm as he counted. "One, two, three."

"Firm in faith," his audience repeated.

"Louder. Firm in faith."

Esther had tried in the past to resist her father's commands, but it was impossible. One part of her mind looked on in admiration while the other part fought to remain independent.

"Let's take the roof off."

Hundreds of voices thundered in unison. "Firm in faith."

In a long-established pattern, the audience repeated the phrase five times until the auditorium plunged into an orchestrated darkness. Her father would be pleased, so why did she feel a niggle of discomfort? Before she could reflect further, the music swelled and the vague thought vanished like a pebble dropped down a deep, deep well.

"Today we have one extra announcement. It's something Blanche and I have believed firm in faith." Her father was incredible. Even the announcements underscored his sermon.

"We have not doubted God would give the best to our family."

Surely he wasn't about to ... she thought they'd made their desire for privacy, crystal clear.

"I'm delighted to announce the Lord has heard and provided. Esther and Nick have announced their engagement. Please stand up and let us see you both."

Esther ground her teeth. Had she not been clear? Or had her father decided to ignore her? Now Esther understood why her father had wanted her sitting at the back. It made a better show for Nick to come from the musicians' pit at the front, run up the aisle, and grab her hand.

He grimaced at her as though in apology, even as he held their hands above their heads like politicians on the campaign trail. So he'd been pressured too. They were both puppets in her father's play. Even now she must smile. She was the puppet, and her strings had been tugged.

CHAPTER 4

January, 1995

*T*wo months later, Esther stood in her half-finished wedding dress in her mother's sewing studio. She raised her right arm to allow her mother to attach the long sleeve, the silk falling in fluid folds to the floor. Outside, it was thirty degrees Celsius. Inside, the air conditioner streamed cool air, so sweat wouldn't stain the expensive white fabric.

Esther could see her mother's tongue protruding from the corner of her mouth. Blanche attached the sleeve, one pin after another, each precisely inserted to avoid holes in the visible panels of the gown. Esther knew better than to distract her. Silk didn't forgive mistakes.

"Good. Now bend your knees a little."

Esther bent.

"Perfect. Raise your arm a bit more—good."

Esther stood as silent and still as someone playing musical statues, moving only when allowed to 'go' and freezing on 'stop'. Her arms and legs were obedient, but her mind was free to roam.

Choosing a dress pattern from the thousands on offer had been a month-long marathon. Her mother was a legendary seamstress, and her experience had guided Esther through the maze of choices. It had been an education in organdie and organza, chiffon, satin and silk.

This wedding wasn't going to be the cozy and casual celebration she'd dreamed of. Not as the senior pastor's only daughter. Not marrying Nick, another conspicuous member of a megachurch. Their wedding was going to be a big deal, requiring the standards of a cordon bleu chef and the organisation of a quartermaster to coordinate the army of volunteers.

She'd hoped to avoid a lengthy train but her father had said her dress had to look right in the auditorium. Considering the enormous size of the room it was a miracle she'd avoided having a cathedral train. No matter what her father thought, this wasn't a royal wedding. They'd compromised on a chapel-length train. Nick had manoeuvred himself out of most of their planning powwows. A wise decision.

Her mother stepped back. "Now, let me see that sleeve. Move your arm slowly up and down. Is it pulling anywhere?"

Esther moved her arm up and down and side to side. The silk slid sensuously over Esther's skin and raised goosebumps. "Seems fine to me." She remained motionless as her mother continued to circle, tugging here and there on the silk.

"This first sleeve is right. Can you turn around so I can do the other one? The light on this side is better."

Esther turned as instructed, careful to avoid being pricked by pins. "I hope this isn't too much for you, Mum."

"I wouldn't miss it for anything." Her mother's gaze remained glued on the dress as Esther moved into position. "Don't worry about me. I love sewing. I wish I had more time for it." She tweaked a fold of fabric.

Sewing was one hobby Esther didn't share with her mother. The creativity gene seemed to have missed her. She also didn't have a tenth of her mother's sense of style.

"Mum, I do appreciate all you're doing. I had no idea of all the rigmarole. It feels like I'm being carried on a brakeless bus, lurching along with no idea of what I'm doing."

"That's why girls have mothers." Her mother's tone was brisk as she pinned the left sleeve and then circled to check her work. "Now, how does that feel?"

Esther lifted her arms. "Ouch."

"What are you ouching about?"

Esther held herself rigid, trying to avoid a repeat of the pain. "A pin must've stabbed me."

"I doubt it. Where's the problem?"

"Somewhere here." Esther's hand fluttered in the general region of her armpit.

Blanche patted the area. "I can't find anything. Maybe you turned awkwardly. You can slip out of the dress now, so I can sew the sleeves on." She helped ease Esther out of the dress, and Esther changed back into her ordinary clothes.

Her mother handed her the almost completed veil and pointed to the chair nearest the window. "Why don't you sit there and do the hem? I'd like the company."

"Okay." The two of them seldom worked in tandem on anything. Maybe working together might help her get to know her mother better. Her mother's opinions, dreams, and background remained a total mystery to her.

Her mother settled herself at her deluxe model sewing machine, humming along with its busy whirr. She seemed to love her task. Esther couldn't understand the attraction. Why sew when you could be out in the fresh air doing something more active?

There was a knock. Her father peered around the door, then came into the room and looked around. "Hate to miss out on all the fun. You look like you're making progress." He patted Blanche on the shoulder. "As I'd expect, with my wife as director of operations. How many bridesmaids have you chosen, Esther?"

Of course. He had to be here to express his opinions on something. Why did she have the sinking feeling she was about to lose another battle?

"I thought two would be plenty. The wedding's going to cost a bomb."

"Two?" Her father's voice rose. "They'll disappear in that vast space. You'd better have four or five." No one could ever accuse her father of stinginess.

"Dad, you'll kill Mum having to make all those dresses."

Her father held up his palm as though refuting the idea. "Your mother loves all the fuss." Leaning towards the floor, he plucked up some discarded threads. "Only the best is good enough for our only daughter."

A look flashed across Mum's face, a look Esther had never seen before. Was it hurt? Anger? Or something else? Whatever it was, it made her feel a desire to protect and comfort her. "You okay, Mum?"

"Of course, and I've got plenty of time to make the extra dresses." Had her mother deliberately answered the wrong question?

"Does it have to be five, Dad? I had two bridesmaids chosen—but five? Nick's only chosen two groomsmen."

"Make sure they're your best-looking friends."

"This isn't some sort of beauty contest." Esther spoke without thinking. Something in her revolted at the implications of his comment.

What was the fleeting look on her father's face? Shame? Or annoyance, quickly stifled, that she'd spoken against him?

"I want the best for you—talking of contests, have you done

your crossword? I've nearly finished mine." The Macdonald family subscribed to two copies of the paper, and Esther and her father had been having a daily contest for three years. Her father usually won. He took it more seriously.

"Please, don't distract Esther." Blanche flapped her hand as though to sweep him out of the room. "We still have lots to do, and you know how much Esther struggles to sit still and sew."

Her father left, no doubt to finish the crossword before Esther even got a chance to start.

Esther sat and gnawed her lip as she sewed. Had her father suspected that one of her bridesmaid choices would be Gina? She'd been at the church a while but it wasn't until she started playing the oboe at the night service that Esther got to know her. Sure, she was overweight, but what was the big deal? It wasn't as if Jesus required everyone to look like a model. Jesus focused on the heart and Gina's was platinum.

"I hope neither of you change your mind." Her mother's words broke through Esther's rambling thoughts.

"What do you mean?"

Blanche's eyes flicked towards the door and then back to her sewing. "Nothing in particular."

It was so unusual for her mother to offer an opinion that Esther was determined to pursue it. "Come on, Mum, what are you trying to say?"

"Marrying someone like Nick—you know."

Something was going on. Was her mother giving veiled marriage advice? "Mum, I don't get what you're trying to say. You'll have to be clearer."

Her mother lifted her head and looked directly at Esther. "It's not easy being married to someone who pastors a large church."

"He won't be head pastor for years. And anyway, it might not happen. Maybe we'll go somewhere smaller."

"I don't think your father will let Nick go. He's preparing him as his successor."

"That's something that Nick and I will have to talk about. I don't want to be on show—too much pressure." She'd known Nick succeeding Dad was a possibility, but was it normal for her parents to already be discussing it?

Her mother looked up. "How's your sewing going?"

Why did Mum always change the topic when she was about to say something significant?

CHAPTER 5

*E*sther opened the door of the clinic and released a torrent of sound. Babies, toddlers and distracted parents crammed the room to bursting point. Every seat was filled and several people leaned against the walls. A pungent smell of lemon antiseptic failed to override less pleasant odours.

Esther hesitated in the doorway. Perhaps she should give up and return to her car. But her hand throbbed and the pain wasn't improving fast enough on its own.

She concentrated on not treading on toys, nor a tiny hand, or foot. The last thing she needed was an irate parent, a screaming baby, or a sprained ankle. The receptionist juggled the phone and attempted to organise a towering pile of files. Once the phone was hung up she tucked her hair behind her ear and said in an undertone, "Sorry about all this, normally we run an orderly operation but one of the doctors had to go home early—"

"Should I reschedule my appointment?" Esther asked.

"No. Dr Arnold will see you, if you're prepared to wait a little longer. He's running behind time because he's covering both sets of appointments."

Esther squeezed into a seat offered by an older man, opened a well-thumbed magazine and attempted to block out the hubbub. Fat chance.

The clinic emptied of mothers and babies, and filled with adults.

"Esther, the doctor will see you now." Esther checked her watch —ninety minutes. What would Sue say if the physio clinic kept patients waiting so long?

Esther placed her magazine in the rack and gathered up her bag and umbrella. As she entered the doctor's room he was sitting, head down, scribbling. He looked up over his bifocals.

"Ahh, Esther. Haven't seen you for several years. How are your parents? Still fighting fit? A good ad for their church…" Esther gave a ghost of a smile. He'd been making the same joke for as long as she could remember.

"Now, what seems to be the problem?"

"Well…"

The intercom buzzed. "Dr Claude ringing back on line one."

Dr Arnold reached for the phone. "Sorry, have to take this one." Was she ever going to get to her dress fitting? Esther sat motionless, endeavouring not to listen to the one-sided call. Five minutes later, he ended the call.

"Sorry for the interruption. I don't usually take calls during appointments but I've been playing telephone tag with that doctor all day." He glanced at her open file again. "Now, where were we?"

Esther held up her swollen left hand.

"Oh, that doesn't look comfortable. What happened?"

"I went hiking last weekend, and put my hand onto a wasp nest."

Dr Arnold stood up and gestured towards the treatment table. "Sit there and let me look." His hand felt cool against the heat of her hand. "Nothing out of the ordinary. I'll give you the name of some antihistamine tablets and a cream." He wrote on the notepad in front of him and ripped off the sheet of paper. "If this isn't improving in three days, please make another appointment. If that's all—"

"I've also had some twinges in my left armpit." The intercom buzzed yet again. Esther stifled a sigh. More waiting. There were two more calls before Dr Arnold could ask more questions.

"How long have you been getting this pain?"

"The first time I noticed it I was trying on my wedding dress—that would make it more than a month ago. Since then, I've had occasional twinges when I raise my arms above my head or stretch out to the side."

Dr Arnold looked towards the clock behind her head. "Sounds like you might have strained a muscle or something. I suggest you put a hot pack on it each evening. If it's still bothering you in a month, come back."

He'd forgotten he was talking to a physiotherapist, and was trying to palm her off and get on with the next person. Now she'd finally gained his attention, she wasn't ready to leave.

"I feel a little silly, but I wondered if it might be something more serious."

"Now let's see, how old are you?" He looked back at the front page of the file, pursed his lips and said, "Twenty-seven, nearly twenty-eight. It's unlikely to be anything serious at your age—"

Buzz-zz. If that intercom buzzed again, Esther was ready to drop-kick it across the car park. The call finished, but before Dr Arnold could open his mouth, the intercom buzzed yet again. And again.

Enough was enough. Esther stood up, turned her back on Dr Arnold, and gathered her bag. She didn't want him to see her annoyance. She gave a sketchy wave and left. What a waste of time.

CHAPTER 6

April 1995

*T*he wedding was now only four months away. Nick and Esther needed every minute of their nine-month engagement.

They'd started by plodding through the major decisions like date and reception venue. Finding a date had been a nightmare, as her father was usually booked eighteen months in advance. He'd vetoed every reception centre they'd considered until he'd had a brain wave and suggested the church side halls. Few reception centres could match their new decor. That decision took the pressure off confirming numbers, and the job list became more of a waltz than a plod, a matter of finding caterers, then enjoying the fun decisions like colours, flowers, and music.

Esther might not have any married siblings, but her parents had organised dozens of weddings. Together they made a great team and she'd come to appreciate them in a new way.

Mid-Sunday afternoon was one of the few times they could find for preparation. Every week her parents invited Nick to come for a late lunch, during the brief lull before the busyness of two evening services. Dad would take the first one, and she and Nick helped with the second. Today they planned to work on the final guest list and the wedding invitations.

Nick placed a towel on top of the highly polished surface of the cedar dining table. Then he positioned Esther's laptop, opened a new file and headed it, 'Wedding Guests'. Esther perched beside him on a matching upholstered balloon-back chair, her hand resting on Nick's shoulder.

Poor Nick had braved several nervous months before he'd adjusted himself to the formality of their dining and living areas, with their cream carpets and Persian rugs in maroon and gold. At least now he remembered not to tilt back on his chair and strain its antique legs.

Her father sat behind them in the leather lounge chair doing his crossword. Her mother stitched the hem of her mother-of-the-bride dress in the nook of the bow window. Why couldn't her parents go away so she could put her arms around Nick? Since her parents never showed affection in public, she hesitated to do so in front of them.

Had Nick guessed her thoughts? He turned his head, smiled a secret smile and winked before typing the headers for each column of his file. "Okay, I've made various columns so we can keep track of those who accept or reject their invitations. I've already thought through my list of priority guests, so I'll type those in first."

He muttered as he typed. "Mum ... Grandma and grandpa one, grandma two ... brother one and his wife ... brother two and his girlfriend ... six uncles and six aunts and ten cousins. I'll type their names in later."

Esther jotted her own list of names inside the leather-bound scrapbook she'd bought to preserve all her wedding memories.

These days of preparation sometimes blurred together, but one day, when she was old and grey, she wanted to be able to turn the pages and treasure the memories. Maybe she'd do so with her own daughter.

Nick typed his final name. "I've got plenty of relatives but not so many workmates and other friends. Most of them are already at Victory." He glanced across at her father. "Besides, I've been working so hard, I've been a bit cut off from old friends."

"Completely natural, Nick," her father said. "What about you, Esther? How many workmates and friends are you thinking of asking?"

"My boss, Sue, is a definite but I'd better ask the whole department. If I only ask one or two I'm sure to insult somebody." She checked her scrapbook. "I also have five uni friends I want to ask, but two are bridesmaids anyway."

"Can you start by giving me your workmates' names?" Nick asked.

Esther stood and leaned over Nick's shoulder and briefly put her hand on top of his.

"Are you trying to distract me?" he whispered with a cheeky half-grin.

Esther put her mouth next to his ear. "Would love to, but we'd better get this done." More loudly she said, "Sue, Alan, Jane, Mark." Esther paused between each name so Nick could keep up. "Richard, Jen, and Jeannine—that's the outpatient group. Then there are about eight others outside the physio department who I'm close to."

Nick's fingers tapped on the keyboard. "You'll have to find me their addresses once we're ready to send out invitations."

"No need. I'll hand them out at work." Esther sighed with enough breath to blow Nick's hair.

"What was that loud sigh for?"

Esther straightened up but kept a hand on each of Nick's shoulders. "Hearing you list all of your relatives makes me realise how few I have. Mum's parents are both dead, and she isn't in contact with any other family members." If only she had a sister. Someone to journey through life with. Someone to giggle and cry with. All her life, Esther had daydreamed about having a sister.

"What about your other grandparents?" Nick asked.

Her father interjected, "My father's dead—"

Esther leaned forward to lay a warning hand on Nick's arm but she was too slow.

"And your mother?"

Esther stifled an anxious hiss. Would the question lead to an angry outburst from her father? She'd forgotten to warn Nick. She herself hadn't dared to raise this topic since she was in primary school.

Back then she'd writhed in embarrassment at the annual 'Grandparents' Day'. She never had a guest. No grandparent to look smug and applaud her accomplishments. No one to make her look normal. No one, year after year. When she was eight she'd finally raised the topic. She'd never forgotten her father's voice of steel, a voice that said the topic was never to be mentioned again.

Now Nick had strayed onto forbidden ground. She held her breath. Would her father be as angry at Nick as he'd been with her in the past? If so, it would be the first time Nick had earned her father's displeasure.

"You don't want to invite my mother. We don't have anything to do with her."

Esther peered over her shoulder at her father. His jaw was clenched. With small issues he was all sweetness, but with some things he'd dig in his heels. As a child she hadn't always known what issues to avoid. But she'd learned to skirt around the dangerous swamps of work, reputation and family background.

It had been years since she'd even remembered she had a grand-mother. Suddenly it mattered.

"Dad, wouldn't a wedding be a chance for a new start?"

Her father laid aside his crossword pencil. "Believe me, my mother is incapable of new starts. If you want your wedding wrecked, go ahead and ask her."

How had her grandparent-less family become normal? Why? Nick seemed to be a restraining influence on her father. Maybe now it would be safe to do a little digging. "I've never met her. How terrible can she be?"

Her father continued to stare at the crossword page of the newspaper. "You didn't grow up with her. She made my life miserable." He snapped the paper closed, stood and grabbed his pencil. "If you need me, I'll be in my study."

Esther glanced at her mother near the bow window, keeping silent as she hemmed. Fat lot of good she'd ever be in an argument. Esther shelved the whole conversation to think about later and turned back to their planning. Their file consisted of three lists: the 'definites', the 'perhaps' and the 'ask-only-if-other-people-can't-come'.

Nick yawned. "We still need to finish looking at the samples of the wedding invitation designs and wording. We're down to five choices. Let's go line by line and try to narrow it down to two choices. Then your parents can have the casting vote."

Nick was wise. Giving her parents the casting vote kept her father off her back. Not stirring up sleeping lions had become a habit.

"Mum, would I be right that Dad would prefer the formal, 'Reverend Doctor William and Mrs Blanche Macdonald request the pleasure of your company' rather than merely 'Mr and Mrs' or 'William and Blanche Macdonald'?"

"Probably, but I could go and check." Her mother got up and left the room. She returned so quickly she almost caught Esther sitting on Nick's knee. They ploughed on with their task, determined to get it over with, and after another hour, they'd finally whittled their choices down to two. Nick stretched his arms up towards the ceiling. "Enough for today. My brother warned me to steer clear of wedding stuff."

"Not having regrets, I hope."

Nick pantomimed scratching his head and screwing up his face like an actor in a cheap melodrama. Esther giggled. She wasn't worried about Nick backing out.

"No, sorry. You're stuck with me. But I do wish there was less to do."

"I know exactly what you mean. Want to go out for a quick walk? There's time before the service."

Although it was early, a crescent moon cruised through clusters of cloud, intermittently illuminating cloud edges to coffee and cream before disappearing. The deciduous trees rattled their almost leafless twigs. A cold breeze hinted of early snow on the distant mountains. Esther tugged her scarf up around her tingling ears and Nick's warm hand encircled hers as they strolled round the block.

"I can't believe Dad won't let me ask Gina to be a bridesmaid." Esther hadn't really taken her father's comments about choosing only beautiful bridesmaids seriously. Or maybe she hadn't wanted to, because his words hinted at buried ugliness she didn't want to confront.

"Does it matter?"

"I feel terrible every time I see Gina. She must have known she was a likely choice. How am I going to be able to explain it to her? I mean, I wanted to tell him no, but you know how he is." Esther stopped walking and turned to look at Nick. "Doesn't it bother you that Dad wants everyone to look perfect?"

"I'm sure he has his reasons."

Now Nick seemed to be annoyed at her too.

"It's not a beauty contest."

"Look." Nick tugged her arm. "This wedding is dominating

everything at the moment. Is it possible to talk about something else for the next thirty minutes?"

The last thing she needed was to alienate Nick. Esther slipped her arm around Nick's waist and leaned her head against him. "Oh, I think I can manage it."

He chuckled. "About time."

They meandered along the road for several minutes.

Nick put his arm around her shoulder and hugged her close. "Do you remember me mentioning the special apprenticeship with John Watson in Melbourne?"

"Vaguely," Esther said. "Was he the guy who mentors preachers and church leaders?"

"Yes." Nick stopped and looked at her. "Your father suggested I apply for it. What do you think?"

What did she think? She thought it was a terrible idea. "It's a tremendous opportunity, but didn't you say the first intake for the year was in September?"

Nick started to walk forward. "Yes, would that be a problem?"

The problem seemed obvious, considering they were getting married on the twenty-sixth of August. "September would be almost immediately after our honeymoon and you'd be away four days a week for over five months."

"I don't think you need to worry. Only ten are chosen, and most of those will be from overseas. It's highly unlikely I'd win the scholarship the first time I applied."

Esther resisted making an exaggerated sigh to show her relief. Winning the scholarship would mean so much to both her father and Nick. Whatever she personally thought about only seeing Nick on weekends, if he won, she'd have to lump it. He didn't sound too confident of his chances and she wasn't going to worry about something that might never happen. She squeezed his hand.

"Sure, go ahead and apply."

They walked the last two hundred metres to her parents' gate in silence. Nick probably thought about the scholarship but Esther thought about the wedding. Her mind simmered with awkward questions. Why was her Dad so insistent about Gina? Why had he cut off all contact with his mother? And would she dare to pursue answers, or would keeping the peace remain her habitual choice?

CHAPTER 7

$\mathcal{W}$ ednesdays were busy at the physiotherapy clinic. The department clerk had stacked the day's files in order in each therapist's inbox, and Esther opened the first one on her pile to refamiliarise herself with the case and its treatment. At nine o'clock, she called in her first client.

"Whatever you did last time worked a treat," the client said. "Things were stirred up a little for one night, but it's been much better since and I'm no longer waking in the morning with headaches."

Esther recorded the comments using the shorthand she'd learned at university. "Is there any time of day that it's still a problem?"

"Late evening, but going to bed early with a hot pack helps."

"Okay, lie on your stomach and I'll get to work." It looked like being one of those client-every-thirty-minutes-no-cancellation days. Mrs Brown with a sore leg. Mr Chong with headaches. A child with a stiff ankle post cast removal. The usual stream of aches and pains. Esther prided herself on running to time. An efficient rhythm of question, examine, treat. Question, examine, treat. Today most patients were improving, and she discharged two beaming customers, freeing up space for new clients.

Treating clients who'd been before gave Esther more time to think as she worked. She loved her work. Maybe she loved it even more because she almost didn't become a physiotherapist.

As Esther had approached the end of high-school, she'd had no idea about what to do next. She was more of an all-rounder than a specialist. She hadn't even known what physiotherapy was when her favourite teacher suggested it, but when she investigated, things seemed to fall into place. It combined her interest in science with her love of people, and it wouldn't take as long as becoming a doctor.

The problem was that she couldn't imagine her father ever saying proudly. "Meet my daughter. She's a physiotherapist." Physiotherapy had no status, no fancy titles, and no high salary to make anyone envious.

She was a Daddy's girl, even if he was often too busy to pay attention to her. One of her high-school friends had asked why she adored her father, since he was as aloof as the gods on Mount Olympus. Perhaps that was part of his mystique. She'd worked hard at music and academics to make him proud of her.

Esther had needed to be subtle to get her way. No childish blurting out. In the end, she was saved because she didn't get the marks for medical school, and she won a scholarship for physiotherapy. It was the only scholarship available, which allowed her father to convince himself physiotherapy was okay. Esther smiled to herself as she mobilised the joints of her client's back. The whole experience had taught her it was possible to beat her father, but it required stealth and patience and a sprinkling of good luck.

The first client after lunch was an elderly woman with a painful lower back. Midway through the treatment, Esther asked the woman to turn from her stomach to her side.

"Can you help me please, dear?" Mrs Barclay asked. "I'm afraid I might roll off this narrow table."

Esther leaned forward to give assistance. Mrs Barclay over-balanced, flung out her hand, and hit Esther in the chest. A stab of pain shot through Esther's left breast. She gasped and tears welled in her eyes.

"So, so sorry. I'm not usually clumsy." The client tried to sit up.

"It wasn't your fault. Just one of those things." Esther rubbed the flat of her hand over the painful spot.

After Mrs Barclay left, still apologising, Esther hurried to the bathroom. Why was there still a dull throb where she'd been hit? She locked the door of the two-cubicle bathroom and untucked her shirt so she could raise it and look in the mirror. She couldn't see any visible bruising. She touched the skin and pushed deeper. Ouch. She sucked in her breath as her fingers connected with one painful spot. Her fingers probed around the area. There was defi-nitely a lump in her breast, and not a small one. Her breathing accelerated.

She checked her right breast—nothing. There was no way that knock had caused the lump. Clammy skin, shaky legs. She leaned on the sink. Surely not? Not something serious. She was too young. Too healthy. Too—too blessed. After all, she was the daughter of William Macdonald. The man with a direct line to God.

Calm down. Nothing has been proven yet. But logic didn't lower her hurtling heart rate. Telling herself to calm down didn't stop her sweating. Her mind zoomed through possible scenarios, each more horrible than the last. She tottered into the toilet cubicle, lowered the cover, and slumped on the seat.

Get a hold of yourself, Esther.
Breathe.

She filled her lungs and held her breath. One-two-three-four. Exhale. Again. Deep breath. In-two-three-four. Hold-two-three-four. Out-two-three-four. Two more cycles and she had to put her head between her knees. Talk about a rush of adrenaline. This was more a surging flood of panic.

The breathing helped, but she still felt weak and trembly.

Thank goodness her next client had cancelled. She had about twenty minutes to pull herself together. Still shaky, she splashed water on her face and dabbed her skin with a paper towel. She couldn't possibly concentrate on writing up treatment notes now. Instead, she went and knocked on her boss's door.

"Sue, got a minute?"

Esther tried to keep her voice steady and bright. She must have failed because Sue peered at her over the top of her reading glasses.

"You alright? You sound terrible."

"The last client accidentally hit me on my chest, and I've discovered a lump."

"You mean she hit you so hard it raised a lump?"

"No." Esther shook her head. "I mean that she hit a lump that must have been there for a while."

Sue's forehead furrowed. "Have you noticed the problem before?"

"Not really." Esther stepped fully into the room and closed the door, not wanting her private business audible to anyone passing by. "I went to my doctor months ago, but he fobbed me off. Told me I was too young for any major problems. And I've been distracted since." Esther grimaced. "Wedding preparations." It sounded lame.

"People can have breast cancer in their twenties. I've even known someone who was seventeen." Sue sat up straight. "If it was me, I'd find it difficult to concentrate the rest of the afternoon. My doctor is excellent, and she's only just around the corner. Would you like me to call and see if she's got a cancellation?"

"I've still got five clients to see."

"Let's call and ask if there's a vacancy." Sue lifted several piles of papers. "If she does, there's no reason I can't see your clients. Any excuse to avoid paperwork." She pulled out her diary, reached across her desk for the phone, and dialled.

Forty-five minutes later, Esther took off her name badge and put a jacket over her uniform. She drew the jacket across her chest to ward off the cold clutching at her with icy tentacles. Her stomach seemed to be hosting a butterfly's garden party. Desperate, pleading prayers tumbled through her mind.

CHAPTER 8

*A*fter her previous experience at Dr Arnold's clinic, Esther was reassured to see this reception area almost empty. At least the doctor should be able to concentrate on what she was saying. She gave her details to the receptionist and opened a magazine, but didn't read it. Instead, she stared unseeing towards the window. Random thoughts flitted through the crevices of her mind. Was she worrying unnecessarily? Not all lumps were cancer. Not all cancers were malignant. Perhaps she'd be one of the lucky ones. The receptionist's long nails clicked on her keyboard. Was this a small problem or a much bigger one? Should she have called Nick? Her parents?

Outside, a car's brakes squealed masking the clickety-clack of a local train switching tracks. If she had cancer, how would it affect her work? What if it dragged on? And worst of all, what if it interfered with her wedding? Bubbles of worry popped on the surface of her consciousness.

"Esther? The doctor will see you now." Jerked out of her reverie, Esther laid the magazine aside and walked through the door. The doctor waited until Esther took a seat.

"I'm Dr Singh. My receptionist said Sue Powers sent you here. How can I help?"

Esther related the story of her mishap with the client.

"Have you felt other twinges before?" Dr Singh opened a clean new file.

"Six months ago, but it didn't seem urgent." Esther blushed. She was still berating herself about her stupidity. She was supposed to be a health professional. Why hadn't she followed up on that twinge in her armpit? Why had she let the clinic's chaos distract her from pursuing the issue? Better to have been sure.

"Has anyone in your family had breast cancer?"

"I've no idea. I have never known any of my extended family."

"That's something we need to follow up." Dr Singh made a note in the file, asked a few more questions, then gestured for Esther to get on the examination table. "Let's not assume this is a major problem. Lots of people have non-malignant cysts and lumps." She rubbed her hands vigorously on a rough towel to warm them and examined Esther's right side. "Nothing unusual this side. Let's check the other side." The physical examination was thorough and Esther gritted her teeth as the doctor gently felt around the area where she'd found the lump.

Dr Singh had gone quiet. Esther sweated. "Can you feel it?" Stupid question. She must be nervous to blurt out something so superfluous.

"Yes, it's hard to miss. Sorry for causing you discomfort. Put on your blouse, and we'll talk."

Dr Singh wrote as Esther dressed. Once Esther sat down, Dr Singh said, "You've got at least one large lump."

The too-gentle tone and the words, 'at least' made Esther's pulse rocket.

"I'm going to send you across the road to get an ultrasound and mammogram. Depending on the number of people waiting, they might be able to do the tests today." Dr Singh wrote the referral, signed it, and sealed the letter in an envelope. "They'll also be able to do fine needle biopsies there, but you'll probably have to wait a few days for those. I'll write a separate referral for that." She took half a minute to do so, opened a drawer, and selected a pamphlet. "This gives you some information about the biopsy."

Esther scanned the main points. "So I shouldn't need to take extra time off work?"

"No, you'll only have a little pain and bruising as the local anaesthetic wears off. As you pass the reception desk, could you please book another appointment for two weeks from now?" Dr Singh closed her file. "Whatever you do, be kind to yourself and don't assume the worst. Let's wait until we have the results."

How could she not assume the worst? The 'what ifs' and criss-crossed rabbit tracks of possibility were all she could think of.

Across the road, she only had to wait a short while. The first two tests went by in a blur. A biopsy was scheduled for Friday. Before she knew it, Esther was out the door and headed back to the hospital to collect her bike. The physiotherapy department was already dark and silent, so she'd have to wait until tomorrow to update Sue.

At home, there was a note on the kitchen bench.

DINNER IN THE FRIDGE. WE'LL BE HOME BY 9:30.

Thank goodness. At least she wouldn't be forced to make conversation.

When she was a child, her parents always said they could tell when she had a secret. Could they still? Esther toyed with the circlets of carrot on her dinner plate. Should she remain quiet about what she was going through until she had a definite diagnosis? Or was it better to tell everyone now, in case they felt hurt about being excluded?

Esther squared her shoulders. She'd keep quiet. That way they'd be spared unnecessary stress. The problem with this decision was it left her alone, teetering on a tightrope, threatening to fall into gnawing worry, or pointless denial.

CHAPTER 9

*T*ime slowed to an excruciating drawn-out waiting, freeze-framed, advancing one slow-motion frame at a time. Flick. Did Esther have cancer? Flick. Was it malignant? Flick. How serious?

It was difficult to be enthusiastic about the wedding. Had anyone noticed? She hung back on printing the wedding invitations, and she'd checked the cancellation terms for the caterer. There was minimal penalty as long as she gave them six weeks' notice.

On Wednesday morning, one week after her discovery of the lump, Esther found a hand-delivered card in the mailbox. Who would be writing to her? She tore open the envelope and scanned to the bottom to check the signature. Gina. Guilt flooded over her —she hadn't dared stand up to Dad about Gina being a bridesmaid. She'd chickened out of talking to her directly and sent a note. A note she'd laboured over. How do you come up with an excuse that isn't a lie, yet doesn't hurt a friend too deeply? They'd barely talked since, so why was Gina writing to her now?

DEAR ESTHER,

I NOTICED ON SUNDAY THAT YOU SEEMED DISTRACTED BUT WASN'T SURE IF I WAS IMAGINING IT. LAST NIGHT, I WAS SURE SOMETHING WAS WRONG. I DON'T KNOW WHAT'S HAPPENING BUT I'LL BE PRAYING. IF YOU WANT TO TALK, I'M ALWAYS AVAILABLE.

YOUR FRIEND, GINA

A tear trickled down Esther's cheek. Talk about heaping coals of fire on someone's head. She would have understood if Gina had cut off all contact, and now here she was being more sensitive than Esther's own family. How she longed to share her burden. But Nick and her parents must be told first. Perhaps she'd been wrong in going this alone. Was her silence a form of denial? As if speaking the words out loud would make the situation real.

Esther distracted herself with hard work.

Surely any news was better than this loitering in limbo. Yet she was terrified of bad news.

She was unprepared. She would always be unprepared.

At night, she had recurring nightmares of swimming in a strong current. She pumped her arms and legs, yet made no forward progress. Millimetre by millimetre, she was dragged towards the edge. Finally, she plunged over the waterfall with a scream that woke her. Sweating and shivering.

Saturday.

Sunday.

Monday.

Each day drawn out like a wire, stretched to its maximum. Dread settled like lead in her limbs. Dread worse than the minutes before music exams. Dread worse than confronting the dentist's drill. Trying not to speak. Trying not to worry. Trying just to appear normal.

Tuesday inevitably arrived. Too soon. Much too soon.

"Come in, Esther. Come in, sit down." Dr Singh ushered Esther into the room.

Was the welcome falsely hearty? Was the repetition a sign that there was good news or bad?

"Are you in a rush to get back to work?"

That was an ominous question. Esther's heart galloped like a runaway horse. "No, I cancelled ninety minutes' worth of appointments." Why, oh why, did they have to play the politeness game? All she wanted was to know the news. No. That wasn't right. She only wanted to know if it was good news. If the news was bad, it was the last thing she wanted to know. But bad news of some sort must be a given. For if the news had been good, wouldn't the clinic have phoned and cancelled her appointment?

Her jitters made her blurt, "Please, put me out of my misery and tell me the results."

Dr Singh put on her reading glasses and looked at the sheets spread in front of her. Even that seemed worrying. "Unfortunately, it's bad news. You have cancer."

A one-two punch to her chest. The runaway horse in her heart was now a cheetah stretched out in full pursuit. What if she lost her breakfast right on the office floor? She wrapped her arms round her stomach.

"… definitely a tumour … malignant … breast cancer." The doctor's words faded in and out.

Breast cancer.

The words she'd never wanted to hear. The words she'd tried not to say out loud. The words she hardly even dared to think about.

As though denial ever kept anything at bay.

Now the cheetah was loose. Snarling and snapping at her heels. Sending alarms of panic along every nerve fibre.

"Getting married ... end of August. What will I do?"

"I can't pretend the next months will be easy."

Not easy. Now there was a euphemism. Esther put her head between her knees.

"Take your time. This news hits people in different ways." Esther heard Dr Singh rise and walk across the room. Water splashed in the sink, then more steps. She looked up and took the glass of water out of Dr Singh's hand, nodded her thanks and took a long drink.

"Sorry, I feel horrible."

"Your reaction is perfectly normal. Take a few deep breaths and another drink."

Esther obeyed. Her energy had leaked out her feet. She trembled like a ninety-year-old with poorly medicated Parkinson's. There was a rushing in her head, swirling confusion and darkness. She closed her eyes and concentrated on her breathing. It had helped last time.

After a long moment, she managed to lift her head and open her eyes.

"What happens next?"

"We'll register you at a specialist cancer centre. They'll do further tests to find out how serious the problem is."

"How many centres are there?"

"Lots, but there are two local ones, and one is next door to your hospital."

"Of the two, which would you recommend if you weren't thinking about convenience?"

"They're both excellent, which is why I'm suggesting the closer one."

"I presume I'll need surgery and chemo." Wow, she could still function. This ping-pong of questions kept reality far away.

"The specialist will advise you about surgery and chemo."

"How long will I have to wait before I see them?" The words still slipped out on auto-pilot, as though she was functioning on two levels—the efficient, outer professional level spoke and breathed. The inner level curled in a ball of denial, trying not to move in case she shattered into a million pieces and was never whole again.

"They'll want to see you as soon as possible. Why don't I call them now?"

Esther sat rigid as Dr Singh phoned. The words being read off her biopsy report seemed distant, as if describing a stranger. The news settled on her shoulders, an Everest of implications.

If only she'd brought someone with her. She needed a kind word, a gentle touch, a hug. The phone clicked and Esther jumped.

"Sorry, I've been in a trance."

"These things are always a shock." Dr Singh handed over a piece of paper. "I've written down your appointment with Dr Webster, a week from today, ten o'clock. You haven't told your family yet, have you?"

"I'll have to tell them tonight."

Dr Singh put her elbows on her desk. "It's a tough time. Some people can't handle this kind of news."

"Mum should be fine, once she gets over the shock, but I'm not sure about my fiancé. We've never bumped up against any real challenges." And this one should be temporary too. Once her Dad sprang into action surely God would too. Wasn't that his job?

"Unfortunately, men often find it more difficult than women."

A few tears overflowed and ran towards Esther's chin.

"Crying is therapeutic." Dr Singh handed over a box of tissues. "We keep the tissue companies in business."

Esther cried harder. The tears dripped off her nose and chin. She took one tissue and then another and another. It took a full two minutes before she blew her nose and hiccuped.

"I'm so glad Sue recommended you. I hope the cancer centre

will be half as good."

"Are you okay to walk back to work?" They both stood up.

"Yes, I'll be fine. Work will distract me."

Outside, the sun was shining. How dare it shine? Surely the world should be grey and depressing, to match her news and the winter season. Esther glanced at her watch. Still forty-five minutes until her next appointment. A walk around the block would be better than sitting and staring at her office wall. She walked vigorously, as if her pounding steps could crush the situation underfoot.

It was impossible to keep her mind blank. Questions and worries intruded. How was she going to bring the topic up with Nick? With her parents? She mentally rehearsed one possible lead-in, then another. Was this how the next few months would be, exhaustion both from treatment and mental gymnastics?

She crept back into the department. If anyone asked how she was she'd dissolve in a puddle. But Sue's door was open and she called out as Esther walked past. Sue took one look at her face.

"So —it wasn't good news."

"No." Esther choked.

"I'm so sorry."

Sue's sympathy started Esther sobbing again. Without fuss, Sue handed her the tissues and let her cry.

Esther sniffed. "It's going to be a week of waterworks. I'll have to tell my family tonight."

"Who did Dr Singh recommend you see?"

"Dr Webster."

"He's an excellent specialist, but don't expect frills." Dr Webster sounded grim. "Look, would you like to head home?"

This was a question Esther could answer. "I'd prefer to stay. If I go home now, my parents will know something is wrong." And they'd dig it out of her. "I need to talk to Nick first. This concerns him the most."

But how would he handle it?

CHAPTER 10

*W*hen Esther arrived home, her father wasn't there, but Mum called from the kitchen, "Welcome home. How was your day?"

"Busy." Esther hurried past the kitchen door. "I'll have a shower and change. Nick is coming at six thirty. After dinner, we'll go for a walk." She might feel full of cracks but somehow her learned patterns of behaviour were holding her together. Like a broken egg bound with string.

The shower covered her tears. Maybe she'd use up all her tears and wouldn't break down during the meal. Esther lingered under the hot jets of water.

Lord, make this nightmare go away. I want to get married and have a family. I want a future—a long, long future. Why do I have cancer at twenty-eight?

She dug her finger ends into her scalp as she shampooed her hair. If her scalp hurt enough she might not notice the ache in her stomach. Did God even care? Or did he sit up there and move the chess pieces where he wanted, regardless of the pain it caused? Lots of Australians thought God was like that. Were they right?

GRACE IN STRANGE DISGUISE

It wasn't fair. Hadn't they always honoured God? Hadn't her father promised she would be blessed? Cancer wasn't a blessing, it was a curse. Where was God, and what was he doing?

There was no answer, only the whirr of the exhaust fan as it gobbled up the billowing steam. No comfort, no peace, no surge of hope.

When Esther went downstairs, she found Nick and her father deep in conversation about Dad's new book. Neither man seemed to notice her unusual lack of participation in their discussion. Instead, she laid the table and helped her mother serve the meal.

Nick and her father were still talking as she stacked the dishwasher. Did Nick even register that she was in the room? Was it normal that her father could so distract him from her? Her question left a bitter taste in her mouth. She'd always despised jealousy.

"Ready for our walk?"

"Oh. Um, yes. Let me get my jacket. See you later, Dr —sorry William." After their engagement, her father had insisted Nick use the less formal title, although few other staff members had the privilege.

As they set off for their walk, Esther was still debating the best conversation starter. She took a big breath. Start with something innocuous.

"You seemed to have plenty to talk about with Dad."

"A good thing if I'm gonna be his son-in-law." Nick took her hand. "You seemed quiet tonight."

"I've got loads on my mind." And she was about to dump the load on Nick.

"Is the wedding stressing you out?"

"No, not directly." She squeezed Nick's hand. How could she transition to her topic? "Have I seemed distracted to you these last few weeks?"

"I assumed wedding planning was getting to you."

"No, not particularly." Here goes. Time to step off the cliff. "I've been having some medical tests."

"Oh, why's that?" Nick swivelled his head to look at her.

"I had some strange twinges of pain in my armpit." Her news lumped in her throat, choking her.

"What did the doctor say?" His voice was still relaxed. He had no idea what was coming. She was about to blast his world into smithereens.

"Oh, Nick. Th … there's no easy way to say it. I've got breast cancer."

"Wha—at?" He dropped her hand. "Impossible. You're way too young."

This was horrible. She mustn't cry. "I thought so too."

"How serious is it?"

"I don't know. They might have to wait until after more tests or surgery—" She saw his eyes widen in the glimmer of the streetlight.

"Surgery? What—"

Had she been wrong not to tell Nick from the first day? At least then their reactions would have been in tune. Now they were out of sync, like radio waves interfering with each other. One wave up while the other wave was down. "Nick, this is serious. I have a large lump. I'm seeing a specialist next Tuesday and surgery is a possibility."

"What kind of surgery?"

If only Nick had some sort of medical background, but she could hardly blame him for not knowing these things. "A mastectomy, I presume."

"What? You mean, chop off your breast?"

Ouch. Esther gritted her teeth. She still had another conversation to follow and it might be worse. "Possibly, and maybe chemotherapy as well."

"But we're getting married soon."

Nick had unintentionally stamped on her tender spot. She dug her teeth into her lower lip. "We might have to delay the wedding." Her voice trembled. "If I have surgery and chemo, it might be months until I get the all clear."

Nick cracked his knuckles. "Do your parents know?"

"I wanted to tell you first. I'm hoping you're going to help me tell them."

"Whoa—" Nick took a step back. "That's a big ask. I'm reeling. You've had longer to get used to the idea."

They walked in silence, a wide space between them. Was it symbolic?

Thud. Thud. Thud. Their footsteps were a regular beat on the footpath. Who would break the silence?

"You're fit. You eat right. You live right. Why?" Nick slapped his thigh. "Why is this happening?"

Esther turned to face him. "Look, I don't know any more than you. The one thing I do know is, I need your support." She reached out and grasped his coat, the cloth rough between her fingers. "This is the hardest thing I've ever had to deal with. I've spent half the day crying."

"Maybe—maybe God is testing us. To see how we'll respond."

"If it's a test, I sure hope it's a temporary one."

Nick lapsed into silence. He was probably doing what she had done, scrolling through the implications. She should have told him sooner.

They approached the imposing sandstone gate posts of her home. "Will you come in?"

"Can you go ahead without me?" Nick rubbed the back of his head. "I need to go home—get used to the idea. I wouldn't be any use tonight."

Disappointment seeped into her heart. Dr Singh's words were proving prophetic. Well, she refused to beg. She had no energy for it.

"I'm sorry." Why was she apologising? It wasn't her choice to have cancer. "Please pray. I'm going to need all the help I can get."

Nick opened the door of his car and clicked in his seatbelt. He hadn't even remembered to kiss her goodnight. She would have to be patient with him. He'd work through the situation, given time.

She wasn't nearly so confident about her father.

Nick drove off and Esther opened the front door.

"Is Nick coming in?" her father called from the living room.

"No, he's had to head home." She'd known he'd ask.

"We're having a cup of tea. Come and join us." Esther went to the kitchen for another cup. Once settled on the couch she took a few sips to give her time to muster up her courage.

"Mum, do you remember when I thought a pin had jabbed me while I was trying on my dress?"

"I'm too careful to leave stray pins—"

This was no time to head down side paths. She had to spit out the words and get it over with. "Yes, I know—well, I had more of those twinges and went to Dr Arnold. He didn't pay much attention to my concerns." No need for a rambling story. "Two weeks ago, a client accidentally hit me in the chest. The pain was excruciating, so I visited another doctor near the hospital."

"Why didn't you mention this to us before?"

"I didn't want to bother you." The tears were rising in her throat, like a blow hole not yet at a high enough pressure to shoot out. "I've had some tests and ..." The tears burst out of her. Paroxysms of grief.

Her parents sat rigid in their seats.

"... hoped ... I wouldn't ... cry."

"What are you trying to say, sweetheart?"

"... got ... breast cancer."

Blanche let out a strangled cry and dashed from the room. Her father jumped out of his chair so fast, he staggered.

"That's impossible. You're far too young."

It was like she was caught in an endless action replay. This was worse, much worse than she'd expected. She'd relied on her mother, and now her mother had abandoned her.

"There must be some mistake." Her father collapsed back into his chair.

"I don't think so. All the tests confirm it." Esther dabbed her face with an already sodden tissue. Little shreds stuck to her nose. Why hadn't she brought more tissues? And why was she thinking about such inconsequentialities?

"Why didn't you tell us earlier?"

Good question. "You're such busy people—" Her voice trailed off. Her reasons now seemed feeble. "I didn't want to worry you if the tests proved negative." Why must she face this inquisition?

She stood and fled to the kitchen. She needed the space. Otherwise she'd start screaming. Or worse. And once she started, could she stop? She used to pride herself on her emotional stability. But recently she was like a yo-yo on stimulants.

She ripped some kitchen towel off the roll, leaned over the sink, and splashed water on her heated face. Was the tightness in her chest anger or something else? Whatever it was, she would have to face her father sometime. Might as well be now.

"I only found out today for sure. I told Nick first and now you."

"How healthy is your faith?" He speared her with his gaze.

"What do you mean?" Esther was tired of answering questions. All she wanted to do was to escape to her room and slam the door on life. But that wasn't a possibility. She still had to find and comfort her mother.

"Only unwavering faith results in healing. We'll mobilise the church leadership to pray and anoint you with oil." Now her father had an action plan, his voice had returned to its usual decisive confidence.

Oh, if only it might be that easy, like a magic wand that could wave away all her fears with one swoop and some abracadabras.

But the person who'd believed in abracadabras was long gone. Gone with the child who'd once believed in tooth fairies and Santa Claus. Now she lived in the cruel world outside of the golden fairy tale, where doubts multiplied like evil spells. "What if it's not that easy?"

Her father flinched. "That's not the question you should ask."

Why not? She wanted to ask the question, but didn't dare annoy him any further. She remembered only too well what happened when she overstepped his invisible line.

"You need to be like the bleeding woman—her faith made her well. Your faith must be firm."

Why did he have to launch into sermon mode? She was his daughter, not a member of his radio audience.

"I'll do my best." Her platitude sounded hollow even to herself. She stood. "Hadn't one of us better go and see how Mum is?"

"Why don't you go? I'll start working out who to call." He left the room to head to his office at the back of the house. His comfort place. The place from which he could control his world.

The men in her life were frustrating. No, not frustrating, it was more than that. More like betrayal. The bluntness of the word scared her. It seemed too strong a word for Nick's reaction and her father's actions. She needed support. Nick should be here, with his arms around her.

Esther found Mum face down on the spare bed, broken sobs shaking her upper body. Esther sat down beside her and laid a tentative hand on her shoulder. Tentative, because her mother had never been a touchy-feely person. Now wasn't the time to speculate why.

"Mum, don't take it so hard."

Her mother partially rolled over. Mascara had run down her cheeks and her foundation was blotchy. She rubbed her eyes with the heel of her hand, worsening the smears.

"I can't help it. It's my mother all over again. What have I done to deserve this?"

"What are you talking about?"

Blanche pulled a pillow under her head. "My mother died at forty-five—of breast cancer."

Esther didn't cry but a great weariness settled on her. Perhaps she no longer had the emotional strength to absorb any more. She wanted to show some empathy, but her voice and tear ducts wouldn't cooperate. She could only reach over and stroke her mother's hand. Her mother might not appreciate the touch but Esther needed the comfort.

"Why didn't I know this about my own grandmother? The doctor kept asking me if I had a family history of cancer. I told her I didn't think so."

"Your father doesn't like me to talk about such things." Her words were a mumble.

"But why? Surely I have the right to know."

"Can't you guess? His church is called 'Victory' Church. There wasn't anything victorious about my parents. Mum died young, and Dad was an alcoholic."

Interesting that her mother referred to Victory as 'his' church. "But Mum, wouldn't it be better to know the truth?"

"Maybe, but your father doesn't want to know it." Her mother's eyes widened and her mouth opened into an 'O'. She covered her mouth. "You didn't just hear me say that."

Esther was as surprised as her mother to hear the criticism. Her mother was like a tulip. Graceful and beautiful but always standing rigidly at attention. Had there ever been the disorder of a rambling rose, or had all those tendencies been trained out of her?

Her mother partially turned away. "Leave me alone for a while." Esther stood and tugged her skirt into order.

"When's your next doctor's visit?"

"Next Tuesday."

"I'll come, if you want me to."

"I was hoping you would. This last week has been hard, doing it on my own." She sighed. "Looks like Dad and Nick won't be much use."

"What happened with Nick?"

"He didn't take it much better than Dad." Esther stifled more tears. Maybe she was more like her mother than she'd ever admitted.

CHAPTER 11

*A*t three o'clock on Saturday afternoon, the doorbell rang its two note 'ding-dong'. Church leaders filed in, arriving in ones and twos. They hung up their assortment of coats and came into the warmth. Esther stood in a corner, and Nick came over and squeezed her hand. Then he took the tray off her mother and offered the guests an assortment of drinks.

The leaders talked in muted voices until the room held around twenty people. Once everyone had arrived, her father clapped his hands twice.

"Thank you for coming. As each of you know, Esther has just been diagnosed with cancer. And why should we be surprised? The enemy hates what we're doing at Victory, and the easiest way to discourage us is to strike hard."

Dad's confidence gave Esther courage. She hadn't considered Satan might be linked with her cancer. How could one know for sure? The idea was comforting—more so than wondering if she'd done something to displease God.

"This is a test of our faith. I've called you together to follow the scriptural guidelines, to anoint Esther with oil." William placed a chair in the centre of the room. "Esther, if you'd sit here, we'll gather around and pray."

Esther sat down and the men and women each placed a hand on her. There were so many of them that the hands were not only on her shoulders, but on her back and arms as well.

"Now, let's hold the jar of oil and pour it together, as a sign of our unity."

Help. Was oil about to be spilled all over her? She needn't have worried. Her father had thought through the details, and the container only held a small measure of oil. If it hadn't been such a serious occasion, Esther might have chuckled. It was so in character for her parents to choose extra virgin olive oil instead of a cheaper vegetable oil. The oil's pungent smell filled her nostrils. It oozed down the grooves of her face, leaving sticky snail-trails of goo. Esther twitched her nose to slow its progress. How could she concentrate on the prayers if she was trying to prevent the oil dripping onto her clothes, or the Persian carpet?

Her mother handed her a tissue and Esther mopped up the excess oil on her face.

"Oh Lord, Maker of heaven and earth. Your hands scattered the stars into space." Yes, this was the God Esther believed in. "On earth, you made the lame leap. You made the blind see. You raised the dead. Esther's cancer is child's play to you."

Yes, why was she stressed? God had everything under control.

"Your word says if we ask anything in faith, it will be granted. So today we ask. We, your leaders from Victory Church, ask you for this small miracle on Esther's behalf."

A blanket of peace covered Esther's heart. With such a man as her father, and this group, what was there to fear?

Another leader prayed. "Yes, Lord. This family serves you, to make your name great. You've promised to give us life to the full and no one would say cancer is abundant life. Take it away. Honour your name by healing our sister."

Several other leaders prayed before her father took charge again.

"Let's all pray together. Examine yourself. Make sure there are no seeds of doubt in your minds." He threw his head back like he was issuing a battle charge. "Cast out doubt. Let each of us be firm in faith."

Everyone started praying. The waves of sound surged and soared. Some prayed in unknown tongues. Others shouted. They hammered at heaven's door. Occasionally, Esther could hear her father's voice above the rest, casting out Satan's influence in her life. After ten minutes, the racket receded.

"Now, Esther, it's your turn. Are there any seeds of doubt in your life?"

How was she to know if there were seeds of doubt? A month ago, she would have said not, but now? Now there weren't just seeds, but a whole forest of full-grown trees blocking out the sun.

"I hope not."

"Be clear about it. Confess any doubt now." He waited for Esther to pray silently. "Raise your hands to signify your faith and to claim the healing that God offers." Esther raised her hands. "Now pray and ask for healing."

"Dear great and mighty Creator. You know about this cancer in my body. I ask you to heal me."

"Be more emphatic," her father said. "Sound like you mean it."

Esther steadied her voice. It was hard to pray in front of all these leaders, but she didn't want to embarrass her father. "Heal me. Be glorified in my life. Remove this curse and give us the blessing we ask for in your name."

"Well done. Now, let's all pray the Lord's prayer together to show Satan we mean business."

The hands on Esther's shoulders and head were cumbersome. She braced her stomach muscles and sat up straight. The united voices gave her hope. Of course God would listen to these people. There was such power in their midst.

---

*E*sther and Nick worked together to clear up after the visitors had gone. Nick didn't kiss her goodbye. What was with that? Did he think breast cancer was contagious?

The lock had barely clicked when her father called out, "Esther, come and talk for a bit."

She was tired. A short snooze would have been great but it looked like he still had more to say. She went back into the living room and sat opposite him.

"That went well, I think. A good turn-out considering it was an unscheduled extra."

It would have been hard for anyone to refuse her father's request.

"So we've anointed you with oil and tomorrow we'll recruit the church members to pray."

Privacy was a joke in a situation like hers. By tomorrow, everyone would know her business. God had better hurry and heal her or she'd have to cope with thousands of questions. *Please God, don't let Dad say anything on his radio programme.*

"Now, there are plenty of other things you need to do."

Doing practical things beat wallowing in fear and self-pity.

"Have you ever been around when I taught people to visualise?"

"No."

"It's great for situations like yours." He sat up straight. "Close your eyes and clear your mind."

Esther closed her eyes, but how could she clear her mind?

"Breathe deeply in and out and imagine yourself in utter darkness."

It was almost impossible not to obey her father's commands.

Why couldn't he just tell her about visualisation so she could decide if this was something she wanted to do?

"Come on, I didn't hear you breathe."

Esther stuffed her questions down and breathed deeply. In and out.

"Again."

Dad led her in a minute of breathing until they were both relaxed. The breathing did help clear her mind.

"Okay, now see yourself brimming with health."

She mentally scrubbed out the tumour and pictured herself after summer holidays. Tanned and fit.

Her father's voice was low and steady. "Hold that image."

Esther tried, she really did, but worries encroached on the image. Why couldn't she do this?

After a few minutes, her father said, "There's nothing to it. Morning and evening in bed works best. You've got to do everything you can."

Why? The question leapt into Esther's mind but she wasn't about to ask. How do you question someone so sure of themselves?

"The other thing you need to be doing is fasting. Skip lunch each day. It shows God you mean business."

"Dad, I can't skip lunch. Physiotherapy is hard work and I'm always ravenous. My co-workers often joke about how I love my food. They'll all ask questions."

"And what's wrong with that? You'll get a chance to share your faith."

She'd prefer to do it in another way. One less likely to make her look like she had a screw loose. But if she didn't at least do some fasting, her father would hound her. She'd try and skip breakfast every second day.

*S*unday night, Esther got into bed, visualised for ten minutes and praised God for victory before she drifted off to sleep on a cloud of confidence. No nightmares and the deepest sleep since her diagnosis.

She woke with a smile. What a difference peace of heart made. Now she could get on with her life again. She had a wedding to prepare for.

An enormous yawn and a stretch. A lance of pain seared into her armpit.

Impossible.

The stomach ache of fear was back in an instant, like it had never left. Prickles of sweat dampened her hairline. With her shaking right hand Esther checked for the lump. It was not only there but appeared to have grown. As if it was mocking her.

How could she still have cancer when so many sincere Christians had prayed? Had they missed something out and so negated all their prayers? Could she have committed some sin? Did God have some sort of 'faith gauge' and the needle had wavered and found her wanting?

Tears trickled into her pillow. How was she going to tell her father? Everyone was sure to ask and then look askance at her as if she was at fault. Didn't she have enough to cope with?

Where was God? He wasn't supposed to take holidays.

She'd always been told he was her loving heavenly Father. Well she wasn't feeling the love at the moment. She had friends who believed God was like someone jabbing pins into a butterfly they'd caught for their collection. Were they right? Or was God delaying to test the sincerity of her faith?

Well, she'd be sincere. This was one test she wasn't going to fail.

CHAPTER 12

*T*he car park at the cancer clinic was nearly full as Esther and her mum drove in, even though it was only a quarter to ten. Esther sweated, despite the cool morning. Why was she nervous? She'd had buckets of prayer poured over her. If it was possible, she'd have drowned in prayer.

The décor was surprising. Bright murals of Australian wildflowers, and a hint of lavender instead of the usual antiseptic smells. Men, women, and even children were sitting in the central waiting area. Patients, pale and nervous, and their support people, mostly bored and fidgeting. Classical music played at a tasteful volume, neither so loud as to intrude nor so soft as to be inaudible. Was it meant to calm and distract people? If so, it failed. Esther was sure there was an invisible miasma of fear swirling around her knees ready to invade her heart.

She sat down, clutching her number. Twenty-two. The nurse had just called 'fifteen'. People avoided looking at each other, as though to meet someone else's eyes would mean having to carry their troubles as well. She and her mother attempted to read.

The nurse appeared. "Twenty-one, please."

Twenty minutes later, an older woman stumbled out of the doctor's office, her face pale and a sheen of sweat on her forehead.

"Twenty-two."

Mum gave her hand a swift squeeze, and Esther stood and walked towards the door. A perfectly ordinary kind of door. A wooden-door-with-bronze-plaque kind of door. Yet, matters of life or death were discussed behind that door. In twenty minutes, Esther would know what was next. Was this the moment God would choose to heal her and proclaim his power?

Paul Webster must have been fifty but he didn't look it. He had scant grey in his hair and sported a deep tan.

"Dr Singh sent over your history, scans, and test results. First, I'll need to redo the physical examination. Then we'll talk about your options."

She was simply another person in a long line. At least he didn't make her feel embarrassed. To him, it was just a job. He didn't have time to care that she sweated and her heart pounded.

Come on, God, come on, come on. Show your power, heal me.

Dr Webster examined the right side and began on the left. No pain yet, maybe, maybe, maybe it had happened. Esther squeezed her eyes shut, gritted her teeth and visualised herself healthy.

A stab of pain skewered her hopes.

"That obviously hurt."

"Mmm." She didn't trust herself to speak. Her eyelashes prickled with unshed tears. It wasn't just the physical pain. Hadn't she prayed enough, confessed enough, fasted enough? How much fasting would have been enough? Would missing five breakfasts a week instead of only three have worked?

Dr Webster was writing while Esther dressed. Did he need to write notes or did it give him something to do before his words ripped through people's lives?

"I see that you're a physiotherapist, so you're familiar with medical terms." There was a pause, long enough for her to nod. "You need a left-sided mastectomy as soon as possible."

No. Not maiming for life. What woman didn't want to look beautiful for her husband? Her mouth was dry and she swallowed. "Isn't a lumpectomy enough?"

"No. It would be foolish to mess around, as it's likely your lymph nodes are involved too. The surgery will clarify the extent of your cancer." Dr Webster looked at her as though to check how she was handling the news. "As yet, there's no sign of cancer on the right. A left mastectomy will be enough. Chemotherapy will start when your wounds are healed."

So there was to be no talk about 'if' for chemotherapy. It was a 'when'. "How soon is that?"

"Four to six weeks after the surgery."

Esther had taken out a blank piece of paper and scribbled notes. Scribbling kept her focused and helped her ignore the pounding of her heart, the feeling her veins ran with ice water. "How long will chemo last?"

"We'll need the pathology results first. Then a precise cocktail of drugs will be matched to your specific case."

What would it feel like to have her body become a chemical lab? She'd heard too many horror stories at work to be under any illusions that it would be easy.

"Chemo can last six months." There was an advantage to Dr Webster's emotionless approach. They could have been discussing a stranger. Her life, dissected but without blood or pain. Perhaps that would come later, after the anaesthetic of this clinical discussion wore off.

"What are my options for surgery?"

"That depends on you. I work with two different surgeons. One at the private hospital, and the other at your workplace."

It wasn't going to be a hard choice after all. "I don't have private health insurance, as I've always been satisfied with the public system. Would the chemo be here?"

"Yes. The reason I have my office here is so everything is close by." Dr Webster looked at the clock behind Esther's head. Her time must be nearly up. She still needed to know when all of this would happen so she could rearrange her life.

"How soon can I be booked in for surgery?"

"I'll get our receptionist to telephone the surgeon's office and she'll phone you back today. Any more questions?"

"My head's spinning right now. I'll probably have heaps of questions once I come out of my daze."

Dr Webster signed and dated her file. "The receptionist will give you the information pack on the way out. There's also a booklet written by a social worker. We recommend people make an appointment with them prior to surgery."

Esther collected the hefty information pack and went back into the main room where her mother was waiting.

"What did he say?"

The geyser of emotion threatened to gush again. "Not here," Esther muttered. She told her mother the details in the safety of the car. She broke down twice before she was done.

"Are you sure you're okay to go to work?"

"I'd go crazy waiting at home and I've scheduled an easy afternoon. I'll have to digest all this tonight. Then I'll talk to Nick." Esther dabbed her eyes again. "We've got to make some tough decisions about the wedding. Thank goodness we haven't printed the invitations yet."

There was a telephone call for Esther late that afternoon. "I'm ringing on behalf of Dr Webster. The surgeon can fit you in on Thursday morning, two weeks from now—the sixth of July. Can I confirm that date?"

That was fast. It didn't matter if it was convenient or not—she had to take any spot offered. "Yes, I'll arrange things with work." She gripped the phone tightly. Now wasn't the moment to fall apart.

"Your surgery will be the first of the day. That means you need to be admitted by three p.m. the day before, on Wednesday the fifth." Esther held the phone squeezed between her right shoulder and ear so she could write. The voice spoke slowly so she could keep up. "There'll be an array of pre-surgery checks, and you'll need to fast from midnight before the surgery."

"I'm writing this down, fifth—fast." Esther wrote in her usual shorthand. "Okay, I've got it all."

"All the information is repeated in the pack we gave you."

Esther continued to block out all feelings and concentrate on the call. She was getting good at it. "Yes, I was planning to read it this evening."

"We'll see you again about two weeks after the surgery. I'd like to arrange that follow-up appointment now. Do you prefer mornings or afternoons?"

At last, an easy question. "Mornings. Then it's over for the day."

"Ten a.m. on Wednesday the nineteenth. If you have any concerns, please contact us." The lady repeated the dates and times.

"Yes, I've got all that," Esther said. "Thank you."

Click.

Esther sat and stared at the phone. Her stomach churned. She was being dragged onto the assembly line, and the only way off was if God did his miracle. Without it, she'd be carried along each stage in the process until she was spat out the other end.

Cured or dead.

CHAPTER 13

*E*sther did her best to soldier on as normal at work while she waited the two weeks for surgery. Treatment times were fine because the clients didn't know there was anything wrong, but lunchtimes echoed with loneliness. By now the other therapists knew she'd soon be away for an extended time, and why. Their interactions with her were awkward. Long silences interrupted by clipped, business-like conversations, and avoiding eye contact. Sue was the only one with whom she could talk easily, perhaps because she'd been part of the journey from early on.

Every day Esther continued to pray. She prayed in the morning and before bed. She prayed in the shower and at work. She prayed while she cycled to work, or jogged around the block or swam laps. She slammed the door on any doubt. When her father demanded a daily report she always appeared optimistic. The blame would not rest with her if she wasn't healed.

And every morning, after she'd visualised, Esther checked if the lump was gone. It never was.

What are you doing Lord? Why the delay?

Home was worse than work. At first her father and Nick asked her every day if the lump had disappeared. But since she kept answering in the negative, they asked her less and less often. Both men seemed to spend even more time at work, so their only contact was brief encounters at church meetings and during meals. They were like cars speeding past each other on a race track. When they did stop to talk, it was only to ask if she'd been healed yet.

The question had become a giant rock, squashing her and compounding the daily disappointment that the lump was still present. Where was God? Had he forgotten her? Esther avoided both men rather than cope with their interrogations and their hints that she was somehow at fault. Couldn't there be another explanation?

---

*A*fter ten days of disappointment, Esther went to talk to her father. It was one of his rare days off but he didn't rest. He was outside, swimming laps in their pool. She prepared drinks and waited for him to switch to breaststroke, the signal that he was almost done.

Esther pulled out two of the poolside chairs. It was a winter's day, so even with solar heating the water must have been chilly. Her father rubbed himself vigorously, tied his robe around his waist, sat down and took the offered hot drink.

"Thanks, sweetheart."

Esther waited until he relaxed. "Dad, I've been wanting to talk to you."

"What's troubling you?"

"Dad, I can't help wondering why I'm not being healed? We seem to be doing everything right."

"Everything can't have been done right if you haven't been healed."

Esther swallowed. His abruptness hurt. Like he had become a

machine, popping out an automatic answer but forgetting he was talking to his daughter.

William slurped his drink and stared off over the back fence. "Maybe God has delayed healing so it will make more of an impact. Those medical people don't believe in God or healing, not with all their science and research. A last-minute miracle would be something for my *Hour of Victory* programme."

"Dad, I don't want to be an exhibit on your radio show."

"There's nothing wrong with being on my show."

Maybe exhibit had been too strong a word. Esther didn't want to make him angry. She needed him on her side, for wouldn't God be more likely to listen to her father?

"I never said there was, but I'd prefer not to be on it. I'd be happier to discover the whole thing wasn't as serious as expected."

"There's still time before your surgery. Maybe God is testing how much you want to be healed. Why don't you spend extra time in prayer? And step up the fasting."

"It feels like all I've been doing is praying. I'm already skipping every second breakfast."

"Why don't you skip lunches on the in-between days."

How could she skip any more meals? She'd lost a kilo in the last week.

"How can you expect God to work if you can't sacrifice yourself? The rest of us will do our part. We'll keep praying, and Nick and I will anoint you with oil again." He drank another mouthful of tea. "Most of all, you'll have to work on digging up those troublesome seeds of doubt." He stared at her over the rim of his mug. "Keep going with the visualisation. Make sure you can see yourself healthy and cancer free."

"I'll try, Dad." She mustn't squirm under the directness of his stare.

"Don't just try. Make sure you do it. We don't want Satan

winning this round." He put down his mug, grabbed his towel, and headed in for a hot shower. Obviously the conversation was at an end. Esther stood up, tidied away their chairs, and took the dirty mugs inside.

For the next week she skipped more meals. She prayed in multiple positions. She confessed every sin that came to mind and even some that didn't. Just in case. She visualised to the point of tensing her face and stomach muscles into knotted kinks. Could she at last see an ethereal vision of a beaming, healthy physiotherapist about to get married?

It had to work. It just had to.

* * *

*A*s Esther and Blanche headed for the door on their way to the hospital, William said, "I'll send another group this evening to pray for healing."

"Dad, I'd be much happier if you came on your own." How could she make him understand?

"You know Wednesday is my night to pre-record my radio broadcast." Before she could say anything more he rushed on, "I've hand-picked people with strong faith. Do remember to ask the doctors to re-examine you before surgery."

Esther squirmed inwardly. "Dad, I'd be embarrassed to bother them."

"Honey, you sound like you're not interested in being healed."

Why did he always make it sound like she was at fault? "Of course I want to be healed. Who wouldn't?"

"Well, remember to ask." He nodded several times. "After all, I only want the best for you." Esther allowed herself to be rounded up and herded out of the house. Sometimes it was easier to go along with her father's wishes. But how was she going to explain her request for a last-minute examination to the anaesthetist? Dad always made things sound so easy. What would she do if news of her last minute request leaked out throughout the hospital? They'd think she was some kind of religious lunatic.

Blanche gripped the steering wheel, her face tight and pale.

"Don't worry, Mum. Dad is convinced God will heal me. Although, at this late stage, I'd almost feel like I'd wasted everyone's time."

"They're not going to go bankrupt if one person is healed." Her mother rolled her eyes. Was it a good sign that her mother could joke, or was she joking to prevent herself crying? It was almost impossible to know. Was she as disappointed, confused and full of doubts as Esther was herself?

Arriving at the hospital, they parked and prayed before they got out of the car. After check-in —more forms—they went up to the ward. How had Esther ended up the only person in a two-bed room? Perhaps her father knew the head of the hospital? That wasn't out of the question. He had wanted to pay for her to go to a private hospital, but Esther had insisted that she worked in the public system and wanted to be in a familiar environment. Maybe she'd drawn the prize because she was a hospital employee.

Two matching mechanised beds, two matching side cupboards, a double-sized built-in wardrobe and two functional chairs. Bleak. Her mother had brought a bunch of purple orchids which she put in a vase on the side table. Then she opened all the doors and drawers before going to stand by the window. What was her mother doing? Was she nervous, or merely worried about hygiene?

"Mum, you'd think it was you facing this surgery. You're making me nervous."

"Sorry. I can't seem to help it." She'd guessed correctly. Her mother was nervous but not talking about it. No surprise there.

"It's natural for you to be thinking about your mother, and what happened to her, but the situation isn't the same. Medicine has made great strides since those days." Her mother still stood with her arms clasped across her body. "Why don't you go and check out the cafeteria? If there are no miracles, you might spend more time there than you want to."

"Shh." Her mother held a finger up to her lips. "Don't even suggest such a thing."

"Do you think God won't heal me if we joke about doubt?"

Her mother's voice was hushed. "I don't know what to think. I'm trying to follow your father's instructions." She twirled a lock of hair around her finger. "I don't want to be blamed for failures."

Blame? Would Dad blame Mum if Esther wasn't healed? If so, there was something seriously wrong in her parents' marriage. Come to think of it, her mother was always careful not to offend Dad. Why? What was she frightened of? Esther was getting tired of tiptoeing around issues.

"You seem overly concerned about Dad's opinion. I don't want Nick to think I'll do everything he wants just because he wants it."

"Oh, I was Miss Independence once, too." Blanche waggled her head and mimicked a swagger. "Once. Before I was married. It didn't last long. Marriage isn't a breeze."

There was a long silence. What should she say? Was she shocked at her Mum's outburst, or embarrassed? Sure, she wanted to dig beneath the too-perfect surface of her mother's life and get to know her, but she didn't want to wound her along the way.

"I didn't mean to hurt you, Mum." Her mother gave a brief nod. An acceptance of her apology or for some other reason? There seemed to be invisible tension hanging in the air between them. Time to lighten the mood.

"Mum, why don't you go and check out the menu in this top-class establishment."

Mum seemed relieved to go off by herself. While she was away, the anaesthetist and nurses all came by. Esther was questioned and examined, checked, and labelled. The nurses left, leaving her alone with the anaesthetist. This was her chance.

"Have you ever seen a miracle happen?" she asked.

He pulled a face, as if she'd had an adverse drug reaction and was hallucinating purple-spotted pigs flying past the hospital windows.

She tried again. "I mean, have you ever seen someone healed so they don't need surgery?"

"You mean because of prayer or some other hocus pocus? Nope. Can't say I have."

Great. He was going to love it when she insisted on having someone redo the physical examination tomorrow.

All the preparations for her surgery were finished too early. How would she fill the evening? If she'd had a roommate, there would at least have been someone to talk to. However, her 7.45 p.m. visitors and the ensuing prayer meeting made her change her mind—it was better to be on her own. They were so loud, a nurse had to come in and ask them to tone things down.

The prayers had to work this time. Avoiding surgery and chemo were high on her list of priorities. The thought of losing a breast filled her with trepidation, however urgent the need.

After the visitors left, ancient television reruns failed to distract her from her rumbling stomach, empty from fasting. Esther wriggled all night and woke far too early. The wait for the hospital orderly to take her to theatre seemed interminable. At last she heard him. He swore softly as he ran the wheelchair into the door. Hospital protocol was strange. After all, judging by the steering skills he'd displayed as he'd entered her room, she could walk better than he steered.

Waiting in the room outside the operating theatre, she clasped her hands, and prayed.

Lord, please, please hear our prayers. Heal me. I want to get married next month. Don't let me doubt.

"Well, here we are. Ready to get on with it?"

Esther dropped her voice to as low a volume as she could. "I'm sorry, but I need to ask a favour." Goodness, she sounded like an idiot already. "This might make me sound like I belong in a lunatic asylum." She looked to check that the nurses were far enough away not to hear. "All my friends have been praying for a miracle. They want me to insist on having a final check, in case I no longer need surgery."

The doctor's eyes widened and he seemed to choke back something, probably a laugh. He too checked there was no one within hearing distance.

"I do think you're somewhat crazy but you're lucky. We're running ahead of schedule so I'm willing to humour you." Despite his scepticism, he examined her thoroughly.

Esther held her breath ... her gasp was the gasp of disappointment. Why hadn't God come through for her? What had she done wrong? And who would her father blame? She stuffed the questions down into the basement of her subconscious. The bitter taste accompanying her doubts was her last conscious memory.

---

*T*he next thing she knew, a light was shining in her eyes and a voice said, "Esther ... Esther can you open your eyes? The operation is over and you're in the recovery room."

"Go away, don't want to wake up." Was that her voice?

She went back to sleep and woke intermittently. Later, she felt her mother's presence. It was reassuring to have her hand held. But she had no energy to talk.

Nick turned up much later and leaned down to kiss her cheek.

"Brought you these."

Esther turned her head towards the extravagant bunch of flowers. "Thanks, sorry. Too sleepy… to talk."

Did he stick around? He certainly never held her hand. She'd have remembered that. As she slid back into the shoals of sleep, one question hovered in the murky waters of her mind.

Where was her father?

CHAPTER 14

*G*ummed-up eyes, cracked lips, scratchy throat, leathery tongue. Esther swallowed what felt like shards of glass and squinted. Pale pearl-grey light filtered through the venetian blinds. What time was it? Voices murmured somewhere outside her room.

Esther pointed her toes, wriggled each foot and jiggled each knee. Those parts of her worked. What about her arms? The right was fine. She moved her left elbow and stretched her fingers. No major pain, but she wasn't about to stretch too far. Gentle exploration revealed she had a catheter, an intravenous line, and some drainage tubes. She was tethered to the bed.

As long as Esther lay still, there was no physical pain from the surgery, but no drug on earth could dull the emotional pain. She was less of a woman than yesterday. How ridiculous. As though being a woman required certain parts, and without them she was sexless. It wasn't as if she'd lost an arm or a leg or something important, like her sight or hearing.

She could ridicule herself, but logic was powerless beside her feelings. Today she was ugly and depressed. As though she no longer had anything to offer. She shied away from the word 'mastectomy'. Would thinking the word make her surgery real? It was real, whatever she did. In the pearlescent dawn she whispered to herself, "mastectomy, mastectomy, mastectomy." It didn't make her feel better, but perhaps it made things a little more real.

She'd been sure God would come through for her. So many had prayed, and her father's confidence had smothered any doubts. During her obligatory appointment with the social worker she'd paid almost no attention to comments about post-surgery emotional trauma. Why should she pay attention to something she wouldn't need to know? Esther had gone under the anaesthetic so fast that she hadn't had time to scream her protest at God. Her father had promised God would heal her but God had failed. All her life she'd trusted blindly. Now she'd have to learn to wander in dense forest without a compass.

Using her right hand, Esther pushed up her pillows and wriggled higher in the bed. Now was not the time to dig too deep. Instead, she'd prepare for visitors. She must look a fright. Her scalp itched even though she'd washed her hair the night before she came in. She manoeuvred herself so she could stretch her right hand towards the bedside drawer. Fishing around inside, she found a brush and did her best to tidy her hair. There was no mirror to reveal the result. Probably a good thing.

Now that she was a little more comfortable, she was not only thirsty but ravenously hungry. When could she eat or drink? Would a shower be possible? She was sick of lying in bed. How long should she wait before it would be acceptable to call a nurse to help her get up?

Where was the television remote? Esther patted her bed and found it dangling by its long cord. The six o'clock breakfast show was halfway through. The inane chatter soothed her until the crumpled bed became too uncomfortable. She should ring the buzzer. Nurses were employed to look after patients.

The nurse strode into the room, and drew back the curtain around the bed.

"Good morning. What seems to be the problem?"

Esther winced. Was this hearty cheeriness a job requirement? "I feel revolting. What are the chances of being able to get up and have a hair wash?"

"I can set you up for a sponge wash and help you with your hair. It won't be comfortable, but the doctor will be pleased if you exercise your arms. Once you're up we can also whisk out the catheter."

The wash was as uncomfortable as predicted. However, it was worth it. The nurse helped her dress in a clean gown.

Once she was up and dressed, Esther couldn't bear to go back to bed. Could she manage to sit in the armchair for a few hours? Sitting made her feel a little woozy but she could lean her head back on the chair. How much longer until visitors arrived to distract her?

She peered at the flowers Nick had brought. Showy, but not her style. A hand-picked posy would have been better. She knew he'd visited yesterday, but he hadn't stayed long. Perhaps he was uncomfortable in hospitals. As a pastor, he'd better get used to it. Although, come to think of it, her father seldom did hospital visitation. He said it didn't look right for someone who believed in divine healing. Was that why she hadn't seen him yet?

Time passed. Minute by weary minute.

At last she heard footsteps and her mother's neat figure appeared. She beamed, obviously determined to cheer Esther up.

"How are you?" Her voice faded out. "Sorry, that was an automatic question. Not the best one for today."

Two tears trickled down Esther's cheek. She wiped the back of her hand across her eyes, not wanting to start the visit by crying. "Yes, not feeling too tip-top."

"Has the doctor said when you can go home?"

"The medical team haven't done their rounds yet. They'll let me know if it'll be Monday or later. It depends on how well the wound heals."

Esther pushed the wheeled table to the side so there was no barrier between them. "I've been looking forward to your visit. Otherwise I think too much and end up feeling sorry for myself. The room is great for undisturbed sleep, but there's no one to talk to."

"Your father was pleased you had your own room."

"Speaking of Dad, where is he?"

Her mother looked down at her hands folded in her lap. "Ahh—" Her mouth opened and closed a few times without any other sound coming out. "He's been especially busy these few days, preparing for the special radio interview he has coming up early next week."

Poor Mum, always attempting to be the middle person. "Mum, you don't need to cover for him. If he wanted to be here he would be." Esther rested her head on the back of the chair and looked up at the ceiling. "I guess I'm almost an embarrassment for him. All that prayer, yet I wasn't healed."

"Are you upset about not being healed?"

Esther blew out through her nose. "I'm trying not to think about it. I have enough to deal with. But I am a little bewildered." She moved her head upright again. "I'm sure we did everything right. Why didn't God do his bit?"

"I don't know. Do you think God might have other purposes?"

"Mum, I don't know. Let's talk about something cheerful."

"Noelene has—" Blanche stopped. "Margie and Rob —"

"Mum, you don't have to censor good news."

"But I don't want to talk about topics that might upset you."

"Thanks for your consideration." Esther laid her hand over her mother's. "But much as I'd like to, I can't live my life without hearing of babies and engagements. Did Noelene have a boy or girl?"

"A girl, seven and a half pounds."

"After four miscarriages, she must be over the moon." They continued casual conversation. The kind which fills the air but is neither satisfying nor encouraging. Blanche stayed until after lunch, then Esther asked for help to get back into bed. It was good to lie down. When would life be normal again? She had ten days to wait until the pathology reports were back. Ten days to wonder about the seriousness of her cancer. Although she was more likely to be worrying than wondering.

At three o'clock, she heard firm steps outside her room. Nick entered with a basket of fruit clutched in front of him like a shield. Perhaps it was the easiest way to carry the basket and she was imagining his need for a barrier. He perched on the edge of the chair, looking everywhere but at her face.

"Work has been busy..." His voice wound down as though he'd lost battery power. Was he unsure if this sounded like an excuse for not visiting, or a topic best avoided with someone who couldn't work at the moment? They'd always loved doing youth group together, and now she was missing out.

"Your dad has..." He stopped again. Now he seemed preoccupied with a spot on the wall. A dull flush stained his cheeks. These conversational false starts and long pauses had never happened before. Where was their ease with each other? Was this awkwardness to be their new normal? Potentially distressing topics lay like a minefield across their path and Nick didn't seem equipped to navigate them.

He kept looking away—was it embarrassment? What was *he* embarrassed about? She'd had surgery. She'd been maimed. A surge of anger coursed through her. She didn't think of herself as an angry person. Had she changed, or had anger been long-buried waiting for certain conditions before it spouted?

She clasped her hands together and closed her eyes to gain the time to calm herself. Maybe he'd think she'd drifted off. It was one way to avoid talking, although they were going to have to talk about the wedding sooner or later. It would have to be delayed, but if she mentioned the wedding today, she'd start yowling and not be able to stop. And that would be embarrassing. Nick admired her strength—what would he think if she collapsed? Was there anyone who could be normal around cancer patients?

"There's no need to come back tonight. I know you're busy with youth group."

"No one's expecting me to go tonight." His sense of duty was strong, so she'd have to try again.

"You'd be better being there than worrying if your co-leaders are managing without you. Besides, I'll likely be sleeping." The white lie rolled off her tongue.

Nick hung around a few minutes more. Then stood up, leaned over, and kissed her cheek before shooting out of her room. Esther's relief made her feel guilty.

The rest of the day passed far too slowly. Any time Esther started to think about her situation she stomped on the thought. She surfed through the four available TV channels far longer than they deserved. When the nurse turned up to teach her how to manage the wounds, she greeted her like a saviour. Anything to keep her mind focused on humdrum, everyday things.

*G*ina was the best of the weekend visitors. She breezed in on Saturday morning holding an African violet.

"I liked the white edgings on the purple petals." She placed it on the side table. "I brought my knitting—hope you don't mind."

What a relief to have someone talking to her like she was a human being and not someone with three heads and a tail.

"Not at all. Tell me about your week."

After catching up, Gina pulled a box out of her over-sized bag. "I remembered an old family favourite. Did you play Mastermind when you were a kid?"

"Only at friends' places but it was a long time ago and I'll be rusty." What did that matter? This was the first person who'd come up with a creative idea to distract her. "I'll give it a go."

Gina proved competitive and beat Esther three times in a row. By the end of Gina's visit, Esther was much more cheerful.

"Thank you so much for coming, this was better than wallowing in self-pity."

"Glad you enjoyed it. I'll come back tomorrow afternoon."

Esther grinned. "Bring Mastermind, and prepare to be beaten."

***

$\mathcal{N}$ick came again Saturday afternoon but was still ill at ease. They could manage mundane conversation but it was obvious he wasn't prepared to tackle any hard topics. If he wouldn't, or couldn't, then Esther would have to try. She sat up straight.

"Nick, it looks like we'll have to delay the wedding."

"I'm trying not to think about it." He tucked his feet under his chair.

"Me too, but we can't avoid it for long. Can you at least ask the printers not to print the invitations until after my appointment on the nineteenth?" They'd already notified everyone of the wedding date, so late invitations shouldn't be a problem.

"That's easy enough. They told me the actual printing only takes a day or two."

She'd made a mental 'to do' list while lying in bed last night. "I guess I'll have to call the bridesmaids." The bridesmaids' dresses were all finished, but as none of her bridesmaids were the kind to gain weight, they should be fine. And the fabric and style would suit almost any season. "I've already warned the caterers. I'll have to confirm in the next week."

Esther paused before asking the question most on her heart. "Have you seen Dad?"

"He's about." Nick didn't look at her. "Doing all his usual things."

"Except he hasn't been to see me."

"I'm sure he has his reasons." The phrase sounded prerecorded and it was becoming Nick's standard response to any criticism of her father. She understood the awkwardness of his position, trying to be loyal to his boss while responding to her, but it concerned her that his loyalty to her father seemed to triumph over his loyalty to her.

"I would have thought visiting his only daughter might be a priority." That came out sounding peeved. It was hardly Nick's fault.

"There's nothing I can do about it."

"I wasn't blaming you. I'm just disappointed—cut up, really. My father, who has time for everyone else, hasn't made time to visit his daughter. Why not?"

CHAPTER 15

*E*sther lay in the quiet darkness of her own bedroom the Thursday after her discharge from the hospital. Surgical pain wasn't an issue, but every night she struggled to sleep. Couldn't someone stab her with a syringe of something and send her into dreamland? Or knock her over the head and give her the gift of unconsciousness for a few weeks?

What if her cancer was serious? Had they caught it early enough? Her stomach ached even thinking about it. She clenched her fists. *Please, please help it to have been caught early enough.* She wasn't sure who she was pleading with, as she hadn't talked to God since her surgery. All those prayers beforehand hadn't made an iota of difference, so why keep praying?

What if the cancer meant that she couldn't have children? She'd checked up on that when she was first diagnosed. Medical research suggested it would still be possible, but getting pregnant might take longer than usual. Would Nick be prepared to take the risk? If the cancer was serious, should she free Nick from their engagement?

Esther threw off her blankets and stuck her leg out into the cold air. If only she could sleep and escape her thoughts. She still hadn't dared look at her wound. She didn't want to see the network of stitches across her chest and continuing under her arm. Young guys often wolf-whistled her in the street. They wouldn't give her a second glance now.

She'd seen plenty of scars when she worked on the surgical ward. For every patient with good results there was another that looked revolting. Most surgeons were men. Did they understand the impact of scars on women in a society which demanded Barbie doll-like perfection? What if she had to wear loose, frumpy clothing for months? She'd always been a water baby, so when would she be able to wear a swimsuit? What if Nick found her repulsive? He didn't seem to be able to bear to look at her so far.

Her stunning fitted wedding dress hung over a dressmaker's dummy in the sewing room. Her mother had laboured over every stitch. What if Nick changed his mind and cancelled the wedding rather than delaying it?

Stop it. Stop thinking like this. It doesn't help.

Rebuking herself didn't seem to work. The questions kept sliding into her mind in an endless stream. Bedtime was a mental battle—a battle she was losing, an endless war to escape her own imagination.

Her father's behaviour didn't help. He avoided her whenever possible. She would need to talk to him sooner or later.

They were all avoiders.

Her father and Nick used work as an excuse. Her mother busied herself cooking delicious meals that Esther choked down. And Esther avoided talking with Nick about the future. No one said anything beyond conventional mumblings. Meaningless. Comfortless. They were all skirting the big-C in the room. Cancer's towering presence overshadowed everything. Everyone waited for diagnosis day, looming like the ominous atmospheric pressure before a major storm. Meanwhile all of them busied themselves with endless nothings.

Why couldn't she talk to Nick?

*E*sther's first post-surgery appointment arrived all too soon. After a short wait, she was summoned into Dr Webster's office. He was seated behind his desk scanning a medical file, presumably hers. He looked up.

"Any ongoing problems from the surgery?"

"Some numbness and twinges from the wound." She rubbed her left upper arm. "Nothing unexpected. The drain came out at the usual time, and Mum changes the bandages every day." She was babbling. He didn't need to know all these details.

"Stand up please. Let's look at your shoulder movement." Esther pushed her chair back and put her shoulder automatically through its movements. Dr Webster grunted. "It's obvious you're a physio." He jotted some notes. "Most people don't have full range of movement until two months after the surgery. Keep doing whatever you've been doing." He shuffled the papers on his desk. "Now, I have your pathology report here."

Esther sat down, with her blank notebook ready. She could check the details later.

"I'll explain it line by line." He placed the tip of his pen on the page. "First, they found multiple cancers in a square of fifty millimetres."

She squeezed her pen. An awareness of impending disaster dawned.

"Some of the cancers were tiny but others were up to twelve millimetres long." He paused. What bad news was he delaying? What could be worse than what he'd already shared? "Seven out of twenty lymph nodes contained cancer."

Esther's stomach plummeted and bile rose in her throat. That was why he'd paused. This was worse than expected, much worse. The cancer had already spread out of its original area.

Medical knowledge could be a curse.

She clenched her fists in an attempt to keep control. She must not cry here. How strange to be reluctant to cry in front of strangers. Cancer specialists must be used to it.

Dr Webster looked over his glasses at her. "You would know that seven out of twenty lymph nodes is not good news."

Esther clicked the end of her pen as Dr Webster continued talking. Did he want to get this over as much as she did?

"There are some other technical measures. Do you want me to summarise or give you the full details?"

"Full details, please."

"The first of these is the mitotic rate which is how fast the cancer cells are dividing. The second is called the Ki-67 rate."

Esther's hand shook as she wrote the words in her notebook.

"Your mitotic rate is seventy-five and Ki-67 is seventy-two percent."

She recorded the numbers, having no idea what they meant.

"These numbers mean yours is a rapidly dividing tumour. Your tumour increased in size between your first tests and your surgery." He looked directly at her and thumped four fingertips together on his desk. "Your mastectomy was one hundred percent necessary."

Esther's pen scrawled across her paper.

"The lab also tested your cancer's response to various hormones. Yours is what is called 'triple negative'. It didn't respond to oestrogen, progesterone or HER2."

Esther kept writing.

"You can look up some of these specifics later," he said.

Esther took a deep breath. Her voice came out with only the tiniest of wobbles. "What does all this mean in terms of the four stages?"

Dr Webster squinted at her. Was he measuring her up to see if she could handle the information? "All these factors taken together gives you an overall stage III."

Esther gasped. Tears spilled down her cheeks. She rummaged in her bag for tissues to gain time to control herself. Dr Webster sat silent. Esther dabbed her cheeks with the tissue.

"—worse, much worse than I expected."

"It is a high stage—and a high threat—but treatment in Australia is first-rate. Triple negative does mean treatment will have to be more aggressive because the cancer is less responsive."

Esther blew her nose. "What are my chances?"

"It's much too early to tell, but I've seen plenty of stage III's live past five years."

Five years. Esther swallowed. Five years didn't seem much of a chance when you were twenty-eight. She needed to know more. Yet she dreaded knowing more. She fought a quick see-sawing battle between these contrasting desires. "If you were to give me a percentage, what chance would I have?"

"Ahh—" Even Dr Webster sounded conflicted. Was she right to put him on the spot?

"Reality, please." Her mother had wanted to come and support her. But Esther had declined the offer, and left Blanche reading in the car. If her mother had been here she'd have been inhibited about asking these questions. Being alone she could absorb things first, and soften the blows for others.

"Without treatment, your survival rate after ten years would only be about thirty-five percent. With treatment, it rises to about seventy percent."

Thank goodness Mum wasn't here. Stated positively it sounded bearable. Stated negatively, it meant that even with treatment there was a thirty percent chance she'd die within ten years. Esther clenched her teeth. She would not cry. If she started, she'd never stop. She'd drown in waves of self-pity and flounder in boggy swamps of fear. The only way to prevent crying was to keep asking questions and keep writing answers, as though the mechanics of writing blocked her tear ducts.

"When will treatment start and what will it involve?"

"My receptionist will find you a slot in the next two to three weeks. You'll receive what is known as F.A.C. chemotherapy, named for the initials of the three drugs. Each cycle will involve approximately one day of therapy, then twenty days' rest." Dr Webster waited as Esther wrote. "The cycle is repeated a maximum of six times. Sister O'Reilly, my specialist nurse, will tell you more about the whole process. On chemo days, you'll be here at least half a day."

"Will I see you each time?"

"Yes, unless I'm away for some reason. Let's see if Sister O'Reilly is ready." He pressed the buzzer on his desk. "She'll give you all the practical details and the brochures with the information you'll need."

*S*ister O'Reilly was straight-backed, starched and worth her weight in rubies. No wonder she merited the old-fashioned title of 'Sister'. Her red hair had faded, but her eyes held a twinkle in their grey-green depths. They'd obviously given the tough job to the right person. She was empathetic without being cloying, practical and efficient without being too clinical. Esther's tears trickled as the practical details were discussed. The news was sinking in.

"Why don't you pop into the private waiting room next door to compose yourself. Get a cup of something to drink and sit for a few minutes. Did you bring someone with you?"

"—Mum—in the car park."

"Do you remember where? I can send our volunteer to go and get her if you'd like."

"I'd prefer to get myself together first."

The waiting room was quiet. Too quiet. Only the ticking of a clock on the wall. It was a soothing, subconscious sound that soon became irritating. Wasn't that the issue? Here she was, twenty-eight, with stage III cancer. Her life was ticking away.

Tick—tock, tick—tock, tick—tock.

She wanted to get up out of her chair and throw the clock across the room. The perpetual ticking became 'why —me, why —me, why —me?' Esther slammed her hand down on the arm of the chair. The pain felt good. A choked whisper erupted.

"Why God? Why have you allowed this? Why haven't you healed me as you've promised?"

"Do you think God promised to heal everyone?"

Esther whirled around. In her self-absorbed state, she hadn't noticed that a middle-aged Asian lady, in a cleaner's uniform, had entered the room and was wiping the coffee stains on the counter.

"What did you say?"

"Excuse me for startling you. I asked, 'Do you think God has promised to heal everyone?'"

Who did this woman think she was? Surely she shouldn't be bothering patients? Maybe if Esther answered her, she'd shut up. "He'll heal those who ask with faith."

"Hmm ... was everyone in the Bible healed?"

It looked like answering had been the wrong policy. "Jesus healed everyone who asked."

The cleaner rinsed her cloth under the tap. "Are you sure Jesus works whenever we ask and in the way we want?"

The woman's persistence was irritating. What would it take to shut her up? Esther repeated her statement more belligerently. "He heals if we have faith."

The cleaner seemed impervious to Esther's tone, or perhaps she was ignoring it. "Jesus had the power to raise the dead, didn't he?"

"Of course." What had this question got to do with anything?

"Then why did he only raise three people?"

Esther had never thought about it. Why should she have to? She blurted out the first thing that came into her head. "Maybe only three families had faith enough to ask."

"Are you sure they asked?" Could she not put this woman on mute? She was unstoppable. "Jairus asked Jesus to heal his daughter, but not to raise her from the dead. The widow is not recorded as asking anything, and Mary and Martha were upset at Jesus for not coming earlier. None of them asked Jesus to raise the dead. They knew it was impossible."

Esther had had enough. Didn't the woman have any sensitivity? She would have thought her red eyes were warning enough that she wanted to be left alone. All her mother's etiquette training deserted her. "I'm not in the mood to talk about theology. Shouldn't you be cleaning or something?"

The corners of the woman's mouth curved upwards. "Yes, probably. But I never could resist answering when someone asks a good question. I'll be praying for you."

This pious platitude was the final straw. Esther didn't want this woman's prayers. Esther glared at her and grabbed her notebook and bag. Then she swept out the door on a swell of indignation. How dare a mere cleaner challenge her, Esther Macdonald, only daughter of Reverend Doctor William B Macdonald, theologian.

CHAPTER 16

*E*sther dialled the phone number. It was picked up on the fifth ring.

"Is that Liz? This is Esther."

They spoke for a minute before Esther could get down to business. This week was the worst of her life so far. Two hours ago, she'd had a tear-filled conversation with Nick about postponing the wedding. The subsequent conversation with her parents hadn't been any easier. Her mother took pity on her and said she'd ring the caterer and the florist, but Esther had to ring the bridesmaids. Liz was the first call. The call she thought would be the easiest.

"Thank you for your concerns about my health but that's not what I'm ringing you about. The cancer is more serious than expected." Esther gripped the phone. "I'm sorry, but we're going to have to delay the wedding … No, we don't know when the new date will be."

Saying the lines once was bad enough but she was going to have to say these things over and over, like a Victorian-era bell tolling bad news. Liz was obviously bursting with questions but Esther wasn't going to oblige her curiosity. She'd have to wait. Her father's insistence on five bridesmaids meant there were still four more calls to make. If she didn't stick to her prepared script, she wouldn't make it through all the calls.

During the day, Esther made all her calls. Each call made her more depressed. The more depressed she became, the more she shut down her emotions, and the more she gave up on communicating with Nick. She was alone in a rudderless boat in thick fog, going around and around in endless circles. For someone who'd always been organised and goal oriented it was a new and bewildering experience. She was barely eating or sleeping.

Everything was exacerbated by having too much time on her hands. Her doctors had told her not to return to work until after her first round of chemotherapy. And her parents and Nick were absorbed with their own lives and couldn't be expected to sit around and keep her company.

Home was too quiet. No matter how hard she tried, Esther couldn't settle down. She often sat with a book open on her lap, staring at nothing. Unable to concentrate, yet unable to rest.

She heard the cleaner's words in her head, over and over, like a record needle stuck in a groove.

Do you think God promised to heal everyone?

Do you think God promised to heal everyone?

Doubts whirled like grey flurries of volcanic ash. Why couldn't she scrub that cleaner out of her mind? How dare she comment so confidently on the Bible, as though she knew more than Esther's father.

Esther flicked on the television but ended up idly switching programmes on the remote. Why did anyone bother with daytime viewing?

There was only one way to deal with the cleaner. She would have to prove her wrong. Esther scrambled up from the reclining chair to find her Bible. It wouldn't take long.

After she had returned to the recliner, Esther turned first to the story most familiar to her, Jairus' daughter—one of her father's favourite stories. She skimmed the story once, and read it again from the beginning. She snorted in disbelief. The cleaner was right. Once Jairus knew his daughter was dead, did he believe, like his servants, that it was too late to bother Jesus?

She reread the story to check, not willing to admit she'd been wrong, then leaned back on the headrest to ponder what she'd read. What had Jairus thought when Jesus still insisted on going to his house? Did he think Jesus was coming to mourn with them?

Did he question Jesus' sanity when he'd said, 'Your daughter is only asleep?' What had they felt when Jesus took the girl by the hand and raised her up? Amazement? Awe? Joy? Or fear? For who *was* this man who could raise the dead?

Round one to the cleaner.

But it didn't mean she was right with the other two cases. It took Esther longer to flick through the pages of her Bible and find the story of the widow of Nain and her son. The account in Luke 7 was so brief, she almost missed it. It took her only half a minute to read before she growled in annoyance.

The cleaner was right again. There was no mention of the widow requesting anything. She might not even have noticed Jesus, as she followed her only son's corpse towards the graveyard. Jesus approached her, not the other way round.

Cleaner two, Esther zero.

But would the cleaner be right a third time? Lazarus' story was a longer account. Perhaps among the details she could find the proof she sought. Lazarus' family must have known Jesus had twice raised the dead. They knew Jesus well and were the most likely to urge him to bring their brother back from the dead.

Esther read John chapter 11. She was unfamiliar with most of the story. Had her father ever preached on the whole chapter? She'd forgotten Jesus had ignored the sisters' urgent request for his pres-ence, and had delayed returning by several days. She'd also forgotten how strongly Mary and Martha expressed their disappointment in Jesus' failure to arrive in time.

Sure, they knew Jesus had the power to heal anything and anyone, but Lazarus had already been buried for four days. His body would have started to decompose. This miracle would require a restoration of more than life.

Esther punched the soft arm of the recliner. She'd lost the argument. Last and final round to the cleaner.

Three separate stories. Three times, and no mention of anyone requesting Jesus to raise the dead. Three times, and no mention of people having faith. The cleaner had been one hundred percent correct. How infuriating.

Two major questions remained. Why did Jesus raise these three? And if he had the power to raise the dead, why did he only use that power three times?

Esther didn't have the answers but did she want to keep researching? She wasn't stupid—she could see where this questioning could lead. Was she prepared to question her father, to question what Victory Church had taught her? Could she deal with the consequences of such a quest? She remembered only too well what had happened the few times she'd disagreed with her father in the past. If Esther began this journey, who else would it hurt? Her mother was loyal to her husband. The last thing she wanted was to put her mother in a difficult position.

Esther closed the Bible with a snap and went to make a sandwich. Now wasn't the time to think about such things. She had more than enough to deal with already.

But when would be a good time? Could she live with what she'd found out and not seek further?

Yes, she must. To do anything else would only lead to trouble, big trouble.

That night, Esther tossed and turned. Turned and tossed. Post-surgical discomfort compounded by troubling thoughts. The next night was no better.

"*Y*ou're looking haggard," her father said at breakfast the next morning. "Are you okay?"

Esther mumbled excuses, not willing to share the real cause of her lack of sleep. It was less to do with cancer than with the fight going on in her heart. Her gut was twisted in knots. She forced herself to eat for Mum's peace of mind, but retreated to her room as soon as possible.

On the third night, Esther did something she'd never done before. She took one of the sleeping supplements she found in the medicine cupboard. Maybe it was out of date, because it failed to work and she lay, almost crying, from sheer exhaustion. One thought came into her mind with crystal clarity.

Jonah tried running away but look at the mess that landed him in—a three-day cruise inside the belly of a fish.

She rolled over and switched on the bedside lamp. The fastest way to get to sleep was to get this off her mind. She'd start at Matthew and read the New Testament right through. Here she was, a pastor's daughter, yet she'd never read the Bible through from beginning to end. Usually she flipped backwards and forwards, or looked at favourite passages. Did she read any other book this way?

The surprises commenced right away. The first few chapters of Matthew were a vast contrast to the values at Victory Church. The stories were so understated. There were only a few foreigners there to honour the birth of Jesus. Even the priests who ought to have been waiting for the birth of the Saviour couldn't be bothered to walk a dozen kilometres to check out the story of the miraculous star.

The miracles were no better. So unsensationalised. Most of the time, when Jesus healed people, he commanded them not to tell others what had happened. These stories would annoy the *Hour of Victory*. Victory Church specialised in blowing trumpets so people would be left in no doubt when miracles occurred.

Esther kept reading. Two o'clock passed. Three o'clock. Four o'clock. Tiredness went disregarded. Absorbed in her task, she read all through Matthew, taking notes as she went. She finished as the first pale light of dawn glimmered around the edges of her window blinds. Esther got out of bed, switched on her lamp and rummaged around in her desk until she found a piece of paper. Then she wrote a note and attached it to the outside of her door.

MUM, ANOTHER SLEEPLESS NIGHT BUT I'M GOING TO TRY TO SLEEP NOW. PLEASE WAKE ME FOR LUNCH.

CHAPTER 17

A gentle tapping on the door woke Esther. The bedside clock said twelve fifteen. "Mum, I'm awake. Have I got time for a shower?"

"No rush. I'll have soup ready when you come down."

The shower and a change of clothes refreshed her. Despite being sleep-deprived, her reading project had been the right thing to do. She went downstairs to the kitchen.

"I was beginning to worry about you but you look like you've had some sleep."

"Not until nearly dawn, but I've had a good sleep since then." Esther took the soup bowl from her mother and sat next to her at the kitchen bench.

"What were you doing until dawn?"

"I couldn't sleep. So I gave up and started reading."

The corners of her mother's mouth twitched. "You used to get absorbed in a book all your teenage years. Dragging you back to real life was nearly impossible." Esther didn't want to go down reminiscence alley. She took a mouthful of her soup before speaking.

"Mum, do you ever read the Bible a whole book at a time?"

There was a tiny hesitation. "I just follow the notes we're given."

"That's all I've ever done too, but I'm always vaguely disappointed."

"What do you mean, disappointed?" Her mother started fiddling with the salt shaker. Was this to be one of those false start conversations her mother would close down before it started?

"I mean empty, and sort of dissatisfied."

"Hmm."

Esther was familiar with these *hmms*. They indicated discomfort. A mass of topics in this family generated hmms. Like her mother feared to go further. What was she afraid of?

Esther didn't linger over lunch. She wanted to get back to her reading. At least today she had the energy to clear up after herself. In recent weeks, her mother had been doing far more than her fair share of household tasks.

By the time her father came home, Esther had finished reading Mark and Luke. It was like walking into an unexplored valley for the first time. The preaching she'd heard suggested people were only healed if they asked 'with faith'. Her father frequently referred to the leper in Luke 17 who was told that his faith had made him well.

It wasn't as simple as Dad had implied. Ten lepers were healed, but only one had been told, 'your faith has made you well.' The other nine were healed whatever their state of faith.

Esther leaned back. What did it mean? Could it mean that one lepers' healing was deeper than the others? Nine received physical healing but nothing more. One, a Samaritan, received emotional and spiritual healing as well.

Dinner was rushed as usual, because her father had evening meetings. Nick was the same. Esther had learned early on that she had to share him. This week she was glad to have the time to herself. Her reading was urgent. A voyage she was impelled to take.

Before bed, she read all of John's gospel. There were new discoveries on every page. The Jesus portrayed in scripture was almost unrecognisable as the Jesus proclaimed week after week at Victory. She'd never heard anyone preach on Jesus washing the disciples' feet. It wasn't hard to see why. The Christians she knew wouldn't want to humbly follow Jesus to the point of sacrificing their own lives.

Imagine if Victory Church was renamed the Humble Service Church. She repeated the name out loud and giggled. It sounded odd. None of the leaders she knew were like this. Again, she was tempted to quit reading. It was like being on splintering ice where cracks opened in front of her feet. She'd inevitably fall in.

What a choice—peace of heart or family harmony.

Why did it have to be a choice? Why couldn't she have both?

Jesus' words later in John rattled her.

'If you belonged to the world it would love you as its own ... the world hates you ... If they persecuted me they will persecute you also.'

If persecution was not only the norm for disciples, but the proof someone was a disciple, why wasn't this her own experience? She closed her eyes to concentrate. Could it be Satan didn't perceive her as a threat? Could it be she wasn't a disciple at all? Had she ever chosen to follow Jesus on the steep, narrow path?

Wasn't there some story about Peter being strongly rebuked by Jesus? Esther opened her eyes. It took her a minute to find the passage at the end of Matthew 16. Jesus had said to Peter, 'Get behind me, Satan. You are a stumbling block to me.' Why? Because, 'you do not have in mind the things of God, but the things of men.'

Why had Jesus said such a thing? She looked for clues in the verses preceding the rebuke. There it was. Peter had rebuked Jesus first by telling him he'd got everything wrong. He was the Saviour of the world. Saviours should be conquerors, and not end up crucified.

Wow, Peter wasn't shy about sharing his opinion. What had he expected of Jesus? Had he hoped Jesus would usher in a new kingdom on earth? That Israel would take over from Rome as a mighty empire? How many of the disciples had wanted to reap the benefits of being Jesus' friends? Did they have grandiose dreams of being prime minister or cabinet leaders? Jesus' death must have shattered all their dreams. They hoped for a triumphant Saviour, but all they saw was a dead failure.

Today, it was like having new eyes. The call to follow Jesus was a daily call to die to self, to pick up the cross and follow him.

Why hadn't she known this? How was she any different to Peter? She was happy to follow a triumphant Jesus who would make life smooth. Happy to follow a miracle worker who blessed her on her terms. But was she willing to follow a crucified Saviour? To walk the narrow road of persecution? Persecution that might start within her own family.

Her clock said eleven.

Past her bedtime.

But first she had to respond to what she'd read. Esther had two clear choices. One would make her life inwardly miserable. The other might cost more than she wanted to give.

Her head and heart tugged her in opposite directions. Her heart was all for maintaining the status quo, for having short-term comfort, but her head urged her to see the implications. She was no longer willing to wander in the wilderness. It was more than time to change.

It seemed appropriate to get out of bed, kneel, and murmur her prayer out loud.

"Lord Jesus." Her tongue felt like a slab of wood but perhaps it would get easier. "I barely know where to start." Surely she should start with a string of sorrys—she had more than enough of those. "Sorry." The word itself stuck in her throat but this was a prayer she must pray. A battle she must win.

"Sorry for believing a lie. Sorry for reducing you, the Creator of the Universe, to a benevolent daddy who patted my head. Sorry for only wanting a heavenly wish-granter and only thanking you when life was good."

She choked as she saw the enormity of her self-absorption. How dare she, a mere human being, treat the King over all kings in such a way? She rested her forehead on the bed. A gloom descended. There seemed to be a scornful voice in her head urging her to take a break from this excessive introspection. What she needed was a good long sleep. Esther nearly gave in. She ached all over and lethargy was making her limbs heavy and her thoughts sluggish. She stopped praying and sank into a half-trance.

Suddenly a thought hit her like a sunbeam piercing a black cloud.

Pray!

Esther jerked awake as though summoned by a trumpet blast in battle. This was no time to stop praying. This was the single most important minute of her life. She was a soldier at war.

"So many things to say sorry for. You haven't heard any word of thanks from me since I was diagnosed with cancer. Oh Lord, I'm so sorry I never bothered to read your word properly. I do want to walk your way—I know it won't be easy, but I want to follow you wherever you lead. Help me to have the courage to take up my cross one day at a time." She shifted on knees that weren't used to kneeling. "And Jesus, thank you for the cleaner's courage. Help me to find her again."

Drained and limp, she rested her head on her bed. Slowly, a trickle of joy seeped into her weary heart. Somehow, she knew her prayer had been heard. New life had come.

Esther collapsed into bed and slept for twelve solid hours. Only her mother was home when she descended the stairs. As they prepared lunch, her mother gazed at her a few times, her forehead furrowed. *How little people truly know each other. She has no idea what has happened to me.*

"There's something different about you," her mother said as they stacked the dishwasher after lunch. "You've been distracted for days, but now you seem calmer."

It would have been better to have a few more days to process what had happened to her. She couldn't blame her mother for asking, yet at the same time she didn't want to stir up trouble because of lack of tact.

"Yes, I am more at peace." She paused. "Reading the Bible has been a huge help."

Her mother tilted her head to one side. "How has it helped?"

Esther's old anxiety was back. A pain in the stomach and nausea every time she confronted conflict that could lead to rejection.

She didn't want to fob her mother off and she didn't want to lie. If only she'd had more time to prepare. Any answers now were sure to come out all garbled, because everything was so new to her. Perhaps she could explain a little of her journey. Not the incident with the cleaner—her mother wouldn't be impressed at the way Esther had treated the woman, or how the cleaner's words sounded like criticism of Victory Church. And any criticism of Victory was criticism of its pastor.

"I'd never read such big chunks of the Bible, and now a whole lot of things make sense. What I'm trying to say—" She still wasn't saying it. "Sorry, I can't seem to express it but I think …. I think I became a Christian last night."

Her mother stopped washing up one of the pans with the brush frozen in mid-air. "What do you mean? You've always been a Christian."

How could she explain this in a helpful way? "I thought so too. But this week I discovered the Jesus I thought I knew isn't the Jesus of the Bible."

Little furrows appeared between her mother's eyes. "I don't understand what you're saying. There is only one Jesus, not two."

Lord, help. I don't know what to say.

"Sorry, I'm being so confusing but it's all a bit foreign to me too." Last night's experience had been wonderful, but it was hard to explain to someone who hadn't gone through the journey with her. "You're right. There aren't two versions of Jesus, but the one I believed in was wrong. What I mean is I believed in a sort of divine Santa Claus but Jesus isn't like that at all."

Her mother stood still and silent. Listening had always been a strength of hers, which was a good thing in a household like theirs.

"I was totally self-centred. Last night I worked out I had everything backwards. Jesus is supposed to be the centre, not me." Now that she'd finally said something that made sense, at least to herself, the joy of the previous night returned. A joy that made her want to jump on the top of the table, to sing or dance or yell from mountain tops, but she knew she mustn't shock or overwhelm her mother.

Her mother wiped her hands on a tea towel. What was she thinking? Did her own mother think she was nuts? She hoped not, or life would indeed be tough.

Her mother peered at her as though gazing at a stranger. "I don't really understand what you're trying to say but I'm glad you're at peace." She half raised a finger towards her lips and then stopped herself. "Please do keep quiet about this in front of your fiancé and your father."

There were times Esther wanted to scream in frustration. Why must she always keep quiet? Her family had so many taboos about what they could and couldn't talk about. Why must no one ripple the surface of the water of her father's life?

What lurked beneath the surface that must not be disturbed?

CHAPTER 18

The receptionist at the chemotherapy unit wore a multi-coloured blouse with a name tag—Michelle.

"Good morning Esther. I believe this is your first time," Michelle said. "Have you read the pamphlets you were given?"

"Yes, thank you." How would she get through today? There was sure to be lots of hanging around. The last thing she wanted to do was dwell on the fact that she should have been getting married nine days from now. "What do I do now?"

"This first time a volunteer will take you around to familiarise you with the set up. Next time, you'll come here first and register for the day, then take yourself to wait at the blood clinic." Michelle gestured towards those sitting around. "As you can see, there's plenty of waiting so I suggest you bring your own reading or something to occupy yourself. We're efficient but it takes time to get blood test results."

Michelle looked down again at the pile of files in front of her. Esther cleared her throat to gain attention. "As there's no one else here, can I ask a few more questions?"

"Of course."

"Will you be here each time?"

"Yes, unless I'm sick or taking time off."

"Then I'd like to introduce myself properly." Esther held her hand out, somewhat awkwardly because of the height of the reception desk.

"Oh, good," Michelle said as they shook hands. "You're one of those."

"One of what?"

"One of those who make an effort." Michelle lowered her voice. "Some clients come and go without any interaction. Perhaps it's their way of dealing with things." Her voice returned to normal volume. "I find it easier when people make an effort."

Esther looked from side to side to check she wasn't being over-heard. "My other question might seem odd. Last time I was here, I met a cleaner who I'd like to talk to again. She was Asian, about mid-fifties." Michelle's eyebrows rose. "She said something helpful, and I'd like to thank her."

"That must be Joy Wong. I can't think of anyone else who fits the description."

"Is there any way I can contact her?"

Michelle scratched her ear. "I could call her on her pager while you're waiting for your blood results. Then she can talk to you if she wants."

"Great. Thanks."

"If you'll take a seat, I'll send a volunteer to show you round." Michelle pointed to the right.

Esther looked for a seat from where she could watch the room. These seats were more comfortable than the usual hard plastic chairs that usually filled waiting rooms. Indoor plants in bright pots were scattered around. She sat down and watched the people coming and going. It looked chaotic but it was obviously a stream-lined system. A sign pointed to the pathology area and many people came back from that direction and took a seat in the waiting room.

Nurses popped out of doors and announced numbers. Those people must have been going to the chemotherapy treatment area, as they didn't reappear.

Esther spotted Michelle's two types of clients. Some were minding their own business. Others interacted with those around them. The man closest to her raised his eyebrows.

"New today, are you?"

Esther laughed. "I was hoping my newness wasn't obvious."

"You don't look as nervous as some," he said. "Mind you, we're all nervous at first, because we don't know what we're facing. You'll get used to it. It's my fourth round and I'm an old hand."

"I'm surprised to see men here. I was expecting only women."

"This is a centre for all varieties of cancer. I'm here for bowel cancer. My name's Rob Boyle." He stretched out his hand and Esther shook it.

"Rob Boyle, Robert Boyle ... quite a name you've got there. Were your parents into science or something?"

"As you'd expect, they were both chemists." He grinned. "It could have been worse. I could have been named Isaac Newton. That reference would be harder to miss. Are you into science?"

"Sort of. Applied science. Physio—my name's Esther. And you, are you into science?"

"Guilty as charged. I teach physics and chemistry at the local high school."

It was good to discover someone friendly on her first day. She had so many questions queuing for attention.

"Do you mind if I ask, are you managing to work full-time while you do your chemo?"

"I usually need to have the second or third day after the chemo off, but haven't missed other times."

"I've already been off work for six weeks since my surgery. I was planning to go back to work half days next week and then full-time the week after. The half days were my boss's suggestion."

"Sounds like you have a good boss. Here comes your volunteer to take you for blood tests."

"Maybe see you again another time." Esther stood as a woman in her sixties approached.

"Esther? Good morning, I'm Lilian. First, I'll take you to the clinic where you'll be weighed and they'll do your baseline blood test." Esther picked up her bag, book, and water bottle, and trotted alongside her guide. As they walked, Lilian talked and talked and talked, instructions streaming out in well-practiced patter until they arrived in a new area.

"You register at the counter first, and they'll give you a number which they'll call when it's your turn." The room was already three-quarters full. "As there's a bit of a traffic jam today, line up there and you should be able to have your weight done while you wait for your blood tests."

Lilian sat in the waiting room while Esther was weighed. The half-hour wait for blood tests gave Lilian time to show Esther numerous photos of her fifteen grandchildren. Esther hadn't wanted to rebuff her oh-so-kind gregariousness, but would she ever have time to read her book? At last, Lilian went off to escort others.

After the blood tests, it was back to the main waiting room to await her summons to chemo. Before sitting down, she went up to the reception desk and asked Michelle to page Joy Wong. Joy obviously consented to talk to her, for Michelle handed over the phone.

Esther stepped to one side. No point broadcasting her business to everyone. "Hello, Joy. My name is Esther." Did she sound like a weirdo? The worst that could happen would be that Joy refused to meet her. "I don't know if you'll remember me, but you spoke to me a few weeks ago when I was crying in Dr Webster's waiting room."

"Yes, I remember you," Joy said.

Well that made things easier.

"I wanted to ask you a favour but it might be too much to ask.

I'm here for my first round of chemotherapy and I wondered if you would have time to meet up with me during your lunchtime?"

Joy hesitated. "Would you still be in the chemotherapy treatment area? Can you check if I can visit you there after your treatment?"

"Hold on a minute, I'll ask." Esther checked with Michelle.

Another minute and the details were worked out. Esther handed the phone back to Michelle and went to wait in the corner with a large fern and views of the whole room.

---

*E*sther sat next to Sister O'Reilly with her arm supported by a small table. While Sister O'Reilly talked, she swabbed Esther's right arm, and inserted the cannula which would be used to deliver the chemo drugs. Esther felt only the tiniest sting.

Then Sister O'Reilly reeled off the possible side effects of the upcoming treatment. There was no time to be nervous.

"I mustn't forget this one," Sister O'Reilly chuckled. "One of the drugs dyes your urine red. We've had some panic-stricken calls from people about that." She pressed a buzzer and a nurse came through the back door of the office to collect Esther.

The nurses's station was surrounded by recliner chairs. People lay back as though they were in their own homes.

Esther sweated as the drug line was connected to her cannula. This was it, the treatment she had dreaded. In the end, there was nothing to brace herself for. Nothing dramatic, only a mild coldness as the drugs entered her arm, and later some small hot flushes. She read her book and occasionally looked up to nod towards others. She wanted some sort of connection with those in the room. There was no need for, and nothing desirable about, self-imposed isolation.

As she'd been promised, there were free drinks and sandwiches. Even wholemeal bread. Next time she'd bring her own fruit.

A few minutes after midday, the nurse came over. "You've got a visitor."

The lady she remembered, and now knew as Joy, entered and smiled as though not yet sure of her welcome. Considering how rude Esther had been at their last meeting, it wouldn't have been strange if Joy had come armed with pepper spray.

Esther smiled to try and make Joy feel at ease. It must have worked, because Joy smiled back.

"Yes, you are the person I was thinking of. I've been praying for you."

Thank goodness Joy didn't seem to hold a grudge against her. "If you've been praying it might explain a lot of what has happened. Have you got time for me to tell you about it?"

Joy found an extra chair, checked it was available, and moved it next to Esther. She settled herself and leaned over to pull a plastic lunch box out of her bag. "My lunchtime is only forty minutes, so I'll have to eat as I listen."

"No problem. Before we go any further, I want to say sorry. The last time we met, I was angry and rude."

Joy looked up and smiled the kind of smile that showed she had heard, but was also waiting for anything more Esther might say.

"Your questions made me angry. I'm a pastor's daughter and it hurt my pride to be challenged on biblical things." Esther swallowed. Apologies were never easy. "But I couldn't forget what you said. You were right. I am biblically illiterate."

"Thank you for your apology. I'm relieved. After we met, I went home expecting to be fired." Joy laid the lunch box aside, and shook her head. "We Chinese aren't usually so direct. It was almost as if the words I spoke that day just came out of my mouth."

Esther dropped the footrest on the recliner so she was more upright. "Maybe they did. I can be pig-headed on some issues. I needed a direct rebuke, or I would have ignored what God wanted to say to me. Since I finally opened the Bible for myself I've been reading it non-stop. It's like entering a new world."

Joy opened her container of food, and Esther shared her story. As she did she remembered the jumble of emotions since they'd last met. The confusion, the anger, the tears and finally the joy that permeated her heart when she had at last surrendered to Jesus. Joy seemed to welcome the whole story, tears and all.

"Thank you so much for sharing with me."

Esther twitched her nose. "I was afraid it was way too much detail."

"Oh no, it's encouraging. I seldom know if my prayers are answered. Could I pray for you right here?"

Esther glanced to the side. Had anyone overheard them? How strange to be apprehensive. She called herself a Christian, but had she ever prayed with someone in a public place? Now seemed as good a time as any to start a new habit.

She kept her eyes open to make what they were doing less obvious but Joy had no such inhibitions. She bowed her head.

"Dearest heavenly Father. Thank you for my new sister, Esther. I pray you will help her cope with the side effects of her treatment, but most of all keep her reading and thinking about your word. Give her great joy in following you and bless others through her. We pray especially for wisdom within her family context. In the name of Jesus, amen."

Joy opened her eyes and Esther beamed at her. She leaned over and shook Joy's hand.

"Thank you. I know you barely know me, but I'll be back here in three weeks. Could we meet again?" She hesitated, afraid to seem a pest. "I'd love to hear your favourite part of the Bible."

Joy dusted down her uniform. "It will be hard to choose a favourite. I have so many. But it would be my pleasure to share something." She placed her now-empty container back in her bag and withdrew a piece of paper and a pen. "Let me give you my pager and my home phone number. If you let me know the day before you come in, I'll come and have lunch with you."

"I'll look forward to it."

After Joy left, Esther checked the bag of chemo chemicals. It was nearly empty. She reclined her chair again and closed her eyes to snatch a few minutes of rest before she had to head home. Her heart was full. This was what she'd been missing. Someone to share with about things that mattered. She'd hoped Nick would be one such person, but her journey seemed to frighten him.

She must pray for him more. Perhaps she could start praying with Gina, then approach Nick about the idea later. Bible study and prayer had never been a part of their relationship. They would have thought it was mixing work in with their personal time.

Esther managed the walk to the train station. Her mother would have come to pick her up, but Esther wanted to remain independent and appreciated the chance to be out in the fresh air. The brochures encouraged chemo patients to keep exercising. She hoped to get back to cycling to work.

If only her home situation was going to be as easy as the first day of chemo. It was time to confront her fears and tackle Nick.

CHAPTER 19

*T*he day after chemotherapy, Esther felt fine. Maybe chemo wasn't going to be as bad as everyone said. But the second morning, she could barely lift her head. Someone had poured concrete over her during the night. A shower helped, but thank goodness she didn't need to start work until Monday. She should be able to function by then. Meanwhile, she'd have to pace herself.

She snoozed for several hours, then took her Bible and note-book out into the garden. Yesterday she'd read the beginning of Genesis. She jotted down things she noticed about people and God, then chewed over the applications to her life. The second and third chapters of Genesis were so full of treasures she spent two hours on them. Mining deep.

The gate clicked—Nick had arrived. Being a youth worker, his afternoons were freer than evenings and weekends.

"Nick," Esther yelled. "I'm in the garden. Mum has left fruit and drinks just inside the back door."

Nick arrived, carrying the tray. He fiddled around, serving them both drinks, then sat down.

"What have you been doing this week?" That should be a question even Nick could answer.

"You know the youth group boy who keeps saying funny things? This week he said, 'Unleavened bread. Isn't that the bread made without any ingredients'?" Nick chuckled. "I couldn't stop myself laughing when half of the group were already rolling around on the floor."

Esther spent ten minutes trying one conversation lead, then another. Nick was talking, but not saying anything much. What wasn't he telling her? If it was good news, she wanted to hear it as soon as possible. It was more than time for good news.

"Have you got any encouraging news?"

Nick licked his lips. "I haven't known when to tell you. My news somehow seemed inappropriate."

"Inappropriate because it's good news, or bad news?"

"Oh, it's good. At least it is in one sense, but I'm not sure if you'll think so."

She had an inkling what it might be. "Come on, tell me. It's always worse not knowing."

"I had a phone call last week." He hesitated. "I've won the scholarship to go to Melbourne."

Yes, she could see why Nick had been unsure of how she'd respond. She wasn't sure what she felt herself. Numb?

"That's great news for you, and for Dad. You must accept or you might miss your chance." She summoned a smile. She couldn't cry —that would seem like self-pity.

"I can come home every second weekend. We have to do weekly preaching, but they're happy for half the sermons to be in our home church. Your Dad said Victory will pay the airfares."

Of course. Victory would want to have Nick back as often as possible to gain the maximum benefit from his training.

They were barely going to see each other over the next six months. Her emotional thermometer must truly be out of whack, because she felt relieved. Dealing with Nick's lack of reactions to her cancer had been an additional burden. Talking had been nothing but hard work. Maybe distance would help them. Phoning and writing might help Nick express his heart better.

Esther gave a tight smile. "The timing isn't great but I won't be alone. Mum is proving a great support."

Nick leaned back and stretched out his legs in front of him. At least one of them was relaxed. Esther was tempted to let things slide, to distance herself from the emotional rollercoaster that was Nick. But cancer had shown her that avoidance made issues even more difficult to deal with.

She prayed, then used the easiest lead-in she could think of. "What are you finding challenging right now?"

"One of the youth group kids has parents going through a rough patch. He's acting up and has needed extra time."

Was that it? No mention of her cancer. Nick wasn't an idiot. Why wasn't he helping her out?

It was more than time to quit tiptoeing and dig straight through the maze hedge. Otherwise she may as well end their relationship now. She took a deep breath.

"Nick, you've been uncomfortable ever since you found out about my cancer. What's worrying you?"

"I'm not sure I can explain." He shuffled his feet.

This was a conversational maze with far too many dead ends. She clamped her hand under her leg so she wouldn't start tapping her finger in frustration. Getting angry was unlikely to help.

"Can you try?" Esther said. "Why don't you just speak out loud and see what comes out." Did every conversation have to be such hard work? Stop, start, stop, start. Had she been mistaken about their compatibility?

"I don't want to say the wrong thing." He crossed his arms.

Lord, give me patience. "Right now, saying nothing is the wrong thing. Would it help if I asked if you're angry?"

"No-o-o ... I don't think I'm angry."

Did she believe him? Maybe. But it was too late. She was tired of being patient. Patience wasn't getting them anywhere. "Let's face it. Physically, I'm not a whole person any more. I've lost a breast."

His eyebrows went up and he rocked back into his seat. She wasn't going to stop now. "Does that upset you? I know it upsets me."

"No—not really."

Was he for real? She'd try another tack.

"What about disappointed?"

"Partly."

At last, a response she could follow up. "What are you disappointed about?"

"Delaying the wedding—um—cancelling the honeymoon." He wriggled in his seat. "I've wanted to go to Tasmania for years."

He wasn't the only one.

Nick subsided into silence. A silence that threatened to lengthen into even more awkwardness.

"I can tell you what I was disappointed about. First and most obviously, being diagnosed with cancer." Was Nick leaning forward a fraction? "I was disappointed and angry at my family doctor for dismissing my concerns. I was disappointed and angry at myself for not pursuing things. Most of all, I was disappointed and angry at God."

At last Nick was looking at her. Maybe something was getting through. "That was my biggest issue. Why did God allow the cancer and why didn't he heal me when we prayed so earnestly?"

"Yeah, why has this happened to us? We're serving God, yet he doesn't protect you from this." Nick leaned forward fully, elbows on his knees. "It's embarrassing, having such a prominent person in our church having chemo. It makes the church—and your father—a bit of a joke."

Hurray. Nick had started talking. Anything was better than the uncomfortable silences that had been between them.

"I'd wondered if that was bothering Dad." She crossed her ankles and looked at the cloudless sky. "What do you think? Does God owe us?"

"I wouldn't put it like that."

"How would you put it?" She'd been too direct, for Nick's shoulders rose, hunching towards his ears.

"Ahh...not sure."

It seemed to work better if she shared her emotions, and allowed him to respond. Emotions probably hadn't been discussed in his family, what with his Dad dying and all the family responsibilities being dumped onto his seventeen-year-old shoulders.

"Look, shall I tell you how I've been feeling and why I haven't felt the same these last few days?"

"Yeah, that'd be great." Nick's shoulders relaxed.

Where should she start? She prayed it wouldn't be an incoherent jumble of disconnected ideas. "Like most of those around me, I presumed my cancer was a temporary problem. Surely God would respond to our prayers, right? After all, since I was a little girl I've heard that God is the God of miracles." Now she'd started talking the words flowed.

"When the lump refused to disappear, I became upset. Why wasn't God healing me? I was doing my part—but what was he doing? Dad convinced me that God was waiting for the dramatic eleventh hour to heal me, like giving Abraham and Sarah a son in their nineties. Finding that the lump was still there before I went into surgery, was devastating." She clasped her knees and hugged them close to her body. "I felt like the heavens were stone and God didn't care. When I finally heard the seriousness of my cancer, I kept my anger dammed in until I thought I was alone. Then I exploded." She'd been a calm person before cancer. Now the outbursts of anger scared her, like magma under pressure, coming up from some hidden place inside of her. She'd only had that one outburst, but she was aware that more anger bubbled under the surface. How was she to deal with it? Where had it come from?

"Then what?" Nick asked.

"A cleaner overheard me, and she didn't let me get away with my outburst. She peppered me with questions. Persistently irritating like a buzzing mosquito." Esther slapped the back of her fingers into her palm. "She asked me, 'Why did Jesus only raise three people from the dead'?" Slap. "'Why didn't he make life smooth for everybody'?" Slap. "'Why did I believe he'd heal me?' Her questions made me so boiling mad, I was rude to her and rushed out of there."

Nick was looking directly at her for the first time in way too long. She wasn't about to waste the moment.

"I guess my pride was hurt because I had no answers to her questions. The next few days were hell. No matter how hard I tried, I couldn't block out that woman's questions. But I was also scared to go searching for answers. Deep down, I was afraid of the consequences of knowing."

What did the expression in Nick's eyes mean? Was he having second thoughts? She'd never shared like this with him before. There'd been little reason for it. Would he understand what happened after she met Joy?

"Ultimately, I had to be honest with myself and seek answers, no matter the cost."

Nick remained silent.

"I've been reading my Bible constantly ever since. Book by book. I started with all four Gospels and Acts, and yesterday I began Genesis."

The wrinkles on Nick's forehead deepened. "But you know your Bible. You've been reading it all your life."

"That's what I thought. But I've discovered I've mostly relied on others telling me what the Bible said. I've been familiar with some bits and skipped many others. Did you know the story of Peter being rescued by the angel in prison follows a verse where it says James was killed?"

"What does it matter? The focus is on Peter's rescue."

"It matters, because if we only talk about Peter's rescue we imply that God only rescues. But he didn't rescue James. Why not?"

"Perhaps James didn't trust God for release. Perhaps he'd committed some sin or something."

She couldn't blame Nick for such objections. After all, she'd used many of the same ones. "The text gives no suggestions of failure on James' part. In fact, it looks like neither Peter nor the praying Christians were expecting a miracle."

"I'm not sure where you're going with all of this."

"I've realised I've never read my Bible consistently. I presumed a Christian is victorious, blessed with stable marriages, pots of money, and perfect health. But my reading has shown me the opposite. The Bible emphasises denying self, carrying a cross, climbing a steep road, and facing persecution."

Nick drew in a soft whistling breath. "What are you saying? That your Dad and everything he teaches is wrong? Isn't that arrogant?"

Her heart sped up. She'd been afraid Nick would react like this. "I'm not saying anything about Dad. I'm still doing my own research. My life has taken a one hundred and eighty degree turn. Even the cancer isn't as important any more."

Nick's eyes widened and his eyebrows nearly hit his hairline. "I don't understand that at all. Your cancer is a big deal to me."

He could have fooled her all these weeks. "Yes, it seems strange, but it's my cancer that forced me to re-examine what I believe. It's all still so new. Could you pray for me?"

Nick grunted, presumably in assent, then stretched out his hand to take her empty cup and gather their plates. Obviously their conversation was at an end. Probably a good thing, as she was past exhausted. He stood and picked up the tray, ready to take it back to the kitchen.

"Don't come and see me off. I'll think about all you've said, but now I've got to head off and do youth group prep."

Their conversation had dragged at the beginning but in the middle it had seemed they'd begun to truly communicate. Hadn't they? At least they'd talked about her cancer. At last. It was the first glimmer of hope regarding their relationship in weeks. Surely things were now moving in the right direction.

CHAPTER 20

*E*sther woke on the morning of the twenty-sixth of August with a wet face and damp pillow. She'd dreamed she'd walked down the aisle in her gorgeous wedding gown. Nick waited for her with a look of joy and expectation. But even in the dream she'd known today was no longer her wedding day. A keening wail jerked her awake.

"Are you alright?" Mum called from the passageway.

Esther jumped out of bed and padded over to the door. "A nightmare."

"It must have been a bad one. You scared me."

"Sorry."

"What about breakfast in bed?"

Esther didn't have the heart to say that eating was the last thing she wanted. Her stomach churned and acid burned her throat.

Her digital clock said 8:00. Somehow she'd slept in after a restless night. If today had still been her big day, she'd have already been at the hairdresser surrounded by a giggling gaggle of bridesmaids. Would the whole day be like this? Vivid tableaus of what should have been happening. Hair and makeup, flowers and friends, mayhem and music.

During the week Nick had phoned, and suggested they do something special for what should have been their wedding. Esther had agreed. Anything had to be better than sitting at home and moping. Being out in God's creation seemed the best option, but Esther doubted she could handle a real hike. Nick had done some research and discovered a nature reserve only twenty kilometres away. They could tag along with a guided walk, and have a picnic.

*N*o guide in the world would have kept Esther's thoughts on track today. She took pictures of the flowers like any good sightseer, but flowers reminded her of weddings. Everything reminded her of weddings. She blew her nose. Would the other walkers think she had hay fever? She'd already had to turn her head aside three times in the last hour, and Nick had lagged back at one point.

They set up their picnic rug under a tree, away from others. They barely talked—they couldn't. Midway through lunch, Esther put her head down on Nick's knee and cried. He rubbed her back. A minute later tears fell on her hair.

During the last weeks, Esther had sometimes doubted Nick cared. She'd felt abandoned to grieve in isolation. But maybe past griefs had put his emotions in the deep freeze. *Lord, help this to be the start of something new.*

As they loaded their picnic gear in the back of the car, Nick's mobile phone rang. Her father had insisted the staff all have the latest means of communication.

"I'm on my way. I'll drop Esther off at home first. Should take me about thirty minutes." Nick looked grim as he hung up. "John tried to commit suicide but they found him before the pills took effect." John was in the youth group.

Now they had someone else to think about other than themselves.

---

*T*hree weeks later, Esther walked up to the reception desk for her second round of chemo.

"Good morning, Esther," Michelle said. "Glad you've made it."

"I'm impressed. Called by name on my second visit."

"Well, I do have the list of everyone who has chemo today and you were particularly friendly last time." Michelle leaned forward as though to share a secret. "It's a game I play. Match the right name with the right client." She straightened up. "Now, do you know what you're doing this morning?"

"Bloods and weight first?"

"Yes, that's right. The blood results will take about an hour." She glanced down. "There's a note here saying that Dr Webster would like to see you while you wait for your blood results, so please come back here when you've finished at the blood clinic."

Esther spotted Rob Boyle in the pathology area. He raised his hand in greeting so she drifted in his direction, not forgetting to get her number from the counter.

"I see you've still got your hair," he said running his fingers across his skull. "Not ready to join the glamorous bald club yet."

"Something I'm not looking forward to."

"I lost all mine after the second treatment. Not that I had much to lose." He grinned. "Are you going to get a wig?"

Esther wasn't yet sure if she liked Rob's blunt realism. "You know, so much has been going on in my life, I haven't had time to think about it. I did get my hair cut. Perhaps I hoped it would make the next step easier." Since Rob was keen to chat, Esther sat down.

"What's been happening in your life? It's boring sitting here month after month. Half of us cope by ignoring everyone, but the rest of us love to be nosy."

She wouldn't mention the day of the picnic. Much too personal. The day had ended in more tears when flowers had been delivered in the late afternoon—a sheaf of blue irises from Gina, and a bunch of multi-coloured freesias from Sue. So kind.

Esther relaxed back into her seat. "Work's fine, but neither of the men in my life have coped well with my diagnosis."

"We seldom do. I'm grateful for my wife, and even my kids are doing well."

"How old are your children?"

Rob assumed the smug expression of a proud parent. "My son's in his first year at Uni, studying science. My daughter's in Year 11."

"I'm hoping my family gets used to my situation. Dad ignores it, as though his denial means cancer doesn't exist in his household." She felt the stab of regret as she added, "And my fiancé has taken a while to adjust. He tries a mixture of avoidance and burying me in expensive flowers."

"Give them time."

How much time?

"My wife initially dealt with my cancer by trying to feed me every good thing on the planet. I told her I wasn't enduring chemo so she could kill me by overfeeding."

Esther laughed. It was amusing to picture Rob as obese rather than pencil-thin. "No one's tried that on me yet. They do try to stop me cycling to and from work, but I've rebelled on that issue."

"Oh." Rob rolled his eyes. "One of those fitness freaks."

"If I'm going to lose my hair, I'd like to feel good about some aspect of my life."

"Can't say I'm fit but my family still loves me." He pointed to his head. "It helps that I'm much more handsome bald than I was before."

Esther laughed. "Chemo obviously hasn't poisoned your sense of humour. What's been happening with you since we last met?"

"I've had a shocking few weeks and had to miss ten days of work." He shook his head. "Only began to feel better two days ago."

"I thought you looked a bit pale."

Rob frowned. "Hope my blood results are okay."

"What happens if they're not?"

"They'll delay chemo until they bounce back."

"Is it common for people to have to delay a round of chemo?"

Rob shrugged. "I don't know. Don't think it normally happens more than once. I just want to be out of here as fast as possible and never have to go through it again."

"That's one hope we all have in common. Can I also be nosy and ask your original cancer stage?"

"II."

"Better than mine. I'm a III. My family doctor told me I was far too young for cancer." Esther clicked her tongue. "Stupid me. I didn't follow up my gut feeling."

"What are you going to do about that doctor?"

"He's about to retire. I'm not going to ruin his life."

"You're more forgiving than I would be in your place."

Was this the opportunity she'd been praying for? Could she say something about why she was willing to forgive? Before she could work out what to say or summon the courage to say it the nurse came out and announced, "Number fifteen, number fifteen."

"There's my number," Rob said, and the opportunity for more meaningful conversation was gone.

---

*W*hen she was called in to see Dr Webster, Esther was struck again by the contrast between his office and the rest of the clinic. Professionally framed originals of his certificates were proof of his qualifications. Everything was neat to the point of obsession. Stark and cold. No colour, no life, no personal photos or objects. Even his pen was unembellished silver, functional but soulless. His manner matched the room. Was there some humanity buried there somewhere? What did he do besides work? Did he have a family, or had he sprung fully formed out of the ground?

Dr Webster jumped straight to business. "Any side effects after the first treatment?"

"Just a couple of days of tiredness." The questions were routine. Esther could have written the script herself. Sue had been correct in her assessment of Dr Webster as 'excellent but don't expect frills'.

"You seem different from when I last saw you."

Esther nearly fell out of her seat. He wasn't an automaton after all. Perhaps these visits could be more than robotic dialogue. Here was her chance to share the reasons for the change in her life. But how could she do it in a meaningful way? She inwardly rehearsed one way to start the topic and then another. And another.

And the opportunity was gone. She mentally kicked herself as she left Dr Webster's office. She'd blown it. What if she never had another chance?

*R*ob Boyle was returning from the pathology results counter. He looked lousy. When he saw her, he came over.

"Argh—I knew if the white cells were ever going to be too low, it would be this time. Now this round of treatment has to be delayed."

"I'm sorry. Guess this means we'll be out of sync for future treatments. Pity, because you're the friendliest person here."

Rob delved into his pocket. "Of course, my blood count means

I'm also going to have to be careful of infections. It's face mask time." He whipped one out of its sterile wrapping.

Esther couldn't help herself, she laughed. "Yes, do take care of yourself."

Rob headed off and Esther sat down to wait, again. No wonder people felt so drained after chemotherapy. It wasn't only the chemical assault on the body. It was the waiting. Waiting for results. Waiting to see if they were healthy enough to have treatment. Waiting for their lives to start again. Few bothered to read. It was too hard to concentrate with all the coughing and sneezing, and random noises like the older woman pushing a rattling trolley across the floor.

The second chemo session was like the first. Hot flushes and a peculiar taste in her mouth. Sometimes Esther's overactive imagination suggested she was submitting herself to deliberate poison. It made her want to rush home and shower, as though the poison needed to be washed off the surface of her skin.

The lady in the chair next to hers lay with her eyes closed most of the time, hair too neat to be natural. They both drank lots of fluids and both stood up at the same time. As they headed towards the bathroom, Esther's IV stand veered sharply and collided with her neighbour's.

"Sorry. Not a good way to introduce myself."

"No harm done. IV stands are like wayward shopping trolleys." The woman pointed to the wall. "That's the reason for the protective metal strip along the base of the wall."

Could Esther ask more? Or would she seem too nosy? "Are you also being treated for breast cancer?"

"Yes. Nearly finished. Thank goodness." The lady spoke in clipped sentences as though long ones would exhaust her. "Last treatment was the worst. Today's my final chemo. Then radiotherapy."

"I've also got radiotherapy afterwards but today is only my second chemo. Where do they do the radiotherapy?"

"Other end of this building. Means we can keep seeing the same specialist."

Back at their chairs, they continued to chat, the first-time conversation where you feel your way, find out the other's name and little more. The woman's name was Anna Agosto. She had a Swiss background and was married to someone of Italian background. They had three primary-school aged daughters. This was her second battle with cancer. Would Esther even meet her again?

Esther's session finished at midday. Time to meet Joy Wong. She'd looked forward all morning to spending time with Joy.

CHAPTER 21

*E*sther and Joy chose seats in the shade, looking across a manicured patch of lawn to a group of bottlebrushes, their scarlet brush-like flowers and gold tips glowed in the sun.

"Ahh." Joy leaned back on the bench. "This is better than mopping floors. How's treatment going?"

"No major problems so far, but I expect to lose my hair any day. That … that will be difficult." How limited human language is. Difficult was too simple a word to describe her complex mess of feelings. She'd always been proud of her thick, glossy hair. Losing it would be like losing another part of herself.

Joy looked at her. "I'm praying for you."

Some people just said the words. With Joy, Esther knew she meant every word. There was something about Joy that hinted at hidden depths. Was it the expression in her eyes? Like she'd seen a lot of suffering. When would she get to hear more of Joy's story?

Although this was only the third time they'd met, Esther owed Joy a deep debt of gratitude. Was there anything she could do in return? Would Joy appreciate being prayed for? This whole praying for each other thing was foreign to her. She was more used to praying privately, or leading more formal prayers in front of a large group.

"I don't want our friendship to be one way," Esther said. "How can I pray for you?"

Joy's eyes lit up. "I'd love you to pray for eyes to see opportunities and courage to grab them."

"I wouldn't have thought you needed such prayers."

"Every believer needs the same things. Even Paul asked the believers to pray for him to have boldness. After all, our enemy uses fear as one of his favourite weapons to prevent us doing God's work."

Joy was one of the few people Esther had heard talk about Satan as though he was real. Her father talked about Satan, but used his name more as a malevolent force to frighten people into doing things.

"I need the same prayer, too. I missed two opportunities this morning—one with a fellow patient, and the second with my specialist." Esther sighed. "I wasn't fast enough to respond with either of them. My specialist made a comment about how much I'd changed from my previous visits." She laughed ruefully. "I was so busy trying to think what to say, I didn't say anything at all."

Joy laid her hand on Esther's shoulder. "Don't be too hard on yourself. At least you desire to share, and you've started noticing opportunities."

Esther hadn't thought of those as improvements. All she could see was how far she had to go to be an effective sharer of God's story. Things were changing internally, but hadn't yet overflowed to be visible externally. She grasped Joy's arm. "Joy, I need help to know what to say."

Joy smiled, the kind of smile a teacher gives an eager student. "You asked me last time to share one of my favourite parts of the Bible. My favourite parts are actually stories. I'd chosen Joseph, but Daniel seems better suited to your current situation."

What kind of pastor's daughter was she? The name meant so little to her. Her Old Testament knowledge was even sketchier than her New Testament. "Daniel. Wasn't he the guy in the lions' den? And something to do with a fiery furnace."

"Yes, that's Daniel. I'll start with some background, but I'll have to eat as I go. Mopping floors is hungry work." Joy took out her container of reheated rice, meat and vegetables, unclipped a pair of chopsticks, and took three mouthfuls of food.

"The Israelites were supposed to obey God, but instead they rejected him as King and ended up worshipping idols. So, of course, they failed to be a witness of God's goodness and power to the surrounding nations." Joy ate another two mouthfuls.

"God sent Nebuchadnezzar, King of Babylon, to conquer them and be the means of God's judgement on his people. Daniel and his three friends were among the captives. Nebuchadnezzar selected them to be educated in his university. It wouldn't have been easy to have been ripped away from home and any family still alive. It's also likely their training included magic and divination. Subjects that would have been forbidden by God. What do you think they struggled with?"

Joy asked questions which forced her to think.

"Oh —the usual questions. Why us? Why does it have to be our generation that's judged?" Esther stared at the tall tree beyond the lawn. "Do you think they ever questioned if following God was worth it?"

"They wouldn't have been human if they didn't ask those kinds of questions," Joy said. "Under pressure, maybe some Jews abandoned God altogether, but Daniel and his friends decided to trust God no matter what. Because they made that choice, God used them to influence others."

Joy had continued to take quick mouthfuls during their conversation. Now she covered the remainder of her meal and laid the chopsticks aside. She angled her body towards Esther. "In the second year of his reign, King Nebuchadnezzar had dreams. He was deeply troubled and couldn't sleep. Finally, he called in his magicians and astrologers."

"The magicians said, 'O King, live forever. Tell us your dream and we will interpret it.'"

"Nebuchadnezzar replied, 'No, you tell me my dream and what it means. If you do, I'll know you truly have the ability to interpret dreams and I'll reward you. If you don't, I'll cut you into pieces.'"

"The magicians said, 'No king in all the earth has ever asked such a thing. No one can tell you what you dreamed except the gods, and they don't live among men.'"

"Well, Nebuchadnezzar ordered the arrest and execution of all the magicians. When they came to arrest Daniel, he asked the king for one night to seek the answer from God."

Esther was mesmerised as Joy shared how God revealed the dream and its meaning to Daniel.

"I don't remember hearing this story before," Esther said when Joy had finished. "It certainly makes me want to read the rest tonight."

"Can you see yet why I shared this story with you?"

"Not really. I can see it's a story about someone sharing about God, but I'm not sure how this helps me."

"Let's dig a little deeper. What opportunities did Daniel have to share with the king?"

"Well, interpreting the dream was a major one."

"Did you notice any other opportunity?"

What was Joy getting at? "Uhh ... Not really."

"Let's think about the bit when Daniel comes before the king. Nebuchadnezzar asks, 'Can you interpret my dream?' Now, what did you expect Daniel to say?"

Esther was still missing something but she could answer the question in front of her. "I'd expect him to say, 'Yes, I can.'"

"But what did Daniel say?"

Esther clapped her hands together. "I do remember. He kept saying, 'No, I can't. No person has that power. Only God can reveal mysteries.'"

"You've got it. And you've got to remember, Nebuchadnezzar hasn't been sleeping well, so Daniel took a big risk in saying, 'I can't, but God can.'"

"Yes," Esther said. "It would be like poking a wasp nest with a stick."

"So why does Daniel take the risk?"

"He doesn't want Nebuchadnezzar to misunderstand."

"Could we also say that Daniel doesn't want to steal God's glory?"

"Oh —" Understanding burst in like the sun popping above the horizon. "That's what I did with Dr Webster. I stole God's glory." Esther stared towards the bottlebrush and thought back to what she had and hadn't said.

"When I didn't respond to Dr Webster's observation, I gave him the impression I'm mature. But it's not true. In fact, there've been times I've behaved more like a two-year-old having a tantrum as I demanded God's healing instead of waiting for his plan. Any change in me is because God changed me. The credit is one hundred percent his." She swivelled towards Joy. "I messed up my chance. What if I never get another one?"

"Before we talk about Dr Webster, did you notice something else about how Daniel and his friends handled their problem?"

Joy didn't seem eager to rush to application. Instead, she lingered in the actual biblical text, mining it for the mother vein of gold, not content to only skim the surface for tiny nodules. Esther scrolled back in her mind through the scenes of the story.

"You mean their praying?"

"When did they pray?"

That didn't seem too difficult a question. "In their time of crisis. They asked God to reveal the dream to them."

"When else did they pray?"

Had there been other times? "I don't know."

"Let me remind you. God revealed the dream and its meaning to Daniel during the night. In the morning, he gathered his friends together, and they praised God. How many of us in the same situation would have forgotten the praise and rushed off to the king?" The tone Joy used to ask and answer questions never made Esther feel stupid or foolish. She knew Joy cared more about Esther's spiritual growth than being the teacher.

"I would have." How could she have missed that?

Joy looked at her watch. "I've got to get back to work." She tidied her chopsticks and lunchbox, talking as she went. "Regarding your missed opportunities. Every day, I pray for opportunities but I also pray I'll notice them when they come. I pray I'll say the right things in the right way. I used to worry about what to say, but now I ask the Holy Spirit for help. He's promised to give us the words we need."

Joy scattered a few leftover grains of rice for the birds. "Another thing I've learned is that if I miss an opportunity, I can always go back and say, 'Remember the other day when you said such and such? At the time I couldn't think what to say, but I went home and thought about it. Could I share with you what I wish I'd said'?"

"Yes—I think that would work."

Nebuchadnezzar wasn't the only one with a mystery. Joy was a mystery. Why was someone so obviously intelligent working as a hospital cleaner?

CHAPTER 22

*T*wo days later, Esther crawled into the bathroom. Even after emptying her stomach she continued to kneel on the floor and clutch the toilet bowl. The tiles were cold and hard and the pine-fresh deodoriser failed to mask the acrid smell of vomit.

This was the pits.

After twenty minutes, her knees were going numb. She stood up warily. Head woozy, she reached out a trembling hand, shuffled over to the bath and splashed cold water over her head. The bottom of the bath filled with clumps of hair. Esther sank back to the floor, put her head down on the edge of the bath, and cried.

Double pits. Triple pits. The hair moved towards the plughole and spun round and round before clogging up the hole. Esther sniffed.

How could such insignificant things as strands of hair mean so much? Their loss was far out of proportion to their weight. She reached down and scooped out the hair to allow the rest of the water to drain. Tossing the heavy clump towards the bin started her crying again.

How many long minutes passed before she heard her mother's steps coming up the hallway?

"Are you alright? We didn't wait for you for breakfast."

"Come in." Esther lurched to her feet.

Her mother took one look at Esther's head and blotchy face. "Honey, oh honey. I'm so sorry."

Esther sat on the edge of the bath and welcomed her mother's hug. "I thought I was prepared —but I'm not. I feel gross. Look at me … hair all scraggly, like moths have attacked me." She felt ugly. And Nick was about to leave her and go to Melbourne. This wouldn't be a nice look to leave him with.

Blanche hugged Esther and stroked her back. Oh, the comfort of her mother's arms. Arms that had seldom hugged her in the past. If only she could stay here forever, stilled by the reassuring sound of Mum's heartbeat.

Esther sniffed again and broke out of the hug. "Mum, I'm going to have a shower. Maybe the rest will fall out. Better it all goes than to have ragged clumps."

"Can I do anything to help?"

If only her mother could wave a magic wand and reattach every strand of hair. But magic wands were for little girls. Now Esther lived in the harsh grown-up land where mothers were no longer all-powerful, and requests had to be more mundane.

"Would you put my comfy jeans and checked shirt on the bed and find that headscarf we bought?" The breakfast things were probably still on the table. "Sorry about breakfast. I'll only be able to manage some dry toast with a scraping of Vegemite."

"I'll bring it up to your room. Your father's already gone to work, so it's only the two of us." Blanche kissed Esther's cheek and headed out the door.

Esther tripped over the lip of the shower cubicle and nearly hit her head on the opposite wall. Knocking herself out would top the day off.

Turning the tap on seemed to release her tears too. She cried and she cried and she cried. How could one body hold so much water? And why did crying make her whole body ache, as if her heart was breaking and its disintegration somehow affected every other limb. This fountain of emotion was embarrassing. It was only hair. In a world full of pain and suffering it felt selfish to make such a fuss.

But her thoughts didn't impact her feelings. There was a vast difference between reading, 'chemotherapy also attacks the fast-growing hair cells' and the reality. The brochure stated facts positively, insignificant sacrifice for greater gain. Only it didn't feel insignificant. It was overwhelming. A tsunami of emotion.

After lunch, Esther rang the hospital and asked for an extra day off.

She stayed in the garden most of the afternoon, and popped upstairs to tidy up. Her father was sure to notice the headscarf. Would he be tactful and ask her mother afterwards, or would he blurt something out? He was tactful with outsiders, but he lacked the same quality when dealing with his own family.

She went downstairs and into the dining room. Her father was there.

"Why on earth are you wearing that scarf? Not your style at all."

Esther tightened her jaw so she wouldn't howl. *Thanks, Dad. Just what I didn't need.* Out of the corner of her eye, Esther saw her mother glare at her father.

"I'm trying to work out the best option for this." Esther yanked off the scarf.

Her father gaped. "Th … that happened fast."

"Much too fast." Maybe she needed to spell it out for him, help him understand. "I've been shattered all day."

"Well, you can't walk around looking like that."

"What would you like me to do, stay locked in my room?" If this was how her father did pastoral care, it wasn't his strong point.

"There's no need to be rude."

"I'm not intending to be rude, but we have to face the facts." He thought she was the one being rude? Esther slowed down her words, no longer caring if it sounded like she was talking down to him. "I have cancer and I'm having chemotherapy. Chemotherapy makes hair fall out."

"Can't you get a wig or something?"

Would he never notice his questions were hurting her? She'd focus on the question and try not to take offence. The last thing she wanted was to destroy her relationship with the man she'd always looked up to.

"I wasn't planning to get a wig but it would be better for work." And for relating to her father and Nick. Although she wasn't going to say that out loud. Her mother looked pale and strained. Maintaining the harmony was taking its toll.

*I*nside the shop was a long counter displaying wigs. Stands with wigs in multiple styles and colours were also scattered round the room. Blond and brunette. Auburn and black. Short, flowing, or mid-length. The saleslady bustled towards Blanche and Esther.

"Welcome ladies. Don't be in a rush. This is your once-in-a-lifetime chance to try out new looks. If you've secretly hankered to be a blond or a redhead, seize the day."

What an original sales spiel.

"Losing your hair is tough but we're determined to make this part of the process fun. Why don't both of you choose from the catalogue?"

"Both of us?" Esther and Blanche chorused in unison.

The saleslady laughed. "Why not?"

"Shall we?" Esther raised an eyebrow at her mother. To her surprise, her mother grinned.

"Lead the way. Show us your most outrageous creation, and we'll start from there."

They chose a selection they had no intention of buying. They posed and made faces into the mirror, giggling the whole time. Esther had never seen her mother behave like a teenager. Where had her sense of fun been buried all these years? And what had made it burst out at this most unlikely of times? They'd have proof of this outrageous hour, because the saleslady took Polaroids of them as redheads and blonds, with black, frizzy hair, and even a joke shot with a fluorescent green mohawk, pulled out of a private cupboard. Did the saleslady reserve it for those customers most into the spirit of the thing?

"So glad I came." Esther bent over and clutched her sides. "It's been too long since I've laughed this hard."

In fact, laughter wasn't something that had been a part of her childhood. Her parents were too formal and too hands-off in their parenting. Playing games and being silly wasn't their thing. Anyway, their appointment time must be nearly over so they'd better make their choice.

"Part of me would love to shock people with the mohawk." Esther shook her head. "But I'll have to regretfully decline. It'll be easier for everyone if I don't go too radical. What about that dark wig there?"

Esther pulled on a wig in a short style, and the sales woman adjusted it for her.

"Wow—stunning," her mother said. "It's surprising how real it looks." Blanche turned to the saleslady. "Do you ever have people buying wigs for a change rather than because they've had chemo?"

"Oh yes, some people buy them like having new clothes or a new hat."

"I can't imagine it." Her mother made an unladylike snort.

Esther thought it unlikely as well, but perhaps coming here was fun if you didn't have cancer.

Esther also wanted a headscarf to wear around the house. She picked up two and held them up to her face. "What do you think—this style or that?"

"Why don't you get both? They look much better than what you were wearing when you came in."

Esther grinned. "I suspect I'll be wearing them long after I need to." On the way to the car, Esther laughed again, remembering their morning. "I can't wait to show Gina the pictures. She'll think they're a hoot. Maybe even Nick will get a laugh."

"Please don't show anyone else. What will Nick think about his future mother-in-law?"

"I'll be discreet." Nick couldn't possibly be more surprised than she had been to see her mother behave like a carefree girl. Her mother had always seemed so rigid, the ice queen herself.

"That saleslady is a genius," Esther said as they drove out of the car park. "She should have a super high salary for the undervalued skill of making people forget themselves." She put on the car's indicator and changed lanes. "We women are funny creatures. Yesterday, I was in despair over the loss of a little hair. Today, I'm ready to brave the world."

CHAPTER 23

*F*riday night, and Esther was well enough to help with youth group. She looked across at Nick and he wriggled his eyebrows at her. She grinned and a warmth settled into her stomach. It was wonderful to be back and working in tandem again. The way Nick related to teenagers always stirred something in her heart. It hadn't been hard to fall in love with him.

Esther had chosen mini-Olympic style competitions for the senior high school youth group. Unlike Nick's old church, Victory was big enough to have both junior and senior groups. The university group was separate again, although several of their members helped with the younger groups.

Nick blew a whistle. The first member of each of twelve teams turned around and ran to the line of tables. Each person had fifteen paper cups stacked together. They had to use them all to make a pyramid. Some tried to work out how many cups for the bottom row and others simply started stacking, adjusting as they went. Esther had a team of spotters to make sure they had a pyramid of five on the bottom, then four, three, two, one. Two of them knocked over their pyramid and had to start again.

"Hurry, hurry," yelled the other youth group members. They couldn't see, as they had to stand with their backs to the activity, so each person had to work out how to make the pyramid for themselves.

Once the pyramid was up, the builder undid it and left the fifteen cups in a single stack for the next team member. They dashed back to their team and the second team member ran forward for their turn. Each round someone knocked over at least one cup. One of the runners knocked another team's table, and their whole pyramid collapsed.

"Unfair, unfair! He knocked our table," the boy said.

Esther hurried over. "Okay, you were close. Just restack them into the single pile and run back to your team."

"Sit down when your team is finished," Nick yelled over the cheering.

Three teams were neck and neck, each with two runners to go. Their team members were jumping up and down. One of the girls stumbled and crashed into another runner, and they went down in a heap. Esther leaped forward to intervene, but stopped when she saw no one was hurt.

Now it was down to two teams. Their team mates watched. "Run, run," yelled half the group. "Not too fast. Steady," shouted the more conservative ones.

The last runner for the two teams ran to their table.

The two teams screamed, "Sit down. Quick." Good thing their gym was surrounded by car parks and not homes. Friday night was loud. Loud but fun.

Nick clapped twice to gain attention. The first activity was usually the most active, before they moved to quieter activities. Tonight they'd do two activities before the Bible session and two after. Next was a design game involving a lot of teamwork. Later they'd do a memory game, and one spelling kind of activity. Would the teens see the connection between the four activities and the

Bible session?

Over the two years since Nick had arrived, they'd worked together to train an impressive set of leaders. Each leader led one group the whole year.

Tonight's topic, planned months before, was self-esteem. Bible study was foreign to the group but Esther was keen to get the teens into the Bible. She'd rung Gina for suggestions. Each group had a bucket of apples and each leader had a list of instructions. The second game ended, and Esther's group of ten sixteen to eighteen-year-old girls came over and sat on the floor around the bucket.

"What are the apples for?" asked one of the bolder girls.

"I'll explain in a minute. Before we start, why don't you tell me something you've enjoyed doing while I've been away."

Her wig must look natural because none of the girls asked about it. Even Nick had seemed at ease when he picked her up. Maybe he was adjusting. Being at Friday night youth group certainly made her life more normal, although she'd pay for it tomorrow. At least she had two days break before work. She hadn't helped with Sunday evening services since her surgery.

"Okay, everyone take an apple," Esther said.

Each girl reached into the bucket and took one, half were green and the rest red. A squabble erupted between two who wanted the same apple.

"It doesn't matter which apple you take," Esther said. "This isn't a competition."

They held their apples and looked at her.

"I want you to look at your apple. You need to know it well. Really well. Notice its bumps and any flaws. Look at its colour variations."

"What's the point of this?" one girl asked.

"The point is that you're about to put your apple back onto this cloth in the middle. Then you'll close your eyes while I shuffle the apples. Your job is to find your apple."

"Impossible," the group extrovert said. "We'll get them mixed up."

"No," the most artistic one in the group said. "There's plenty of colour variation."

"And mine has two spots on it."

"Half a minute more to get to know your apples. Then please put them on the cloth and close your eyes."

When all the apples were on the cloth, Esther checked their eyes were closed and moved the apples around.

"Open your eyes."

Each girl reached out. Some rolled the apples around before picking up one. Some picked up one and then put it down and chose another. At last everyone had an apple.

"You've got an apple, but is it your apple?"

"Yes, mine had this weird squiggle," one group member said.

"And mine had a pinkish side," said another.

All over the auditorium, groups were working through the tasks. The guys were rowdier with more horsing around. Nick saw her looking across and winked. He never had much trouble in his group. The guys knew how far they could push him, and he never objected to fun.

"Round two," Esther said. "Feel your apple with your eyes closed. Will you be able to recognise it by touch alone?"

"Doubt it," Chloe muttered. She was the hardest one to lead, but she wasn't as negative as a year ago.

Esther had tried all these activities at home. It was no use asking people to do anything impossible. Once they'd completed the second round one of the girls said, "What about by smell? Is that possible?"

"I don't know. Do you want to try it?"

Other groups saw them sniffing their apples and followed their lead. Half the group succeeded. It was easier to differentiate the red apples.

"Now what?"

Esther looked across at Nick who was waiting for her signal. They were in tune tonight, yet on Monday he would fly to Melbourne and only be here five days a month. Why hadn't he delayed going? Their relationship was under enough strain already.

Nick stood and clicked on the microphone. "Is there any group that still needs more time?" No one raised their hands. "Could everyone put their apples back into the bucket? We have a team of parents in the kitchen who should have time to turn your apples into apple crumble for snack time."

"Yuck, we've had our hands all over them," one of the boys in Nick's group said. His voice was loud enough to carry around the auditorium. Nick gave him a playful punch on the shoulder. "They'll wash and cook them, bozo."

Then it was back to their groups to finish the study. "What did we learn about apples?" Esther asked.

The girls talked about what they'd noticed, and how surprised they'd been at how easily they could identify their own apple.

Esther had photocopied the Bible passage. She had wanted to hand Bibles around, but she'd been outvoted because the other leaders were concerned about how the teens would react. Esther prayed this would soon change. How could anyone expect teens to read the Bible on their own if they never handled one, even in youth group?

"The paragraphs at the top of your sheet are from Psalm 139, verses thirteen to sixteen. A psalm is a kind of poem or song, and this one was written by King David about three and a half thousand years ago. You might be surprised how relevant it is. Sarah, could you read it for us?"

"You created my inmost being; you knit me together in my mother's womb. I praise you because I am fearfully and wonderfully made ..."

The words had a timeless rhythm that resulted in a reflective hush. They spent ten minutes discussing God's intimate knowledge of every human being.

For the final question, Esther asked, "If this Psalm is what God thinks of us, what difference might it make to our lives?"

Esther was encouraged at the depth of the discussion. One day soon she hoped the girls would learn to pray for each other. But for today she'd model it.

Most of the group bowed their head. "Dear heavenly Father, you are a great and mighty creator but you also care about the minute details of our lives. Thank you for making each and every one of us unique. Help us to never forget your love and care for us. Help us to treat other people as special and precious too, amen."

Esther looked around at each girl and smiled. "We have two more activities and we're doing them in our small groups but we're competing against the other groups. I chose all four games deliberately. See if you can work out why."

All through the games and final wrap up, the fragrance of apple, cinnamon and baking oats wafted through the gym. Even Esther had no problems devouring a bowl of crisp crumble with ice cream. Nick came over and squeezed her hand.

"That was terrific. Well done."

His praise and affection warmed her right down to her toes. Were they finally over the speed bump in their relationship?

CHAPTER 24

*E*sther sat at the back of Victory's auditorium feeling as if blinkers had been ripped off her eyes. The music was the same. The service was the same.

But she herself was no longer the same.

As usual, the music ended abruptly and the spotlight snapped on, placing her father at the centre of a pool of light. Impressive, but where was the humility of John the Baptist who'd said, 'Jesus must become greater, I must become less.' Her father was the centre of this show, not the one who should be. In fact, Jesus had barely been mentioned and they were thirty-five minutes into the service.

The Bible reading was Hebrews 11. Her father had chosen one verse, 'Without faith it is impossible to please God … he rewards those who earnestly seek him.' Sure, the preacher was allowed to focus on a single verse, but if they did so, what was left out? And did the resultant message match the thrust of the chapter?

Esther opened her Bible to read the verse in context. It mentioned the stories of Adam and Abel, Joseph and Jephthah, Samson and Samuel. Blessed and being a blessing. Most of it she'd never read before.

She read on, fascinated. The chapter built towards a flourish that sounded like Victory church. People who conquered, for they, 'escaped the sword and their dead were raised to life again.'

Then the tone switched. 'They were stoned, sawn in two ... put to death by the sword. They went about in goatskins, destitute, persecuted and mistreated.'

Victory Church had never preached this. The last line transfixed her. She read it three times. 'The world was not worthy of them ... these were all commended for their faith yet none received what had been promised.'

Tears pooled in the corners of her eyes. Wasn't there a similar line earlier? She scanned until she found it in verse thirteen. 'All these people were still living by faith when they died. They did not receive the things promised—they only saw them from afar ... Therefore, God is not ashamed to be called their God.'

Esther stopped reading and closed her eyes. For the people of Hebrews, trusting Jesus meant being willing to die. She wasn't like that. Why? What had made her someone who followed Jesus to gain blessings? Someone who hadn't recognised Jesus was worthy of worship, whether she ever received anything from him or not.

She shivered with the beauty of the last phrase. 'God is not ashamed to be called their God.' Tears spilled over and slid down her cheeks. Oh, if only this line described her. Living a life that made her heavenly Father proud.

Her father thumped the pulpit and Esther jumped. How long had she been in a reverie? She tried to concentrate, but having tasted divine water, her father's words tasted like sawdust.

He said a great deal about people receiving blessing, but a blank cheque was implied. Questions surfaced like a stream of air bubbles. Why were people here? What did they want? What happened when they didn't find it?

And lastly, would she be able to stay at Victory?

At the point of the service where everyone's attention was

focused on the front, Esther slipped out. The only private space she could find was a toilet cubicle. She closed the lid and sat down. *Oh Lord. What do I do? Am I being unfairly critical? Am I being arrogant? Do I need to say something to Dad?* The thought terrified her.

She'd been about three the first time she'd experienced her father's anger. She hadn't dared to ask the question bothering her because Mum was moving about like a silent ghost and there was tension crackling in the air. But at last she'd lost patience and banged her spoon on the table.

"Where's —?" she'd asked. She meant the big girl who'd filled her world with hugs, laughter, and songs. She could no longer remember the girl's name because of what happened afterwards.

Her father had looked at her like the hunter in one of her picture books. He'd gone white all around his mouth. Mum ran away to the kitchen, but Esther was trapped in her high chair. She remembered the sour taste of terror and the desire to run to her bedroom, scuttle under the bed, and put her hands over her eyes.

That day, the silence had gone on and on. The windless hush before a hail storm. Her father's voice had hissed. She'd always been terrified of snakes. "You. Are never. To ask about her. Again."

"Why?"

Her father's face changed from white to red. She'd crossed some invisible line. She hadn't thrown up, but a warm wetness pooled under her bottom. Trapped in her chair. Trapped by her shame and fear. Trapped with this man who terrified her.

She'd done the only thing she could and wailed. As her mother galloped to the rescue, her father had leaned over and spoken in a voice that raised goosebumps all over her body.

"She was just a visiting missionary kid. She's gone back to her parents."

Esther had never worked out why her father had responded in such a way, or why such ordinary words could sound so terrifying. But she had vowed never, ever, ever to provoke her father again.

Anything to keep the peace. Anything to prevent her father transforming into a rabid dog.

And she'd kept her promise, right up to today.

But today she remembered Abraham. Abraham didn't know where he was going. He didn't know how long the journey would take. He only knew the one whom he was following. Was she willing to do the same?

Esther didn't return to the auditorium. Instead, she snuck out and headed home. Her parents were seldom home before two on Sunday afternoons.

At two-thirty, they sat down to eat. Nick hadn't joined them, as he was having lunch with his family. Tomorrow he'd fly to Melbourne to start his course. Esther's emotions had been so bludgeoned lately that she didn't know what she felt about him leaving. The reality would probably hit once he left. He'd already warned her the course would eat into his evenings, so letters were more likely than phone calls.

But first it looked like there'd be more challenges right here at home.

Was she soon to confront her equivalent of Daniel's test about eating Nebuchadnezzar's food? A smaller preliminary test to prepare her for bigger tests to come. Would she please her heavenly Father, or would she settle for pleasing her earthly one?

Her stomach ached and she struggled to eat. She still had time to pray. Her father would wait until the end of the meal before he tackled anything serious. He believed dinners were meant to be enjoyed.

Sure enough, after dessert, he folded his serviette and laid it on the table. "Nick told me you weren't paying much attention today. Said you seemed upset and slipped out early."

Lord, give me the words to speak. Her hands were clammy, so she wiped them on her skirt.

"I was moved by reading the whole of Hebrews 11. It was different from what I was expecting—"

"What do you mean?" His question was a warning volley designed to bring about her immediate surrender.

Remember Daniel. "It's all about people who trusted God but never saw what they were hoping for."

Her father had gone quiet. She wasn't fooled. Only a temporary reprieve while he reloaded.

"I cried when I read about all the people, persecuted and suffering terribly. It made me want to know why we don't—" Her voice cracked. This question would cross a line in their relationship. "Why don't we talk more about suffering in church?"

Esther heard her mother's quick, indrawn breath.

"People don't want to hear about suffering," her father said.

How long had it been since anyone dared to question him? Esther sent up another arrow prayer. "But Dad, Jesus himself promised anyone following him would be persecuted. It was the proof we were his disciples."

"You preach a message of suffering and you won't have a church at all."

"Surely that doesn't matter if it's the truth." *Oh, Dad how come you keep making this about church numbers?*

There was another involuntary sound from her mother. Blanche grabbed a few plates and scurried into the kitchen, an animal fleeing before an earthquake.

"What are you implying?" Her father's voice sounded calm but she'd heard that voice before. The false peace of a north Australian swimming hole with a crocodile lurking beneath the surface.

Did she dare to continue? Daniel risked his head. Her life wasn't on the line. "I'm concerned. Until recently, I believed that if I had enough faith I'd be healed, but I can't find that promise in the Bible. I've been wrong."

Her father's gaze attempted to bore right through her. "So, let me get this straight." His voice dripped sarcasm. "Your reading the Bible for a few weeks is equivalent to my reading it for fifty years?" Again, the quiet, deliberate words.

"I'm not trying to make this a competition. I'm only saying if I was wrong, then other people can be wrong too. Dad, what if Victory is leading people astray?"

There was now a tick in the muscle along her father's jaw. "I can't believe what I'm hearing. Are you suggesting I'm a liar?" His voice was no longer low and level.

"I hope not. I'm questioning whether our church focuses on the things Jesus focused on—the cross, and giving glory to God."

Her father folded his arms. "I'm going to pretend we've never had this conversation. That this is some ghastly side effect of chemotherapy." Bludgeoning hadn't worked, so now her father cast aspersions on her fitness to speak.

"Dad, being sick is what forced me to read the Bible. I can't ignore my doubts and questions. Families should be places where we can disagree and still love each other—"

Her father knifed his arm through the air. "I beg to differ. Families are places where we love by supporting each other through thick and thin."

She wanted to plead tiredness and disappear down a rabbit hole. But would that be loving? She was no longer willing to be a compromiser for the sake of harmony. It was time to start living a life that made her heavenly Father proud. The longer she put off picking up her cross, the harder it would become to start the habit.

"But what if something we believe is wrong? Surely we must raise the issue?"

Her father leaned forward, looming over her like a shadow in a childish nightmare. "Are you accusing me of something? I've grown a successful church and have a vast following through my books and the *Hour of Victory*. Are you suggesting all those people are wrong?"

How devastating that these were his proofs of his righteousness. "All I'm doing is asking questions. Let me tell you, it's not easy to do in this family."

"You sound like your grandmother. I can see Nick was right to come to me and share his concerns about your emotional state."

"I'd have preferred he came to me first." Esther sighed. "Dad, let's leave it now. I'm sorry you're upset, but I do believe I should have the freedom to ask questions."

"It seems to me you're abusing your freedom." He pushed his chair back, went out the door and up the stairs.

Esther sat, her mind a kaleidoscope of chaos. Could she continue to live here if her father couldn't handle doubts or questions? And worst of all, if he could never, ever cope with criticism.

CHAPTER 25

*E*sther arrived for her third round of chemo in better spirits. A long letter and a huge bunch of flowers had arrived from Nick last night. He might not talk about cancer, but he was generous in the gift-giving department. And this morning she'd prayed she'd not only be alert to opportunities to share her faith, but have the wisdom to know how.

Rob Boyle was in the pathology area.

"This is a surprise," Esther said, "I thought our treatment times would be out of sync by now."

He scowled. "The last few weeks have been a shocker. My white cells were low, then I had endless dental trips because of an infection. Just as that was sorted out, my wife got the flu and I had to leave the house to guard against getting it too. I've stayed with my mother and she's a curmudgeon."

"Doesn't sound like much fun."

"Not much fun." His voice rose. "It's been hell. Things only settled at the end of last week. The clinic wanted me to schedule my chemo three days ago, but I preferred to be back in sync with people I know."

Lord, is this my opportunity? Give me the words. "I'm glad you did. It makes it so much easier to have familiar people around."

"Has anything amusing happened?" He indicated her head scarf. "I see you've joined the bald-head club."

"That wasn't amusing, but let me tell you about the sequel in the wig shop."

Rob laughed heartily throughout her story. "Thanks. It's good to have something to laugh about." He put his head on one side. "Must have been strange to see yourself as a blond or redhead."

Esther patted her bag. "I have the photos with me, and I take them out when I need a laugh."

"Laughter does seem to be the best medicine."

Esther's heart raced and her palms were clammy. "I agree laughter is great, but personally I find praying is the best stress relief."

Rob's eyebrows rose. "You mean saying the rosary or something?"

"No, not generic prayers. I mean sharing my heart with Jesus, who knows everything I'm going through and is with me every step of the way." Her nervousness was making her sentences too long and rambling. *Help me, Lord.*

"Seems to me there's some doubt your Jesus exists at all. Surely he would have done better to prevent you getting cancer in the first place."

Thank you, Lord. I can talk about my own journey. "You know, I used to think the same. I assumed I'd be healed before the surgery. When I wasn't, I was angry and disappointed."

"But you're not now, I notice. Not even planning to sue the doctor who said you were too young for cancer."

"No, the last thing I need is extra stress. The doctor knows—Mum told him—but I also told her to reassure him."

"You're a better person than I am. I would have let him stew a little."

Esther laughed. "It was tempting, but I'm not necessarily a better person than you. It's just that my attitude and expectations about my illness changed because I started to study the Bible properly." Joy had been right. The Holy Spirit gave her the words to say, when she needed them.

"I'm flabbergasted. You're a physiotherapist, yet you read an old book packed full of fairy tales."

Esther's neck heated. She must not take his comments personally. He didn't think any differently than most Australians. "You know, if Isaac Newton and his contemporaries heard you talking they'd think you were bonkers. In their day, Christians studied science, and non-Christians rejected it." Her words flowed now as though the block in a water pipe had cleared. "Christians believed God created an orderly world. So they went looking for the rules governing the order."

Rob narrowed his eyes. "You sure of your facts?"

This was fun. Her recent reading was proving handy. "Don't take my word for it. Go and check it out yourself. As for the Bible being full of fairy tales ... have you ever read it?"

"I was forced to go to Sunday School, on and off."

No wonder he was so against the Bible. "Sorry it felt like being forced."

"My parents sent me because Sunday School was free babysitting." He made a face. "I resented being there."

"I can understand your resentment." Could she say anything more without alienating him? "Maybe you should take a gamble and read something like Luke. See if it reads like a fairy tale."

Rob didn't tense up.

"It reads to me like a well-researched historical document."

"Number thirty, number thirty," the announcer called.

"That's me." Rob stood up. "Today's my last day of chemo, but I'll be back every three months or so. I'll look out for you. Maybe I'll check out what you said."

Esther shook, but not from fear. Rather she buzzed with exhilaration. Sharing her faith was like a strong dose of caffeine. The main thing seemed to be, pray hard, face her fears, and open her mouth. She thanked God for the opportunity. Several times it seemed like the words had come out of nowhere.

There were still ten numbers ahead of hers. Was there anyone else she could talk to? No—she seemed to be surrounded by the endure-but-don't-talk-to-anyone attitude group. There was one lady she'd tried to connect with last time, but she'd been rebuffed. Esther couldn't see her here today, but she'd added her to her lengthening prayer list. Why was the woman like that?

With no one to talk to, Esther worked on her cross stitch and prayed for Rob and others she'd talked to, or hoped to talk with soon. At about ten, Anna, the IV stand lady arrived but she only waved and headed straight to have her blood tests.

A minute later, the angry lady stumbled out of a side-room, crying. The woman seated herself as far in the corner as possible.

Esther didn't want to talk to her, didn't want another round of rejection. But how could she pray for her, yet not talk to her? Her habit of placating her father had spilled over into general people-pleasing. The habit would have to be fought. It wouldn't just roll over and die.

A minute passed, then two.

Esther stood, crossed over to the woman, and held out a packet of tissues. "One of those tougher days?"

"When you have breast cancer, every day is tough." The woman glared at her, making Esther wish she hadn't bothered.

Lord, give me the right words. "Any reason today is tougher than usual?"

The woman snorted. "Are you one of those incessant talkers who must pester everyone?"

How was she ever going to do the right thing if she retreated every time? This woman needed help, even if she didn't know it yet.

GRACE IN STRANGE DISGUISE

"We don't have to talk but you seemed so distressed, I thought I'd try."

The woman grunted. "I appreciate the thought but I'm not fit company nowadays."

Here was something she could respond to. "Cancer is challenging and frustrating, and other awful things too numerous to count."

"Yeah, today is a downer because my white cells are too low." A tear dripped off the end of her nose. "I'd psyched myself up for the treatment. Now I'll have to wait."

"I haven't had that happen yet. Do you have to have radiotherapy afterwards?"

"Nope, the cancer was caught early."

"You're lucky." Esther winced. Poor word choice. "Mine was caught late. Stage III."

The lady blew her nose. "You know, you're the first person I've had tell me I'm lucky. Stage II isn't so bad in comparison."

Whew, she hadn't totally blown it. "And we're both better than someone with a stage IV."

The woman gave a rueful laugh. "Yeah. Well, Miss Lucky, my name is Liz. What's yours?"

"Esther." They shook hands. "This journey has been the toughest thing I've faced. The hardest part for me was thinking I was going to be healed. I was devastated when I wasn't."

The woman looked startled. "You mean healed by God or something?"

"Yup." *Thank you, Lord, that she raised the topic, not me. Keep this conversation going.*

"What a coincidence. I used to go to a heavy-duty healing church. I left when I wasn't healed. I got tired of being told it was my fault, and I haven't been near church since."

"Does that mean you've abandoned God along the way?"

"Certainly does. I wanted nothing to do with their god. Victory Church's god only made me feel guilty and inadequate."

Esther wanted to cower behind her seat or run away. This wasn't the time to admit to her connection to Victory Church. "Did it ever occur to you the god you heard about at church might not be the God of the Bible?"

Liz shook her head. "Can't say it did."

"I was told many of the same things you were. I blamed my 'weak faith—'" Esther added air quotes with both hands, "—for the fact that my cancer wasn't cured. It was confusing. Then I read the Bible for myself, whole sections of it instead of tiny bits."

Liz didn't say anything, but she didn't look away either.

"I discovered I'd been taught a distorted view of the truth. Jesus is more than able to handle my doubts. I don't know how I'd cope without him."

Liz wrapped her arms around her waist. "When you've been stung as badly as I have, it takes a long time to get over it."

"I wish I could undo what you were told." How terribly Liz had been hurt by Victory.

"It's not that easy." As Liz was summoned by the reception desk, she said, "Thanks for talking to me."

Anna came back into the waiting room before Esther had even been called to see Sister O'Reilly. She sat down next to Esther.

"There seems to be more people here today than usual. How long have you been waiting?"

"Since nine."

"Nice cross stitch. I like patterns of Australian wildflowers or birds, not cutesy things."

The two chatted about everyday topics for a few minutes.

"I like talking to you," Anna said. "You seem somehow at peace amidst the wreckage of our lives."

"I am at peace." *Give me the words, Lord.* "Do you know why?"

"No idea." Anna scratched her nose. "I'm guessing you don't do drugs. Do you practice yoga or something? If so, tell me about it."

"No." Esther laughed. "No special technique. I follow Jesus. I talk to him and listen. He's the one who gives me peace."

Anna leaned forward and whispered. "You mean you hear him talk to you?"

"Not like you're thinking. He talks to me through his word, the Bible. I guess it's a bit like—" Esther tilted her head. "—like the Bible is God's letter to us."

"I've never heard anyone explain it like that. I'm a Roman Catholic with a super-religious family. Mass every week, et cetera —" She twirled her hand in a circle.

"Do you read the Bible?"

Anna narrowed her eyes. "It does seem strange that we don't."

"Have you ever thought it might be relevant to you?"

"No. How does it help you in a situation like ours?"

Esther prayed for the right words. "Even though some people or religions would say cancer proves I'm cursed, the Bible assures me God loves me. He's with me all the time, which is a great comfort when I worry about the future."

"That's what stresses me. I worry all the time about what might happen to Tony and the girls if I don't beat this thing."

"I understand your concern, but I'm slowly learning to turn my worries over to Jesus. He lifts the burden off me."

"Forty. Number forty," the nurse called.

"That's me. I'll have to go." Esther folded away her cross stitch.

Sister O'Reilly subjected her to the usual stream of questions. Esther showed her the chart on which she'd been asked to note all her side effects. She'd become her own nurse, writing down when she was constipated (often), whether her nails were broken (not so much, but they were not their usual healthy pink), how nauseated she was (very), and whether her periods were normal (usually). It was like being back at school, with daily homework. At least vomiting hadn't been a major part of the package so far.

"Emotionally—how are you going?"

"Well, I think. Mum is helpful and my work has been understanding. I've a great deal to be thankful for." Before Esther could say anything more meaningful, Sister O'Reilly inserted the cannula and buzzed for the next client.

---

*E*sther plopped herself down into her chemo chair and raised the leg rest. She couldn't expect to grasp every chance to talk about Jesus, so why was she annoyed at herself? There was more to it than missing the chance. She didn't want to talk to Sister O'Reilly.

Why not? Anna or Liz had obvious needs. People like Sister O'Reilly or Michelle were so nice it seemed an insult to suggest they needed Jesus. She'd talk with Joy about it. They'd have to meet inside today, as she'd still be tethered to her paraphernalia.

CHAPTER 26

*E*sther barely waited for Joy to sit down. "You won't believe what's happened—I've had three opportunities to share about Jesus today."

Joy smiled like a teacher satisfied their student is applying what they're taught. "Have you been praying for opportunities?"

"Yes, every day."

"Then I'm not surprised. God has simply answered your prayers."

There was silence while Esther chewed the thought over and swallowed it.

"Now, let me see if I can guess who you talked to," Joy said. "Was it the angry lady, Dr Webster, and the science teacher?"

"Two out of three correct. I didn't have a chance with Dr Webster, but the others were amazing conversations. I said things I didn't expect."

"Didn't I tell you the Holy Spirit would give you the words? The only extraordinary thing is your surprise."

"Hmm … yes, it is strange how astonished I am that God answers prayer." After all, what would be the use of praying if she didn't believe this? But there was a vast difference between believing something in her head and believing it in her heart, or wherever it was real belief resided.

What was it about people that even with three successful conversations, it was the unsuccessful one she wanted to talk about? "I missed one opportunity, with Sister O'Reilly. I struggle to chat about my experience with her, and with Michelle at the reception desk. They're such nice people it seems an insult to talk to them about Jesus."

"That is interesting. Do you think nice people don't need saving?"

Esther had known Joy would ask that question so she'd had a little time to think about it. "When you ask like that, I know they need Jesus, but my heart struggles to agree with my head on this issue."

"Can you think of a story in which the good news is told to a good person?"

Esther mentally scrolled through the Bible. "Would … would Nicodemus come into this category?"

"Definitely. But before I tell this story, what do you know about Pharisees?" While Esther took a moment to think, Joy chewed her first mouthfuls of lunch.

"They were a kind of Jewish religious leader. Weren't they fanatical about fasting and praying?"

"Yes," Joy said. "If you wanted to choose a stereotypical 'good' person, then the obvious example was a Pharisee. What about their Bible knowledge?"

"Presumably excellent."

"More than excellent. It has taken me years to learn Bible stories accurately. They could recite whole books of the Bible word for word. So, as I tell the story, don't forget that Jesus is talking to a Pharisee, a morally upright Bible expert."

Something had been puzzling Esther for ages. "Joy, why do you tell Bible stories instead of doing Bible study with me?"

"I was wondering when you'd ask. Firstly, it is because that was the way I was taught. But the real reason is, telling stories allows us to hear and remember them, as though we've never heard them before. The easiest way for you to understand the difference between reading stories and telling them, is to try out both approaches with people."

The suggestion was a good one but Esther wasn't sure who she could ask. Nick wouldn't have the time, at least, not in the next six months.

Joy put her partially finished meal down so she could concentrate on storytelling. "One night, a religious leader came to talk to Jesus. He said, 'Teacher, we know you've come from God because no one could do the miraculous things you are doing if God was not with him.'"

"Jesus replied, 'No one can see the Kingdom of God unless he is born again.'"

"Nicodemus said, 'What do you mean? How can an old man enter his mother's womb and be born a second time?'"

"'You are Israel's teacher and you don't understand this?' Jesus said. 'I've spoken to you about earthly things and you don't believe. How will you believe if I speak about heavenly things?'"

After Joy finished telling the story she said, "Let's go through the story again, and you help me fill in the blanks."

This sounded a bit childish, like the comprehension questions she'd been bored with as a six-year-old. But Esther owed Joy so much she wasn't going to question such a small thing.

"How does the story start?"

That was easy enough. "One night a Pharisee called Nicodemus came to talk to Jesus."

"Can you remember what he said?"

Esther only got half the line right. Joy corrected her, then repeated the whole line. "What did Jesus say you need to do to see the Kingdom of God?"

"Be born again."

"That's right. Jesus said, 'No one can see the Kingdom of God unless he is born again.' What did Nicodemus say in response?"

They continued line by line through the story. This method had seemed simplistic but now it made sense. The story was being laid down in her memory.

"Okay, can you retell the whole story?"

Esther managed about ninety percent accuracy, and Joy added the missing bits. Three times through and Esther felt confident enough to tell the story to someone else, if she kept practicing on her own. It was only a short story, after all.

"Ready to discuss it?"

Esther couldn't work out what part of the process she preferred. Learning the story, or digging deeper in discussion. Learning the story gave a real sense of satisfaction. Joy's lunchtime was so short they only had about a minute to discuss each question. What do you like about this story? What questions do you have? What can we learn about people and Jesus from this story?

After completing the basic discussion questions, Joy said, "If Nicodemus was such a good man, why did Jesus say he needed to be 'born again'?"

Esther stared at the opposite wall to help her think. "Because being a Bible expert and a good person wasn't enough. He needed God's new life."

"Yes, but why? What is the Bible's view of people?" Esther loved the way that Joy always pushed her beyond what she knew. This question wasn't too hard. "We're sinners, rebels against God."

"The Bible uses many words to describe our situation, like walking in darkness or being separated from God. I personally find Paul's description in Ephesians especially clear. It says we're 'dead in our sin.' That's an alarming diagnosis."

"Yes, and most Aussies would reject it."

"It's even more insulting in China. I used to say the Bible declares us to be 'walking corpses'. We look lively, but in our hearts we are like a dead branch—dry and lifeless."

Esther breathed out a gust of air. "That sounds insulting."

"It's certainly an attack on our pride. One of the things I like about the Bible, is that it presents the bad news first. Once we're able to see our need to be rescued, it then presents the good news. Good news is like a diamond. It shows up best against a black background."

"So when someone seems too nice, I need to remind myself of Nicodemus, and remember everyone needs Jesus." The imagery caught her imagination. Esther saw the time on the wall clock. "Time always flies when we meet. I'm going to keep praying for opportunities to talk to Michelle and Sister O'Reilly."

"So is your life more purposeful these days?"

"It certainly is. I'm beginning to understand why I've been allowed to go through this experience. Without cancer, I'd never have met you, and I'd still be deceiving myself that I knew Jesus." Esther shuddered. "It's scary to think of what I used to be like. I wouldn't exchange what I have now with my previous life for a million dollars."

Joy stood up, ready to head back to work.

"Next time we meet," Esther said, "I'd love to hear your story. Of course, I know you're from China, but I've been dying to know how you have such flawless English."

CHAPTER 27

*E*sther had completed the fifth round of chemo. Now Nick was home for the weekend and they'd been invited to a party. His being away in Melbourne was hard, but not as hard as she'd expected. They wrote to each other every few days. Nick still seldom mentioned her cancer, but he always had plenty to write about what he was learning.

She dressed with special care, and prickles of excitement shivered down her spine. A last look in the mirror to check her wig and lipstick and then she slipped a few things into her purse including a mask and a packet of sterile wipes. A chorus of voices warned her of the dangers of infection. What would they think of her going to a party? But she wanted an ordinary life. Like this engagement party.

Nick arrived at seven and smiled the smile that was her old friend, the smile that reminded her of the man she'd fallen in love with. "New dress? It looks terrific."

Wonder of wonders, he even took her arm. Like a flame devouring paper, the warmth of his touch spread to the tips of her fingers and toes. He seldom touched her nowadays. Maybe tonight would be a new start.

The party was well under way when they arrived. Trees were strung with starry blue lights. Drinks fizzed. Ice clinked. Voices buzzed. They went through to the garden. Closed-in spaces housed germs.

"Hey, Nick," someone said.

Another voice said, "Nick, how's it going?"

No one said hello to Esther. This was her daily experience. People didn't know what to say, so they didn't say anything. She'd become an alien in a bubble of invisibility.

Nick was in demand everywhere, but her presence was a dampener. Esther pointed with her chin to indicate she was going to talk to some of her friends. Nick picked up her meaning and nodded.

The group included two of her bridesmaids. She'd barely heard from them since the wedding had been delayed. Her arrival produced an awkward silence, then a babble of greetings. Someone asked, "How are you?" but as soon as the question came out, most of them dropped their eyes as though intent on numbering the blades of grass at their feet.

"Oh, I shouldn't have asked you—not overly tactful."

Esther gave a warm smile to show she wasn't offended. "You were just being polite. I understand." Could they move past the bumpy start? "I'll admit the fourth and fifth rounds of chemo have been a challenge. But I'm glad to be here."

Half the group avoided looking at her. Did they want to ask a question but didn't dare? Finally, one of the others spoke up.

"My cousin's boyfriend had cancer. They found out too late—"

Oh no, not again. "I hope you won't think me rude," Esther said, "but you know what I'd love? I'd love not to mention cancer at all this evening. Cancer dominates my life. I'd prefer to hear what you've been doing lately. Would that be okay?"

She'd been fearful about being so blunt, but the tension relaxed. Maybe if she stuck with this group she wouldn't need to repeat the same speech. The cancer horror stories she'd heard were unbeliev-able. Was there a competition to tell their worst-case scenarios? Then they'd conclude, "they died," as if this was a mere nothing. It would be a relief to talk about trips to the beach, promotions, and new babies.

Waiters circulated with trays of snacks. Chemotherapy had deadened Esther's sense of taste, but eating made her look normal. She didn't feel normal. Had her recent past matured her ahead of her contemporaries? Their talk sounded more like idle prattle than adult conversation.

What she longed for was a real conversation, with someone like Joy Wong. Was there anyone like her here? Esther stood on tiptoe and craned her neck. She spotted Gina standing on her own in the far corner of the garden. She disengaged herself from the original group and headed towards Gina, weaving around chairs, waiters, and groups of people.

"Great to see you, Gina." Esther kissed her cheek. "Thanks for all the cards. I find them a real encouragement."

"I hope I haven't overwhelmed you."

"Not at all. Apart from you, there's been a deafening silence. I'm afraid cancer causes embarrassment in a church like ours."

"I've been meaning to speak to you about church for a while," Gina said. "I want your advice."

"Look," Esther held up a hand. "Before you speak, could I talk to you about something that's been bothering my conscience for far too long?"

"Of course."

"It's about the bridesmaids for my wedding. I've been worried you were hurt not to be asked."

Gina swallowed. Had she been more hurt than Esther had realised? "I confess I was disappointed, but I understood. It's hard to choose when you have umpteen friends."

Gina was putting the whole situation in the kindest possible light. "True friends are rarer than I thought." Esther gripped Gina's forearm. "You've been pure gold. I'm sorry I didn't ask you to be a bridesmaid. I wanted to, but I'm afraid I let my father pressure me into other choices." She shifted her feet. "I should have stood up to him. I'm sorry—it was wrong."

Gina glanced around. "I can guess why your father gave you pressure. Victory is full of people who look like a million dollars. I don't fit in and never will. Some people think I'm doubly cursed. This …" she pointed to her waistline. "And this …" she nodded towards the fused ankle that gave her a limp. "That's what I wanted to talk to you about. I'm going to leave Victory and go somewhere else. Somewhere I'm accepted just as I am."

"Oh, Gina, I'm so sorry." Esther placed her hand on Gina's shoulder. "You're the best thing about Victory right now. I've been putting off my own decision. It's not going to be easy to leave while Nick is the youth pastor."

"Not easy?" Gina blinked. "I had no idea you'd ever think of such a thing. Your leaving would be a major issue for your parents —and Nick." A waiter passed and they each took a mini quiche. Once he moved on, Gina continued, "I'd sensed you were struggling. I feel a bit of a wimp going and leaving you behind."

"Look, would you be willing to pray about the whole thing with me?"

"What about Thursday after work? I'll look forward to it." As Esther was scribbling the time on a scrap of her napkin with a borrowed pen, a large drop of rain fell. Then another and another. Esther lost Gina in the rush towards the house.

She ended up squashed in a space at the bottom of the stairs. She scanned the room for Nick, and worked her way towards him, past dozens of party goers, including one man who was coughing without covering his mouth.

"I'm going to have to ask you to take me home," she said in his ear.

He glanced around the room. "What's wrong?"

Was he paying attention or was he distracted by the people who wanted to speak to him? "It was fine when we were outside, but now everyone is shut in the house and some guy has arrived, coughing all over the place."

Nick raised his hand in acknowledgement to someone behind her. "What's the big deal about a cough?" It was all she could do not to huff in frustration. Did he never listen? She knew he was busy in Melbourne but this lack of basic knowledge about cancer was ridiculous.

"I probably shouldn't have come tonight," she said as patiently as she could. Did she need to spell it out? "I have almost no immune system. Even a cold could give me a fever—" Nick looked blank. She did need to spell it out. "—and a fever will land me in hospital."

Nick finally turned to look at her. "I thought you were nearly finished this chemo thing."

At least now he was listening to her. "I am, but my system is weak right now."

"Isn't there an alternative?"

"Well, I could wear a mask but it certainly won't increase my chances of people talking to me."

He held up both palms. "No masks, please. I'll take you home."

"I'm sorry to wreck your evening."

He grunted. "I want to come back to the party after I've taken you home."

They drove home in silence. Nick barely waited until she was in the door before driving away. Had it been too much to hope that he might hug her goodbye? He'd been treating her like she had leprosy since her diagnosis, even though she'd assured him cancer wasn't contagious. Gifts and flowers were nice enough, but she needed a friend. A friend who loved her through every difficulty. Was that too much to ask?

Esther missed church the next day. She woke on Monday

morning with a fever. By midday, it had shot above the danger threshold.

CHAPTER 28

*E*sther's mother drove her to the hospital. After showing her chemo card, Esther was isolated in a special waiting area. An hour later she was much worse. She ached all over and her teeth chattered.

The doctor did a brief examination. "You need to be admitted for two days of intravenous antibiotics."

Esther felt too sick to argue. She barely noticed the first day, but after twenty-four hours, she'd improved enough to be bored with staring at the wall.

Nick had returned to Melbourne. Were they ever going to have any time together? His course wasn't even halfway through, and already it had taken over everything like a virus. Nowadays their only time together was Friday lunch for her forty-five minute lunch break, and some snatched minutes with the youth group or church members clustered around.

Even Sunday lunches with her parents were dominated by her father quizzing Nick on what he was learning. Esther was being reduced to a bystander with her own fiancé. She was sick of being told how lucky she was by outsiders who didn't know the frustrations of their situation. If only she'd voiced her objections when she had a chance. Her cancer would have been a more than reasonable excuse to delay the Melbourne training.

While Esther waited for visitors to arrive, she switched on the old-fashioned radio built into the bedside table. She twiddled the radio dial. She recognised a familiar voice before she slid past a station, and reversed the dial. It must be a repeat of her father's *Hour of Victory*. He was talking about divine healing. Esther reached out to switch him off. She had no need to hear anything more on this subject.

However, before she could change the station, a woman from the live audience asked, "But what if, despite everything you do, someone isn't healed?"

Her father paused. He never liked to speak in haste. "I know someone in that category right now. From the beginning, it has been obvious they don't believe in healing."

Esther's stomach fluttered. Surely, surely not? The woman's tiny squeak of protest was clearly audible over the radio but her father wasn't finished.

"We need to see ourselves well, then reach out to claim victory in Jesus' name."

Had her father really blamed her 'weak faith' all this time? Did everyone who heard this, everyone who knew them, guess she was the 'someone'?

The woman was persistent. Who'd allowed her on the programme?

"But surely there could be another explanation."

"As I said, if it's not lack of faith, then you must look for whether there is unrepented sin in their life."

Oh, Dad. Esther's heart was wrung in private anguish. She wanted to switch the radio off, but now she was trapped. She couldn't unhear what she'd heard. Her father was steamrolling the woman. Even if she said something worthwhile, would her father back down and say 'sorry' on air? Not likely.

The woman had another question.

"Doctor Macdonald, you seem to place heavy burdens of responsibility on people. Surely there are cases in the Bible where people weren't healed?"

Her father went on the attack, although he masked it with a gentle voice. "Why don't you tell me one?"

"Give me a second."

Her father wasn't going to give the woman any time. "Can you think of any story in the New Testament?" he said in a voice not quite scornful but somehow suggesting it. "No? What about the Old?" Like a boxer battering her from the right and then the left he never allowed her a moment to think. The woman didn't have a chance against such an experienced opponent. "You can't think of any situation, can you?"

"I need a little more time."

"I'm afraid time is what we've run out of," her father said. "Write in if you can think of an instance and we'll be happy to answer your letter."

Esther could picture her father turning his confident smile towards the audience as he concluded the show.

"That's all for today. To all our listeners, let me challenge you. Work on your faith muscles. Do you need healing power? Call the healing hotline on 1-800-555-1234." The programme ended with its victorious-sounding theme song. Her father had sponsored a nation-wide competition to find the ideal music to start and conclude his programme.

Esther reached out a trembling hand to switch off the radio. She could no longer deceive herself about her father's views. He was trapped in the world he'd designed for himself. He believed non-healing equalled failure—a failure of faith or morality. She used to be proud of him. Now she was ashamed.

Esther could think of people who hadn't had their prayers answered. At least not like they'd expected. Joseph, waiting in slavery and jail, not knowing when, or if, he'd ever be released. Abraham, waiting for a son, wondering whether God had forgotten him. What about the countless anonymous men and women who died while Jesus was on earth and weren't raised from the dead?

Esther had undertaken some surreptitious research on people who'd left Victory. It wasn't an insignificant number. Some left because they rejected her father's teaching. Some left because they felt sub-standard. Some had been so hurt they abandoned God altogether. Her father's views influenced thousands, tens of thousands.

Oh, Lord. Help him to see clearly. Don't let him lead others astray. Show me what you want me to do.

Was that her heavenly Father's voice? *"My child, follow me…"*

---

*W*hen Paul Webster poked his head into her room, Esther swallowed a mouthful of water down the wrong way.

"I heard you were here and thought I'd come and check how they were caring for you."

Esther coughed. "I thought people of your status sent their juniors or used the phone."

"Er—yes." He avoided looking at her. "I—I was in the area. We want to have you out of here so you can complete your chemo treatment before Christmas. Everyone blames us if they have a miserable Christmas."

Why had Dr Webster dropped in on her? Did it have something to do with all her prayers for him? "How do you spend Christmas?"

"I take a few days off. My children usually come on the twenty-sixth."

So he did have some normal life. "How old are they?"

"Fourteen and sixteen. We don't see each other much since their mother left."

Goodness, he was sharing personal things. "I'm sorry to hear that. It must be difficult."

He avoided her eyes. "Understandable, really. They barely saw me." He picked up the medical chart on the end of the bed. Was he regretting stepping outside his medical role? "Anyway, I was wanting to check you weren't too low. It's not unusual to have a setback at this stage of treatment."

"I'm feeling much better than the last few days." She'd follow his lead but she prayed that somehow, one day, she'd have an opportunity to talk about deeper things.

"Do you remember what we talked about last time?" he asked.

"Which topic in particular?" She tried to make her tone sound casual. Where was this conversation going?

"I've been mulling over something since I first met you. First, I concluded that all religious types coped better with cancer and its treatment. But I have to concede—very reluctantly—that I was wrong."

Was it happening at last? Was Dr Webster venturing on to deeper subjects? A flicker of fear ran along her nerve endings. What if she messed up? She'd better check what he meant before she got excited. Perhaps he wasn't saying what he seemed to be. "What were you wrong about?"

"I've realised it isn't every religion that makes a difference. Those who had your ... I've been trying to come up with a description for it. Perhaps 'peaceful confidence' or 'contented joy'. They've all been followers of Jesus, not merely churchgoers or followers of other religions."

Unbelievable. An immediate answer to prayer. It was okay to mentally caper in delight but she must not startle him.

"I can spot the people who are using religion as a crutch and one more way to deny what's happening to them. You don't do that."

So he wasn't as impervious as he seemed. *Lord give me courage and wisdom.* "I'm learning to trust my heavenly Father more and more. Even death is no longer a terrible thing to me because I'd only go straight to be with Jesus."

He took a step backwards. "Now, now, don't get carried away. Surely you wouldn't go as far as to believe all that."

"All what?"

"That heaven stuff."

"It's a package deal. I can't pick and choose the bits of the Bible I like. It's either all God's word or it isn't. If it isn't, then I'm wasting my time and deluding others."

Dr Webster edged closer. "I wouldn't have thought you'd be a gambler, trusting in blind faith."

"It's not a gamble when it's based on evidence," Esther said. "You should investigate it sometime. I could lend you a book I've found helpful."

He made a face. "I'm not sure if I'm ready for the challenge."

"I'll pray you'll be ready soon," Esther said with a grin.

"I don't need to worry about your health. You can still hold your own in a debate." He reached into his suit coat pocket. "I nearly forgot. Michelle gave me your appointment card." He handed it over. "You should be able to cope with the final treatment by that date. You'll start six weeks of radiation in the new year."

Back to the harsh realities of life with cancer. Wouldn't it be wonderful if she could forget it for a whole day at a time? "I haven't had time to think about radiotherapy. How often do I do that?"

"Five days a week, but it only takes about fifteen minutes."

"Another delight to look forward to."

"It's nothing like chemotherapy. You won't feel it, and there are only a few side effects."

"You mean my hair might grow again?" Esther touched her head.

"A couple of months from now, you won't recognise yourself." He checked his watch. "Anyway, I have to go. We'll see you soon. Good luck." He strode out of the room.

Miracles did still happen. Had the man who always seemed as resistant as a rock just talked about the Bible? And raised the topic himself? Esther closed her eyes to pray for more conversations to come.

A footstep woke her up from her doze.

"Oh, Dr Singh." Esther wriggled back to an upright position. "To what do I owe this pleasure?"

"You'd better not call me Dr Singh here. This is a personal, not a professional visit. I was having lunch with Sue and she told me you were in here. My name is Sitara."

"It's a beautiful name. What does it mean?"

"Star."

"So does mine. My parents thought Esther sounded beautiful. I guess they hoped I'd shine like a star."

Dr Singh stood next to the bed rather than taking a seat. "Parents the world over have the same desires for their children."

Esther hadn't expected to ever have an opportunity to share with Dr Singh, yet here she was. Maybe she could plant a seed or two, even if she was never able to water them. Couldn't God be trusted to bring someone else into her life to follow up? "I'm named after Esther, a famous queen during the Persian empire. Do you know the story of Esther?"

"Is it in the Bible?"

"In the Old Testament. It's an exciting story of attempted murder, fiendish plots and changed fortunes." Esther used her hands and exaggerated her facial expressions like she was a reporter in a movie.

"Sounds like a best seller, but I'm not sure I have time," Dr Singh said. "I'm up to date with the medical side of what's happening with your situation. I'm more interested in you. How are you coping?"

Esther laughed to herself. It was almost impossible to answer Sitara's question without talking about her spiritual journey. But how to do it in a way that was both brief and to the point?

"The beginning was rough, but I'm doing much better now. I had a sort of spiritual crisis that forced me to rethink my beliefs. It was a bumpy ride, but now I'm starting to see God's plan in it all."

"I suppose you're talking about the God of the Bible."

"Yes, that one. My crisis led to understanding what it means to follow Jesus. That's made all the difference."

Dr Singh sighed. "It's not a place I've come to. I've rejected the gods of my past but am not yet ready to replace them."

Yet another person to pray for. Esther's prayer list was chock-a-block with people who needed to meet Jesus. Her prayers used to be so perfunctory and self-centred. "I'd love everyone to have the peace and joy I've found."

"I'm glad for you." Dr Singh moved sideways towards the end of the bed. "Sorry for the short visit. I'd better get back to work."

Esther praised God for these two opportunities. While she was praying, an orderly transferred a new patient into the room. They were obviously less concerned about her immune system than they'd been yesterday. *And yes Lord, I also pray for the new patient who's just being transferred into my room. Help me to have opportunities to share with her.*

As she finished praying, she looked up at the clock. Almost five. Gina and Joy would arrive soon.

Gina had been begging to meet Joy for weeks. At last, they were going to hear Joy's own story.

CHAPTER 29

*E*sther drew her legs up under the covers so Gina could sit on the end of the bed. That left the only chair available for Joy.

"Joy, why don't you start by telling us a little about your family."

"I am the elder of two sisters. I was ambitious and determined to enter medical school so I became my parent's hope for the future." Joy paused to look at them. "But history was about to destroy my plans."

"Do you mean Chairman Mao?" Esther wrinkled her nose.

"Yes. Most judge him harshly now, but back then we viewed Mao Zedong as a hero worthy of worship because he was making our nation great." Joy spread her arms wide. "I dreamed of being a medical specialist in a glorious country. It was not to be. Mao launched what you know as the Cultural Revolution."

"What year was this?" Gina asked.

"Nineteen sixty-six. I'd just completed high school when all the universities were closed and the authorities sent us into the country." Joy shifted in her seat. "At the time, it seemed a light-hearted adventure—but it soon turned sour. Food was rationed, and, most of the time, the work was pointless."

History Esther had only heard about second-hand, grew skin and walked around in living colour.

"The Cultural Revolution proclaimed it was out to destroy old thinking and traditions. I came under suspicion because both my parents were teachers." Joy grimaced. "The leaders urged their followers to report anyone who valued traditional things. Several of my former classmates saw their chance, not only to tear me down to their level, but to be rewarded for their resentment."

"It must have been terrible."

"Far more than terrible. Much of what was good in my country disappeared. More than one and a half million died in prisons and labour camps."

Esther envisioned long lines of anonymous grey faces marching towards their deaths.

"I was one of the lucky ones," Joy said, her lips in a tight line. "I survived."

Esther clasped her knees. "What helped you survive?"

"Ultimately, it was the grace of God, though I didn't know it then." Joy shook her head, her eyes sad. "Before my time in prison, I despised Christians. I considered them slaves of Western thought and, therefore, traitors. Christians were selected for the worst punishments and the harshest labour. They were everything Communists most feared—people whose allegiance was to a universal king."

"Yes," Gina said. "I can see how they might feel threatened."

"But the more the Christians were persecuted," Joy said, "the more they loved others and radiated Jesus' light." She hesitated for a long moment. "I now consider Mao to be the world's greatest evangelist."

Esther sat up straight. "What do you mean?"

"It's a rather startling viewpoint and it's one I've come to only through years of reflection. Mao's efforts to crush the church created the best conditions for it to grow."

Esther could see her own look of confusion reflected in Gina's expression.

"Let me explain using an illustration from a famous Chinese preacher. When asked if he feared persecution, he picked up a glass from the table and dropped it on the ground." Joy dropped an imaginary glass in front of them. Then she stood, and stamped on the floor.

What on earth was she doing?

"Was he mad?" Gina asked.

"The original listeners certainly thought so, but the preacher said, 'The enemies of God's people will persecute you and try to stamp you out. But the more they stamp, the more pieces there'll be.' Like in Acts, the Christians who were scattered kept spreading the good news."

"That's a great illustration," Esther said. "I'm so encouraged when I hear examples of people who went through persecution and held on to their faith."

"The Christian prisoners baffled me. No matter what was done to them, they overflowed with joy. They sang all the time. They'd use their own blood to write on their cell walls, and it was my job to scrub the words off. They'd write 'Jesus came into the world to save sinners of whom I'm the worst,' or 'This is love, not that we loved him but that he loved us and gave himself up for us.' Who was this Jesus they wrote about? And what was this 'love'?"

Tears prickled the edges of Esther's eyes. Christians were incomprehensible to outsiders.

Joy cleared her throat. "How could I understand love? In my world, love didn't exist. There was only self. In my world, my classmates had survived by condemning me."

"It sounds like a nightmare," Gina said. "What happened?"

"I didn't have to puzzle long about love. A few older Christian ladies shared their blankets and gave me the best of the food. In fact, they starved themselves for me." A tear trickled down Joy's face. She took a clean tissue out of her pocket and blew her nose. "Although I accepted their gifts, I certainly didn't want to become one of them. I intended to survive. I was *not* into self-sacrifice."

"Surely there were Christians who didn't sacrifice themselves?" Esther said.

"Those Christians didn't label themselves Christians for long. Prison soon sifted out the real from the fake. Persecution burnt off the dross until only the real gold was left. And no one could mistake the real thing."

There was silence.

The image of gold described Joy perfectly. Suffering had produced twenty-four carat gold in her life. Bright for all to see.

"We see so little persecution here," Esther said. "It's great to hear God doesn't waste suffering."

"Yes," Gina said. "Why do you think we don't experience much persecution?"

Joy didn't answer.

"Maybe because there really isn't much of a difference between Christians and non-Christians," Esther said. Gina's question would be great for another time. "Joy, how did you become one of those people you despised?"

"Those women unintentionally got me into trouble. They loved me so much the guards assumed I'd become one of them. Three years were added to my sentence because I had 'become a Christian'. I was furious at the false accusation, so I decided to pay more attention to what they were saying. If I had to suffer as a Christian, I might as well enjoy the benefits."

They all laughed. "Sounds like God has a weird sense of humour."

"He does. He often does the exact opposite of what we'd expect. In prison, he used those illiterate old ladies to achieve his purposes.

They told me stories. Each knew only a few, but together they knew hundreds. We organised story schools and I worked out the chronological order. We didn't have much food for our bodies, but those stories gave us food for our hearts."

There was total silence in the other cubicle behind the curtain. Esther hadn't heard a page turning for ages. They weren't the only ones listening to Joy.

"What happened next?" Esther asked.

"We learned a new story every few days, and we'd pass it on to ten people each day. We told stories as we scrubbed floors and stirred the soup. We even told stories as we waited in queues, whispering them to those in front and behind us."

It must have resembled a busy anthill. "The more stories we learned, the faster we learned them. Prison became a sacred place. If we were sent to solitary confinement, we'd tell stories out loud. Sometimes we'd hear a shoe scuffing the ground outside the door."

"Did any of the guards become believers?" Gina's eyes were round.

"They would have lost their jobs if it became public knowledge but we suspected several did, because they treated us more kindly." Joy stared at her feet. "Nearly all those women died in prison."

Gina sniffed, and tears pooled in Esther's eyes. Such faithful women. Would she ever sacrifice herself like this for others? It was easy to be kind and generous when it cost nothing. But true love was costly.

"Before the women died, they made me promise that when I was released, I'd learn English and translate Christian books to make sure the believers were fed good spiritual food."

"How long were you in prison?" Gina asked.

"Twelve years."

Gina gasped. "Twelve years. But that would have made you thirty, and all for no reason."

"It did seem a waste, looking at it from the world's point of view. But looking back, I see it as God's grace to me. Suffering injustice made me search long and hard for real justice. It made me long for a love and a security that couldn't be snatched away."

Esther squeezed Joy's hand. "Thanks for sharing your story. I know it can't be easy reliving it. What happened after your release?"

"It was too late to be a doctor, but I could fulfil other people's dreams for me. So I learned English."

"How was that possible?"

"As I came out of prison, Deng Xiaoping launched his 'Open Door' Policy. This meant I could find old English textbooks, if I was extremely careful—and prison certainly taught me about being careful. Through a series of miracles, we acquired a short-wave radio. A team of us learned together. Finally, my competitiveness could be put to good use. During the day, I worked as a cleaner because Christians were often restricted to labouring jobs. I found it ideal. I'd mop and practice making up English sentences with my new vocabulary. And I'd review ten stories a day."

Esther couldn't resist asking. "Did you listen to the BBC? Because I've always thought you sound like their announcers."

Joy laughed. "Yes, I did. It was a strange way to learn a language. Some of the team hand-copied Bibles, but we concentrated on reference books for pastors."

"I know Westerners used to smuggle Bibles into China," Gina said. "I guess Bibles aren't needed now, since they're officially printed inside the country."

"Many people think like you do but printing is still tightly controlled. The official presses focus on foreign customers. Only government-sponsored churches can buy Bibles, but the majority of believers are in underground churches. There is a vast hunger for God's word in my country."

"I wish Australians were as hungry for God's word," Gina said. "How did you end up in Australia?"

"It wasn't part of my plan." A ghost of a smile tugged at the corner of Joy's mouth. "It happened because I married in prison."

Gina and Esther's eyes widened. Esther said, "How was such a thing possible?"

"Rules aren't evenly applied in China." Joy shrugged. "There was a sudden reversal of policy and they promoted marriage. Not because they were being kind, but to breed soldiers. I was assigned a husband, but we rarely saw each other."

What would it be like to be assigned a husband? How could Esther compare her life of comfort and choices with one of hardship, hunger and confinement?

A smile lit up Joy's face. Was it the glow of treasured memories? "Even with the matter of a husband, God was gracious. My husband was a new Christian too. We spent our first night praising God for his generosity in matching us, even if we were only allowed one night together each month."

What a marriage. And she'd complained about Nick's absence for two weeks at a time. Where was Joy's husband now?

A cloud passed over the lingering sunset of Joy's smile. "We only ever had one child and she was born during my imprisonment. Probably those years of hard labour decreased our fertility. I did have one more pregnancy, but I lost the baby." Joy clenched her jaw, as if fighting tears. "And my husband, my beloved husband ..." The tears won. "He was so weakened by prison, he died ... ten years after our marriage."

Joy wasn't the only one crying. They sat with their heads down and tears dripping off their noses and chins. Behind the curtain there was a sniff. Esther trembled. Life was so unfair. Couldn't God have spared Joy's husband or second child? And why did Joy suffer so much when those at Victory Church seemed to suffer so little?

Gina burrowed into the pocket of her bag and handed around some tissues.

Esther took a shaky breath. "I'm so, so sorry."

"Don't be sorry for me. God has only ever been good and gracious."

"I don't think many people would agree with you."

"Then they'd be wrong. First," Joy held up a finger, "prison stripped me of my pride and brought me to Jesus." She held up a second finger. "Second, I wouldn't exchange my prison friendships for anything." She continued ticking off on her fingers. "Third, a Christian husband with whom I never quarrelled. Not many married people can say that. Fourth, a beautiful daughter who loves Jesus. Even my miscarriage was a mercy. God took our baby to his home before it could be murdered under the government's brand new one-child policy." She sniffed. "God doesn't owe me anything."

Esther turned to Gina. "You can see why I love my times with Joy. She's well-named. Her thankfulness and joy are contagious."

"Hopefully I'll catch this contagious disease too," Gina said. "Joy, you still haven't told us why you're in Australia."

"When my daughter turned eighteen, the Chinese government relaxed the rules about overseas study. She won a scholarship and arrived here a few days before the Tiananmen massacre. You remember? On 4 June 1989. That meant she could stay in Australia, and bring me out to join her. I struggled with whether to leave or stay. I came because of the easy access to books. I'm careful to only choose the best ones. Books that won't harm the church."

"Anyone looking at you would never guess at the pain and difficulties of your life," Esther said. "Your accent made me assume you grew up in a wealthy family."

"Even wealth is no guarantee of an easy life."

"How have you avoided bitterness?" Gina asked.

"I told Esther before that the story of Joseph was significant to me. He refused to let injustice embitter him. Do you remember what Joseph said to the brothers who'd sold him into slavery?"

"Remind us," Esther said.

"He said, 'Don't be angry with yourselves for selling me here, because it was to save lives that God sent me ahead of you.' Later he says, 'So then, it was not you who sent me here but God.' It's hard to hold on to revenge when I've been surrounded by so many examples of forgiveness. Not only the people in the Bible, but my own people in prison. If I'd become a doctor, I might have achieved my goals but ended up wealthy, empty, and lonely."

She got to her feet and placed a hand on Esther and Gina's shoulders. "God's ways are always better than ours."

CHAPTER 30

*E*sther was discharged on Wednesday, and a letter arrived from Nick on Thursday morning. He'd sent a huge bunch of flowers while she'd been in hospital, but they'd barely talked since the night of the party. The flowers made her blood boil. Didn't he get it? She wanted to talk to him, not receive flowers. Every day she prayed Nick would talk with her about things that mattered. God had already answered so many prayers. Why wouldn't he answer this one too?

Esther grabbed the letter, rushed up to her room, and tore open the envelope.

DEAR ESTHER,

AS YOU KNOW, THE NEWS OF YOUR CANCER CAME AS A COLOSSAL SHOCK. I STILL DON'T UNDERSTAND, WHY US?

Progress.

Nick had finally raised the issue of her cancer. His letters had driven her crazy because they focused on his training and snippets of daily life, as though she was perfectly fine and they were two friends out for a stroll in the sunshine. They weren't just friends. They were two people who should have been three months into married life.

Why was Nick still stuck on asking 'why us'? How come he couldn't move past his initial reaction? Should she have insisted that they visit a counsellor together? She turned back to the letter. *Oh Jesus, please help this letter to be the start of his breakthrough.* His silence about her cancer terrified her because it seemed abnormal.

But perhaps his silence signified he was processing things. It wasn't his fault he was slower at processing.

I'VE BEEN THINKING HARD WHILE YOU WERE IN HOSPITAL. IN FACT, I WENT TO TALK TO AN ONCOLOGIST FRIEND OF MINE AND TOLD HIM ABOUT YOUR DIAGNOSIS.

This sounded a positive first step. But had the oncologist helped him move forward?

I WANTED TO KNOW WHAT CHANCE YOU HAD TO BE CURED. HE WASN'T TOO HOPEFUL. TOLD ME YOU HAD ABOUT A SIXTY PERCENT CHANCE OF LIVING PAST TEN YEARS.

That was a punch below the belt. Paul Webster had quoted a figure of seventy percent. Now someone had stolen an extra ten percent. Not ten percent of something abstract like money or possessions, but ten percent of her life.

She laid the letter aside and covered her eyes with both hands. A trembling started, beginning at her legs and progressing up her body. A horrible dread oozed into her heart. A forty percent chance that even if she finished her treatment, she wouldn't live past five years. Would she ever hold her own children? Watch them grow and graduate and marry? The questions piled up and buried her deep.

She'd longed for this letter. Now it depressed her.

Esther squared her shoulders and picked up the letter again.

THAT FIGURE OF SIXTY PERCENT SHOOK ME. I'M THIRTY YEARS OLD. I WANT TO HAVE A FAMILY.

He wasn't the only one who wanted those things, so why didn't he include her?

I ASKED MY FRIEND ABOUT THE CHANCES OF CHILDREN AFTER CHEMO. HE SAID MOST PEOPLE MANAGED TO GET PREGNANT, BUT IT WAS HARDER AND TOOK LONGER. I ASKED MYSELF IF I WAS WILLING TO PAY THE PRICE.

The shaking started again, and the pages she held quivered. Nick's questions didn't sound like someone processing issues. They sounded more like a captain about to jump ship. She clamped one hand under her leg to control her shakes and forced herself to keep reading.

I HAD TO SET MY DREAMS ASIDE FOR TEN YEARS AFTER MY FATHER DIED, AND I'M NOT SURE I CAN DO IT AGAIN. I'VE DELAYED MY DECISION BECAUSE I HOPED I WAS THE KIND OF PERSON WHO COULD. I WANTED TO THINK I WAS SOME KIND OF HERO, BUT I'VE DISCOVERED I'M NOT.

Tears dripped off Esther's chin. She couldn't stop herself thinking back to the day of their engagement and Nick's face after she'd said 'yes' to his proposal. The memory was salt in the open wound of her heart. It didn't seem fair. After all she'd been going through, couldn't God have saved and restored her relationship with Nick?

The question was the first rootlet of bitterness. She swallowed, as if swallowing an unpleasant taste.

Lord, help me to be like Joy and Joseph. Don't let bitterness get its claws into my life. But Lord, please, don't let this letter be headed where it seems to be going. I don't think I can bear any more.

But it looked liked she'd have to bear more, because Nick's letter wasn't finished.

PERSONALLY, I'M ALSO CONCERNED ABOUT THE DOUBTS YOU'VE HAD THAT HAVE LED YOU TO QUESTION YOUR FATHER'S TEACHING. IS YOUR FATHER RIGHT? WAS IT LACK OF FAITH WHICH PREVENTED YOUR HEALING? OR DID UNFORGIVEN SIN BLOCK THE HEALING PROCESS?

No, no, no. Nick was the last person she wanted influenced by her father's teaching. Why hadn't he come to talk these issues through with her? Why, oh why, hadn't she tried harder to communicate with him? They should have gone to proper counselling with someone who'd been through similar situations. She turned back to the letter, miserable.

YOUR ATTITUDE HAS ALSO STRUCK ME AS NOT SUITABLE FOR A PASTOR'S WIFE.

Blow upon blow. What did Nick expect in a wife? Did he only want a yes-woman? She'd been sure Nick was right for her. Now she wasn't sure at all. She wasn't sure of anything.

SO ON ALL COUNTS, IT'S BETTER FOR US TO DISSOLVE OUR ENGAGEMENT. IT SEEMS WE ARE NOT AS SUITED AS WE ORIGINALLY THOUGHT WE WERE. I LEAVE YOU FREE TO PURSUE THE ROAD YOU THINK YOU NEED TO TAKE.

NICK

Esther stared at the tiny blotch in the carpet where she'd once spilled ink, her mind blank. Alone in a dry desert. Thirsty and about to die. How could this be it? Nick made it sound as if she was about to die tomorrow. As if he was doing her a favour.

Just when she most needed a friend, Nick was distancing himself from her suffering. What a weak support he'd turned out to be. Outwardly he appeared strong, but inside his character had been white-anted—an intact exterior eaten away by her father's teaching to leave a mere shell.

What did she feel? Anger and sadness. Frustration and pity. Her poor mother, who'd laboured over a wedding dress that wouldn't be needed. And Dad, who would be devastated to lose the son he'd chosen, mentored, and championed.

She lay down and punched her pillow. Better than weeping. *Lord give me strength to write a letter back. The kind of letter that builds up rather than tears down.*

She didn't have the energy to write immediately, but she kept praying.

The next thing she knew it was dark. What time was it? She'd been closeted in her room for hours. Why hadn't her parents come to investigate? She looked towards the door. A square of white paper protruded underneath.

I KNOCKED, BUT YOU DIDN'T ANSWER. PRESUME YOU'RE STILL FEELING EXHAUSTED. DINNER IN MICROWAVE. DAD AND I HAVE GONE OUT.

Thank goodness. She wasn't ready to face anyone yet. She'd have time to write to Nick and pull herself together. If she had her light off before her parents returned, she might be able to avoid them until tomorrow. If they saw her tonight, they'd have to be blind not to see that something was wrong.

Esther sat down and took a piece of paper from her desk drawer. This was one letter she'd hand write even if she had to rewrite it several times. It wasn't the time for an impersonal typed letter. *Lord, I'm bruised and hurt. Help me to honour you and not lash out in anger.*

She picked up her pen and wrote.

DEAR NICK,

I WAS DISAPPOINTED TO RECEIVE YOUR LETTER. I HOPED YOU

WOULD CLING TO JESUS IN THESE HARD TIMES AND ASK HIM FOR
WISDOM.

Esther read the second line again. No. It sounded too much like criticism. She crossed it out and went on. She'd make a good copy later.

THIS HAS BEEN THE TOUGHEST TIME OF MY LIFE, BUT I WOULDN'T
EXCHANGE IT FOR ANYTHING. I HAVE LEARNED SO MUCH ABOUT
MYSELF. CANCER HAS BROUGHT ME TO JESUS AND TAUGHT ME TO
TRUST HIM IN THE DARKNESS. I DON'T KNOW WHAT THE ROAD
AHEAD HOLDS, BUT I DO KNOW THAT JESUS IS IN CONTROL.

She reread what she'd written. She'd wanted to assure Nick she'd be okay. But she didn't want to avoid writing about their relationship, in case he misinterpreted her as hard-hearted. The first lines of her letter were a reminder to herself of what was important. She'd need them in the days ahead.

THANK YOU FOR MAKING YOURSELF CLEAR. THESE LAST MONTHS
HAVE BEEN PAINFUL TO ME BECAUSE WE DIDN'T SEEM TO BE
COMMUNICATING. PART OF THE BLAME IS MINE. I DON'T THINK I
UNDERSTOOD HOW MUCH YOU WERE STRUGGLING. I WAS TOO TIED
UP WITH DEALING WITH CANCER AND CHEMO, AND I DIDN'T HAVE
ENERGY TO SPARE FOR YOU. I'M SORRY.

Now that she'd started writing, some of her pain flowed via the ink onto the paper.

YOUR FRIEND'S PROGNOSIS OF MY CONDITION IS SOBERING.

A tear dropped onto the paper and smudged two words.

IN SOME WAYS, I UNDERSTAND WHY YOU HAVE MADE THE CHOICE YOU HAVE. WHAT WOULD I HAVE DONE IF OUR SITUATIONS WERE REVERSED? MAY YOU CLING TO JESUS WITH BOTH HANDS.

Esther sat back. She'd covered the essentials, and didn't want to ramble on. She nibbled the end of her pen. How should she end?

I WILL RETURN YOUR RING ONCE MUM AND DAD KNOW OUR NEWS.

By now she should be practiced at breaking bad news to her parents, but practice didn't make it any easier.

NOW WOULD BE A GOOD TIME FOR ME TO FIND ANOTHER CHURCH. I HAVE BEEN CONSIDERING THIS FOR SOME TIME, AND LEAVING VICTORY SHOULD MAKE THINGS EASIER FOR BOTH YOU AND MY PARENTS.
MAY YOU BE A MAN AFTER GOD'S HEART.
ESTHER

She didn't trust herself to write more. Revenge was something she'd always despised, but there were times in life when all a person wanted was the satisfaction of clawing someone's face, punching them, or spitting on them.

With the last of her strength, Esther copied the letter onto a fresh sheet of paper, addressed the envelope and took it out to the mailbox around the corner.

She'd ring Gina before work in the morning and invite herself to dinner.

CHAPTER 31

*A*s Esther pushed Gina's doorbell, a kettle whistled inside. Gina ushered Esther into her studio apartment without asking a single question. The handmade patchwork cushions and Gina's artwork matched the sunflower-yellow feature wall. The homeliness embraced her. Esther curled her feet up under her in one of the two armchairs squeezed into the tiny living room and took the peppermint tea Gina offered.

Gina sat in the other armchair. "Do you want to eat first or talk first?"

"Better talk first, or it will be too awkward—oh bother—" Esther's tears spilled over. "I was hoping to get through this without crying."

Gina reached behind and took a box of tissues off the counter. "Rabbit hutch-sized homes have their benefits."

Esther dabbed her eyes and blew her nose. Her news stuck in her throat, big and solid as a cricket ball.

"Has something happened with Nick?"

Bless Gina for her perception. "The wedding's off." Said bluntly, it didn't sound too bad. Yet those three words were nails driven into her heart. She winced as their implications hit her all over again.

"Permanently?"

"Yes." Another nail pierced her.

"Your decision or his?"

"His." She could manage one word answers.

"Are you okay?"

How could she answer that? What was 'okay'? Was okay being able to get out of bed? Being able to go to work? Being able to answer questions?

"Honestly, I don't know if I'm okay. I'm not even sure I know what being 'okay' is any more. I feel like I've done too many rounds in a boxing ring."

Gina reached over and laid a hand on her shoulder. "I was afraid that might happen. Did he tell you when he was home last weekend?"

"Would you expect him to? Look, read the letter."

Gina took the letter but didn't open it. "Are you sure you want me to do this?"

"It's easier than me trying to tell you. I'd cry the whole time." Esther sat with her hands clutched around her warm cup. The warmth reminded her of Gina—encouraging, perceptive, and a rock of practical kindness and common sense.

Gina read the letter once, then again more slowly. "How have you responded?"

"I wrote a letter back, but don't worry, I didn't dash off a reply." Esther sniffed. "I couldn't. I was too flattened. Then I prayed about what to write."

"How have your parents responded?"

"I haven't even had the guts to tell them yet—I wanted to come here and talk things through with you first."

Gina leaned back in her chair and they both were silent.

"What is the hardest thing for you right now?" Gina asked after a long pause.

Did Esther even know the answer herself? She'd come here because Gina could be depended upon to use her God-given wisdom to help Esther see more clearly.

"I'm not sure whether I can explain, but I'll try. When Nick asked me to marry him, I was on a high. He clicked with our family and it seemed a perfect match."

Gina's eyes were focused on her and she nodded every so often.

"Once we were engaged, we started on the whirling merry-go-round of wedding preparation. So many things to think about. So many people with opinions." Neither of them mentioned her father. They didn't need to. Esther shook her head in frustration. "Sorry to be so roundabout."

"Keep trying. I'm not in a rush."

"Maybe what I'm trying to say is that being engaged seemed to tap into some deep spring in my heart. I began to fantasise about a future that included an adoring husband and delightful children. So maybe, I'm grieving the loss of what might have been." Esther took two sips of her tea.

"God has wired us for family and children, so I understand those griefs."

"Yes, but I ought to be grieving the loss of Nick. His loss should be what devastates me, not the loss of my dreams. I feel guilty because I'm not grieving Nick more." Esther hung her head. "In fact, I'm almost relieved, and that makes me ashamed."

Gina made no comment. The silence was the silence between two friends at ease with each other and not the silence of discomfort.

Why did she feel ashamed? Was it false shame, or was it a warning flag of deeper issues? Had she even loved Nick? Or had she loved something else entirely?

Gina touched her knee. "What are you thinking about?"

"I'm embarrassed to say." Esther swivelled to look at Gina. "Did I even love Nick? Could I have deceived myself?"

"It's an easy thing to do. We can focus on outward things, things that don't matter in the long term."

"Gina—" Esther hugged her knees to her chest. "I think I've been in love with love. Nick and I had so much in common, but we didn't talk about deep stuff. Sure, we worked well together, but that might not mean anything more than we'd make good colleagues."

"Do you think your father's approval was a factor?"

"I'm afraid so. I was tired of being treated as if there was a hedge of thorns around me. The few who dared to push through never gained Dad's approval. I guess it was a relief to have a boyfriend I could invite home. It didn't hurt that he was good-looking, sporty, and drooled over by the other women at church." Esther sighed. "I've been a fool."

"The problems haven't all been on your side."

Esther sighed a sigh of pain and weariness. "I've been so disappointed in him. I kept loving a fantasy man of my dreams." She stared up at the ceiling. "In many ways, our relationship died months ago. Nick's never gotten past the 'why me' phase. He won't consider that my father could be wrong, so he's left believing I sinned, or I didn't have enough faith to be healed. When I suggest other possibilities, he thinks I'm trying to avoid admitting my sin."

"They're both trapped by their own thinking."

"Yes." Esther massaged her aching neck. "Nick's been in denial since we first knew about the cancer. At least his letter finally admits he's no hero. There have been many times since I was diagnosed when I agonised over whether I should break off the engagement. It seemed too big an ask to have Nick stick around someone with stage III cancer. I'm not sure what I'd do in his situation."

"I wish he'd stopped his letter there," Gina said. "I could empathise with that reason, but he lost my respect with the later criticisms."

"Do you think his father's death might impact his ability to see my father's faults?"

Gina raised an eyebrow. "What do you mean?"

"Dad is much more than Nick's boss. He's become his surrogate father. I know only too well how difficult it is to question Dad over anything. I can't say I blame Nick for not wanting to take the risk."

"Sounds like I'd better double my prayer for you."

"Yes, please. We need it. When I look ahead, everything seems dark and confused."

"Can't you see any hope at all?"

"You know the answer. I trust that Jesus is sovereign. I can't see how, but I'm willing to believe he reigns, and he won't abandon me now."

Gina smiled, the slow smile of joy at a new sunrise. "It's a magnificent hope, isn't it?"

"I'm concerned for Mum as well as Nick. Both have deep loyalties to my father. Dad would need a Hiroshima-sized event to change him."

"Let's hope it doesn't come to that. Why don't we pray for them now?"

She and Gina bowed their heads, and Gina prayed.

"Lord, have mercy on Nick. He'll be hurting now, and feeling a failure. Lord, help him not to sweep things under the carpet. Help him to confront any issues buried deep within his heart. Help him to turn to you as Father and not to William. William may fail, but you will never fail."

Prayer was an amazing thing. Even if the words were nothing special, supernatural comfort still flowed.

"And give courage to Esther as she tells her parents this news. Help the whole family to pull together and not splinter apart."

Yes, splintering was what Esther was afraid of. Gina prayed for another minute.

"Amen," Esther said. "I can't thank you enough for listening. You've been such an encouragement to me."

"Well, watching what you've gone through has taught me plenty. Are you ready to eat?" Gina stood up and moved into the kitchen. "Nothing fancy, only steak and vegetables."

They ate with trays balanced on their knees amidst a soothing silence. Soothing because it was between two real friends who trusted and respected each other.

"Have you found another church?" Esther asked after she swallowed her last mouthful.

"I've taken my time and visited a few. Would you like to come with me this week?"

That was exactly what Esther wanted. "It would be much easier for everyone if I wasn't at Victory this Sunday. What time's the service?"

CHAPTER 32

*E*sther arrived at work the next day bleary-eyed from lack of sleep. She'd have taken a mental health day if she hadn't already taken so much time off work. Her emotions were all over the place. Regret and disappointment. Relief, that she didn't have to struggle to keep the relationship limping along. Anger, at herself for not being more proactive in seeking counselling with Nick. And dread, at the thought of breaking the news to her parents. Maybe she should have already told her parents, but they'd barely seen each other.

Besides, she wasn't tackling that conversation without plenty of prayer first.

She opened her locker, put her handbag and cardigan in, closed it, and clicked the lock. Her jaw and neck ached with strain. Esther stretched into a fake yawn and rolled her shoulders. Today was a grit-your teeth-and-get-through-it day. There'd better not be any tricky cases.

As she left the locker area the clinic receptionist called out to her.

"Esther, there's a note here from the palliative care ward."

Who did she know there? Esther tore open the envelope.

DEAR ESTHER, I HOPE YOU STILL REMEMBER ME. MY NAME IS ANNA AGOSTO. WE FIRST MET WHEN OUR IV STANDS COLLIDED IN THE CHEMO SUITE.

Of course she remembered Anna, but why was she writing to someone she barely knew?

AS THIS NOTE IS WRITTEN FROM PALLIATIVE CARE, YOU'LL KNOW THINGS HAVE NOT GONE WELL FOR ME. THE CANCER IS BACK AND I'M TOLD MY TIME IS NUMBERED IN WEEKS, IF NOT DAYS. IT'S A HUGE ASK, BUT WOULD YOU HAVE THE COURAGE TO VISIT ME IN YOUR LUNCH BREAK? I APPRECIATED YOUR KINDNESS BEFORE, AND SOMETHING YOU SAID MADE ME THINK.

Of all days to have an opportunity like this, when she was so low herself. What could she have said in their short conversation that had made such an impact on Anna? Perhaps the prayers she'd prayed achieved more than any actual words she'd said.

Palliative care was the waiting room to death, to visit would be staring death in the eyes. But did it matter what made her comfortable or that she didn't feel at her best? If there was a chance she could share Jesus, even a small chance, then she must not hesitate.

Esther phoned and left a message saying she'd be there at midday. During the morning, her mind was split into three parts. Her clients, praying for Anna, and her own personal pain.

*T*heir hospital excelled in palliative care. Beautiful gardens surrounded the unit, and walls were covered in art donated by grateful families in remembrance of their relatives. All the rooms were private, and visiting hours were according to each individual patient's wishes. Within a minute of arriving at the ward Esther walked into Anna's room. Anna wriggled up higher in the bed and held out her hand.

"Thanks so much for coming. I would have understood if you couldn't handle a visit."

"I wasn't going to let you down, and I only had to cross the street." Thirty minutes to have a conversation. Would it be long enough? *Get this conversation moving, Lord.* Esther remembered what Anna had written and it would be a natural place to start. "You mentioned in your note that something I said the last time we met made you think. I can't recall what I said."

"You said you didn't need to worry about the future because Jesus carried that burden for you. I don't know Jesus like that."

Anna's words stabbed Esther in the heart. Mentally gnawing at a problem wasn't trusting Jesus. And her recent gnawing disturbed her ability to sleep.

"In fact, I'm not sure I've worked out how Jesus fits. Sure, I go to Mass, but it's a tradition I've never thought much about." Anna gestured around the room. "Being here brings all my fears out of the shadows."

How wonderful that a conversation Esther barely remembered had such an impact. And that God could use her despite her weakness. "What do you fear the most?"

"Where do I start? Mostly I worry about my family. How will Tony cope as a single parent with three young daughters? What if he marries again?" The questions poured out of her as though long bottled up inside. "Will his new wife give my girls the love and care they need? They're so young. How will my little girls cope without me?" She started to sob.

"Where are the tissues when they're needed?" Esther asked.

Anna hiccuped. "They fell on the floor."

Esther fumbled under the bed and handed them over. Anna rubbed her cheeks. "I cry all the time on my own, but try not to do it when I'm with others."

"Please feel free to cry when I'm here."

"That's why I wanted you to come. I feel you understand, and I need someone to talk to. My husband's a rock, but he's drowning in grief. And the social workers haven't been through it."

Esther knew what she should offer, but was she ready to handle being so involved in a stranger's problems? Especially when she had more than enough of her own? But she knew what Jesus would want her to do. "Would it help if I came and spent my lunchtimes here?"

"I'm embarrassed to ask. Most people want to avoid me."

"I'm a follower of Jesus," Esther said. "I don't believe in avoidance."

"That's what I noticed about you," Anna said. "You're willing to confront things head on. I don't have to pretend with you—" She clutched Esther's hand. "Esther, I'm so scared. Sometimes the hardest thing is trying to cover my fear. Tony has broad shoulders, but I don't want to add any more burdens."

"Let's make a deal then," Esther said. "When I'm here, we can cry and we can say what we want, no matter how pathetic or outrageous it seems."

"That would be a relief." Anna released Esther's hand. "Sometimes I worry I'm going to explode with keeping everything inside."

Esther patted her hand. "So, apart from worries about your family, what else do you fear?"

"I fear the pain of the final days—and I fear being dependent. I worry I'll lose control of all my body functions." She wrinkled her nose. "That would be too embarrassing. I don't want Tony's last memories of me to be disgust." She shuddered. "I want to die with dignity."

"This place is set up to allow people to die with dignity."

"Yes, they're great with the 'dying with dignity' thing, but they can't deal with my worst fear." Anna lowered her voice. "Esther, I'm afraid of dying alone. And I fear that even if people packed out this room, I'd still feel alone." Anna glanced towards the door. "I find myself asking if this world is all there is." She leaned forward and whispered, "Do I sound bonkers?"

"Not to me," Esther said. "You're asking the right kind of questions. Most people avoid them."

"But you don't fear death, do you?" Anna clenched her fists on top of the bedspread. "Why not? That's what I most want to know. Whatever you've got ... Is it for me too?"

Esther's heart did handsprings. She'd been praying someone she'd met would show a real desire to know more. She still worried she'd mess up but Joy kept reminding her that she'd be given the words she needed. "I don't fear death because I know where I'm going. Better still—I know who I'm going with. Jesus has promised never to abandon me, and I believe him."

"How do I find faith like yours? I've known about Jesus all my life but he's always been kind of distant." She looked out the window. "It never occurred to me that he was relevant to my life."

Please Jesus, keep this conversation going. "It's easy to know about Jesus, but we know him as we know a famous movie star we've seen on the screen." Would Anna connect with the analogy? "Knowing about someone is completely different from knowing them personally."

"How do you get to know Jesus personally?"

Lord, give me the right words. "How did you get to know your husband?"

Anna glowed. "I met him at university and hung around with

him nearly every day. Talking all the time and doing everything together."

Esther nodded. "Getting to know Jesus is similar. The major difference is Jesus isn't physically present, so we get to know him through stories and testimonies."

"I don't get it." Anna's forehead furrowed. "You weren't alive in Jesus' day."

"You're right." Esther laughed. "But four different people wrote accounts of his life. They included not only what his friends thought about him but his enemies too." Could she say more? "Would you like it if I told you some of these stories each time I come to visit?"

"Stories?" Anna said. "Yes, yes, I'm happy to hear stories. They might help me forget about myself for a while." Anna's response suggested she didn't equate 'stories' with 'history'. No problem. The author of the stories was more than able to change Anna's assumptions.

Anna shifted in her bed.

"You're in pain, aren't you?" Esther asked.

"I asked the nurse to delay my midday medication so I'd be more alert for your visit."

Would Anna be able to concentrate on the story at all? "Can you endure another ten minutes? I'll tell a short story about a dying man who met Jesus."

"Short sounds good." Anna tugged her pillows.

"I'll start with a brief introduction. This story is about a criminal who'd been sentenced to death by crucifixion. Our story happens in the last few hours of his life."

"Is this one of the thieves crucified with Jesus?"

"Have you heard this before?"

"Yes, but I never thought it related to me."

"I think you'll find it relevant. My story will be a bit rusty because I haven't specially prepared it, but I'll do my best." Esther sat up straight in her chair. "Let me see—Jesus had been crucified with one thief on his right and one on his left. As Jesus hung there he said, 'Father, forgive them for they don't know what they're doing.'"

Anna sat motionless as Esther continued.

"The religious leaders came and mocked Jesus, 'You saved others. Save yourself if you are God.' One of the criminals joined in. 'Yeah, if you're the Saviour that was to come, save yourself and then save us.' Esther put all the mockery she could into her tone. "But the other criminal said to the first, 'Don't you fear God? We deserve to be here, but this man Jesus has done nothing wrong.' Then he said to Jesus, 'Remember me when you come into your Kingdom.'"

Esther paused. "And Jesus replied, 'Today you will be with me in Paradise.'"

"This story is familiar. It must be part of the Easter readings."

"Yes, probably. Have you got enough energy to discuss it for a few minutes?"

"I think so. There's so much I don't understand."

Joy had modelled how to ask questions so Esther had a fair idea what to do. "What do you think the second thief felt as he hung on that cross?

Anna tilted her head. "Definitely fear. And maybe regret for wasting his life and hurting those he loved."

They were off to a good start as Anna didn't seem uncomfortable answering questions. "What might he have feared?"

"The pain of dying," Anna answered, then pursed her lips. "Maybe he feared … what would happen to him after death? Yes." She nodded. "I think that would have been his major concern. It's mine, and I haven't been nearly as bad as he was. I've always tried to do my best. The strange thing is, I'm not sure it's enough. I'm still afraid." She looked at Esther. "If I was confident where I was going, I wouldn't be afraid, would I?"

Wow, this was exciting, Anna was really engaged. "You're right.

Being saved isn't about being good. I mean, who can reach God's standard of perfection?" Both of them were silent for a long moment.

Then Esther asked, "What happens to the second thief? What does Jesus say to him?"

"Today, you'll be with me in Paradise."

"So is he saved?"

"Yes ..." Anna squinted. "But I don't understand why. He doesn't deserve it."

"This story has puzzled many people, but let's work backwards and see if we can work out why Jesus accepts him." Anna seemed to have forgotten her weariness. "The first thing that second thief said was, 'Don't you fear God? We deserve to be here, but Jesus has done nothing wrong.' What can we learn from what he says?"

"He seems clear, doesn't he? He means that he himself doesn't deserve anything but crucifixion and that Jesus is innocent and doesn't deserve death."

"Yes," Esther said. "But how could he have known Jesus is innocent?"

"Could—could he have heard stories about him?"

"That's an excellent possibility. After all, Jesus travelled all over Israel for three years, teaching and doing miracles. There must have been rumours and gossip flying everywhere. What other opportunities did the thief have to learn?" *Thank you, Lord, for prompting me with everything I need to say or ask.*

"Oh, I know." Anna's fists pounded the bed on either side of her body. "He's watched Jesus all day and seen how he treated others."

"The Roman soldiers must have been mystified by Jesus," Esther said. "They were used to being reviled but Jesus kept quiet. When people abused and mocked him, Jesus forgave them. So, up to this point we've discovered two things." Esther raised her index finger. "This thief knows he's an undeserving sinner." Esther raised another finger. "And secondly, he knows Jesus is an innocent man who forgives those who harm him. Here's the next line, 'Jesus, remember me when you come into your Kingdom.'"

Anna closed her eyes. Had she drifted off? Should Esther wait, or should she sneak out and leave Anna in peace? *Lord, help Anna to connect the dots. She's heard random pieces of the jigsaw for years.*

Anna's eyes snapped open and she grabbed Esther's arm. "I've realised something odd. All the pictures I've ever seen of Jesus, he's bedraggled. His hair hanging limp, and he's covered in wounds and blood. He looks a total failure. Not like a king. Certainly not capable of saving anyone."

"I don't see what you're getting at."

"The thief says, 'Remember me when you come into your Kingdom.' He doesn't see a failure—he sees a king." Anna's voice had risen and all trace of tiredness was gone. "He sees a king coming into his kingdom. How is that possible?"

"I'd never seen that. Surely only God could show him the truth."

"Did God?" Anna's voice was breathy. "Did God just do the same for me?"

"You know, I think he did." Esther grinned at Anna. "Your excitement is contagious. I've just noticed something new too. The thief asks Jesus to remember him. He never asks for salvation." Anna looked at Esther like she'd spoken in a foreign language. "Like most of us, the second thief believes salvation is for the good, and he knows he doesn't measure up."

Anna bounced in excitement. "But Jesus gives him what he doesn't deserve. He's given salvation and that means ..." she looked at the ceiling "... that means salvation isn't based on what we do." Her face lit up with joy. "Life is not an exam with a pass and a fail. It's based on whether Jesus accepts us or not."

"You're getting me all fired up. This guy had no possibility of doing good deeds to earn Jesus' approval. He couldn't say to the soldiers, 'Hey there, let me off this cross. I've got to go and be baptised or donate to the poor or help my parents.' The time for that had passed. All he did was admit his own unworthiness and recognise Jesus' worth." Esther paused to let the truth sink into both their hearts. "Yet Jesus accepted him."

"I've heard the word 'grace'," Anna said. "Is that what you'd say about this story?"

"Grace—undeserved favour," Esther said. "Yes—this story is a perfect illustration of that word."

Anna settled herself back with a weary but contented smile. "Thanks so much for coming. Most of the religion I grew up with has felt like an unknowable black hole. Now I think I've grasped the central piece of the puzzle. That thief would still have suffered, but he wouldn't have been afraid. He knew where he was going—"

"—and he knew who had guaranteed his entry into heaven." Esther was so excited, she completed Anna's sentence. "He went in with the Saviour himself."

"Anna, I'm going to have to go. My next client arrives in five minutes. Would you like me to come again tomorrow?"

"But tomorrow's Saturday."

Telling someone about Jesus beat moping about Nick. "I'm free, and I'd love to come. Tomorrow, we can start from the beginning of God's story."

CHAPTER 33

$\mathcal{T}$wo days later, Esther and her parents were eating their usual late Sunday lunch in their formal dining room.

"Dad, have you heard from Nick?" Esther asked.

Her father didn't look up from buttering his roll. "No, and it's strange as he normally gives me a call midweek. He hasn't eaten with us for a while."

God had given her the lead-in she needed. "I doubt he'll visit for a while."

Her father dropped his knife. "What are you saying?"

"Nick has broken off our engagement." Easy words to say but so hard to accept.

Her mother gave a harsh sob and covered her eyes with her hand, but her father bulldozed on. "You mean permanently?"

"I mean permanently." Why did so many of their recent conversations feel like she was labouring to help an imbecile pick up conversational clues? "He does not want to marry me."

"Why ever not? You'll be well soon, and your looks will return."

Why couldn't he focus on something important? Would she be forced to talk about things she'd prefer to avoid? "He doesn't think so. A friend told him my chances of survival weren't as high as I'd been told. He decided it wasn't worth sticking around."

"Oh, Esther—I'm so sorry." Her mother's face was the colour of cooked pasta.

"Of course he was rattled," her father said.

"Dr Webster is more optimistic."

"Why did you take so long to let us know?" He was unstoppable.

"I've only known a few days myself, and we've barely seen each other this week."

"Was that why you weren't at church this morning?"

Esther's stomach cramped. She'd hoped to avoid having these two conversations simultaneously. But of course her eagle-eyed father noticed her absence. "Actually, I've been considering going elsewhere for a while. Gina and I visited a Baptist church near the hospital."

"What are you saying? Are you intending to leave Victory?" The questions gushed like water from a fire hose. "How's that going to look? My own daughter going elsewhere."

Esther leaned back, bowled over by the barrage. But she would not to be browbeaten. The time for that had passed. "Dad, why does every issue have to relate to how something will look? Aren't we supposed to seek God's approval?"

"I don't know what you're saying. Victory is all about honouring Jesus."

She'd let this issue pass. Everything she said would be taken as a personal attack. "I've struggled to go to Victory these last few months."

"What is there to struggle about?"

Where should she start? "The more I read the Bible, the less comfortable I feel there."

There was a drawn-out silence. Outside, someone's mower buzzed, but inside, the room crackled with unspoken tension. Her mother bolted into the kitchen. Mundane kitchen tasks gave her a socially acceptable excuse to leave whenever she sensed approaching conflict.

Lord, I need your help—now.

Her father flushed. "What are you implying?" His voice was calm, icy calm, the exaggerated calm before the storm.

"Dad, you know I've been struggling with the messages at Victory. We talked about it after the Hebrews sermon."

"It seems to me you're struggling with your attitude to many things. Initially, I dismissed it as the pressure you're under, but your attacks are getting harder to ignore."

So now she was to be placed in the wrong. Somehow, identifying what manipulative technique her father used, helped remove her from its power. Her heart flooded with a deep pity and sadness. She'd known that this conversation would be difficult. Difficult? It was almost impossible.

"I'm sorry you feel my attitude is a problem." She wasn't going to apologise for the content of her comments. "I've tried to show you respect while I worked through my concerns."

"Discontent and doubt can spread like wildfire." The button for his preaching mode clicked on. "You have influence simply because you are my daughter. If you stop coming, people are going to ask questions."

Why did everything come back to his reputation? "I would've thought it would be easier for you if I wasn't at Victory. After all, everyone knows I have cancer."

"If people do ask, which they seldom do, I have ways of answering."

"Yes, I heard your answer a few weeks ago on the *Hour of Victory.*" Esther tried not to sound snarky. "It's easy to blame me for my cancer."

"I never mentioned your name."

There must have been more of the snarky tone than she'd

intended. *Oh, Dad.* This conversation made her sick at heart. She didn't see how this could end well.

"You didn't have to. You made yourself abundantly clear. It's a weighty burden for a cancer sufferer to be told it must be their fault." Her shoulders tensed. "How is that any different to Buddhism's concept of karma? 'If you're good then good will result and if you're wicked then you'll be cursed.' A person can spend forever trying to work out what they've done wrong. The answer might simply be that we live in a broken world."

Her father snorted. "This is the attitude I find difficult to handle."

"You seem to want to live in a world where no one disagrees with you." Esther made her tone as gentle as she could.

A line of red spread up his neck. "Are you suggesting—I force people to agree with me?"

Not a question to answer directly. "I hope not. It does concern me that everyone who disagrees with you leaves the church."

"That's their choice."

"Dad, I don't want to continue this discussion." After all she could see where such a conversation would lead. "I'm able to disagree with people and yet still live with them."

"Not any more you can't." His tone was casual, as though he was discussing doing the laundry.

Esther's breath whistled. Did he mean what she thought he did? "What are you saying?"

"I don't want negative people in this house." He jabbed his finger repeatedly on the table. "People who undermine everything I have built up."

A vacuum cleaner sucked all the air out of her lungs. *Lord, give me wisdom.* "Are you suggesting I find somewhere else to live?"

"I'm merely suggesting you consider your attitude and decide what is most important to you."

So the ultimatum had arrived. Bow to her father's will or leave.

A gear shifted in her mind. She'd spent her life placating her father. Trying to win his approval, then labouring to keep it. She'd been wrong. She'd become part of the reason that her father was like this. How could her father change if everyone around him simply nodded and said 'yes' to his every word?

In front of her were two roads. The wide way of the majority, or the narrow way accompanied by high cost. "Does it need to be a choice between my conscience and my home?"

"I'm not saying that's the choice." Her father sounded so reason-able. "If you learn to be respectful, I'm happy to have you here."

"I can't stay here under those terms." Esther shook her head. To compromise now would be to deny her father a chance to change. The narrow road would be lonely but in her heart soared a steely single-mindedness to walk it anyway. "Dad, no matter what you might think now, I love you."

"You sound just like your grandmother." William shoved back his chair, stalked out the door, and slammed it behind him. Esther gathered the remaining plates and went into the kitchen. Her mother stood, knuckles white as she gripped the bench.

"Mum, I'm sorry, I had hoped we'd be able to talk sensibly but—"

"So I'm to lose you too?" Blanche's voice quavered.

"I don't think I'm thrown out immediately, but I will be looking for a place to live. I'll ask around at work." Her mother started to cry. "Mum, I'm sorry. I was worried this was going to happen. My cancer is an embarrassment to Dad. It'll be easier if I'm not at the church." She put her arms around her mother and held her close.

"Can't you reconsider? I'll never see you, if you don't come to Victory. Smooth the disagreement over."

How she longed to give in but she didn't want to become like her mother. A woman who'd compromised to the point she'd stifled her personality.

"I don't see how I could stay. Ever since the first day I started reading my Bible properly, I've had a growing conviction there were going to be far-reaching consequences." She hugged her mother. The last months had brought them so much closer. "You can come and visit when I've found a place to stay."

"I don't know what your father will say."

"I doubt he'll stop you if you don't make an issue of it." Her mother laid her head on Esther's shoulder. "One day at a time, Mum. We follow Jesus one day at a time and leave the future to him." She was preaching to herself. These were the truths she needed to hear.

Mum smiled wanly as she broke their hug. "Right now, we could both do with a rest."

"I agree. It's been a challenging week." Esther took a few tissues from the box on the counter, ready for later. "Oh, one last question. What is Gran's first name?"

Blanche's eyes widened. "You wouldn't try to find her."

"Dad won't know unless you tell him. He accused me of being like her." The corner of Esther's mouth twitched. "If she's like me, she might be a terrific person."

"Please, don't joke."

If she didn't joke, she'd break down. "Seems to me we need all the humour we can get."

"Her name is Naomi."

"That'll be easier. There must be oodles of Macdonalds in the phone directory."

Upstairs with the phone book, Esther ran her finger down the entries for Macdonald. There were only three 'N's'. One of them was on the route to work. Tomorrow after work, she'd track this first possibility down.

CHAPTER 34

$\mathcal{T}$he house was in a quiet cul-de-sac. An old-fashioned weatherboard, painted a creamy gold with maroon edgings that glowed in the late afternoon sunshine. The garden was a mass of scented plants—white, pink, purple, and blue.

Esther hesitated. How could one knock on a door and say, "I think I might be your granddaughter?" There were no guarantees this was the right N. Macdonald anyway. Probably easier to say, "I'm looking for a Naomi Macdonald who has a son, William."

A passing neighbour peered at her. She'd better get on with it before someone decided she was up to no good. Esther pushed her bike across the road, through the gate and up the path, watching for unfriendly dogs. Placing the bike to one side, she went up two steps onto the verandah and rat-a-tat-tatted with the knocker. Someone moved inside, and the creak of floorboards marked their progress towards the door. The inner door opened and before Esther had time to register much, the old lady gasped.

"Rachel, is it you?"

"No, I'm sorry. My name is Esther Macdonald."

The old woman's hand flew to her mouth. "Surely not William's Esther?"

The impossible had happened, she'd found her grandmother on the first try. "Yes, William and Blanche's daughter," Esther's voice trembled with excitement.

"I can't believe it. Let me get this door unlocked." Naomi fumbled with the lock. "I'm all thumbs. Can you come around the back instead?"

"Can I bring my bicycle?"

"Of course. Head through the side gate."

This woman didn't seem terrifying. Rather ordinary, in fact, like a grandmother should be. She lived close enough to work that they might even have passed each other at the shops.

Soon the two of them were having a cup of tea on the back verandah, looking out at the neat lawn, complete with a raised vegetable garden and fruit trees. A jacaranda tree dropped its purple bell-shaped petals on the lawn. The cicadas pulsed their deafening summer chorus. Neither of them seemed to know how to start. How did she bridge a lifetime?

"You have no idea how long I've hoped for this day," Naomi said. "We must be so full of questions we're about to burst. Why don't we ask them? I'll start. Now, of course I know how old you are, but where do you work?"

"I work at the local hospital as a physiotherapist. How do you know how old I am?"

"I saw your birth notice in the paper." Naomi brushed a hand across Esther's cheek. "But this is the first time I've ever laid eyes on you." A single tear trickled down her face. "Oh, I don't want to cry. I don't want to waste a precious minute."

Esther took her hand. It was impossible to believe this lady could ever have been a tyrant. All she saw was a lonely old woman, deprived of her own family. Naomi squeezed her hand.

"I'm afraid I'll wake up and find out this is a dream. Here is a beautiful granddaughter sitting on my verandah. How on earth did you find me?"

"This is going to sound unbelievable, but I didn't know you were still alive until recently. I've never seen a photo of you or heard you mentioned."

"Sadly, I can believe it. When your father cuts someone out of his life he does it properly. I used to write to him, but every letter came back marked, 'return to sender.'"

Someone was wringing out Esther's heart. Squeezing out the water so that it leaked out her eyes. What was the story behind all this pain?

"Of course, I know what William is up to because I can buy his books or watch his programme, but I seldom do so."

Every one of her grandmother's comments had a back story. The frustration was which of the thousands of threads to tug now?

"How did you find out I existed?"

That was a question she could answer and as good a place to start as any. "Mum's parents are both dead and since you were never mentioned, I assumed Dad's were too. Then last year, I got engaged."

"Congratulations dear. Who is he?"

This wasn't going to be all joy and champagne. "I'm sorry my story is coming out in incoherent bits. I'll come back to Nick." How long was it going to take to catch up on two lifetimes? "We were working out our wedding guest list, and Nick asked Dad if I had any relatives. He ignored the question at first but eventually he mentioned you."

Naomi grunted. "I'm guessing he didn't have anything courteous to say."

"Not particularly." Esther drank a mouthful of tea. "So much has happened in the last six months I don't know where to start." She took another sip. "Life's been a challenge."

"Has something happened to your engagement?"

"Nick broke it off last week. It's complicated. I'll have to go back to the beginning." She put her tea cup on the adjacent table. "Nick and I were supposed to get married the last weekend in August."

"Oh, no," said her grandmother placing her hand on Esther's left cheek. "What happened?"

"I need to give you some more background. Nick is the youth pastor at Victory Church, and he's Dad's protégé." He was much more than a mere protégé but she wouldn't go into that now. "You ask what's happened? There's no easy way to say this. In June, I discovered I had breast cancer."

Naomi's eyes glimmered with tears. Esther turned to stare at the purple tree. If she looked at her grandmother she'd never be able to finish her story. "A month later, I had a mastectomy. I started chemotherapy about ten days before our planned wedding date."

Naomi held herself rigid with her hands clasped together. What if all this avalanche of bad news gave her grandmother a heart attack? Hardly the best way to start a relationship.

"Everyone assumed I'd be healed. Including me."

Her grandmother's shoulders relaxed and she picked up her tea cup. "Sounds like something has changed."

"Yes, it did. Things changed after I lost my temper at God. A bit pointless really, but a lady overheard and questioned my understanding of scripture. I was furious at her. How dare she challenge me? Me, William Macdonald's daughter." Esther chuckled. "As you can see, humility wasn't one of my strengths. After I cooled down, I started on a quest to discover the truth from God's word."

"God's word does change things, doesn't it?"

That answered Esther's unspoken question about whether her grandmother knew Jesus.

Naomi finished the last mouthful of her tea. "I can see where the trouble with your father developed."

"Dad didn't realise until two days ago how much God's word has changed me. For a start, I no longer insist God heals me." Esther stuck her legs straight out in front of her. "Unfortunately, those changes make me a misfit at Victory."

Naomi placed her hands loosely in her lap. "What's happened with your Dad?"

Hmm, interesting question and it implied more back story to unravel. "Why are you presuming something has happened?"

"Well, you're here." Naomi tapped the arm of her chair. "I doubt you'd be here unless something significant had happened."

"You're right." A wave of sadness and loneliness rolled over Esther. "I visited another church yesterday. Dad noticed and asked where I'd been. I couldn't avoid mentioning my concerns about Victory." Esther twirled her right earring. "That did not make him happy."

"Yes, questioning your dad wouldn't go down well."

"You can say that again. Dad was furious and told me I was like you. That intrigued me, so I asked Mum for your name. This address was the closest to my work." Esther reached out and grasped her grandmother's hand. "I can't believe I found you on the first try."

Naomi squeezed Esther's hand back. "I'm so glad you did. Now whatever you do, don't stop visiting. How will I contact you? I can't ring you at home."

"I'm not sure where I'll be. I'm going to have to find accommodation somewhere near work, because Dad has virtually tossed me out."

"What's wrong with here?" Naomi said with a big grin as she gestured behind herself towards the main part of the house.

"Here? You can't mean it. I'm finishing chemo and will soon start radiotherapy. I'm bone-weary in the evenings and sometimes throw up. I'd be a horrible house guest."

"I'd be delighted to have you." Naomi's beaming smile suggested she meant it.

"I still think it's too much." And what if living here destroyed this precious new friendship? "Why don't I come for a week's trial first?"

"I don't think I'll need to reconsider, but if you want a week's trial, okay." Naomi reached out and shook Esther's hand once. "I agree."

"One important question," Esther said. "What am I going to call you?"

"What do you think? Does Gran work? I don't even mind if you call me 'Naomi'. I like the sound of my own name."

"Having lived without a single grandparent for far too long, I'm excited to discover I have a Gran."

"I'm so glad." Naomi pushed on the arms of her chair and stood up. "Now come and give me a hug."

Esther rushed to do so. Their hug was a homecoming.

Esther helped her grandmother take in the afternoon tea things. The clock said seven fifteen. "I didn't realise it was so late. Daylight saving always tricks me. I'd better ring Mum and let her know I'm okay. What if I bring my car, bike, and a week's worth of luggage tomorrow?"

"What will you tell your mother?"

"I'll tell her I've found somewhere and I'm having a week's trial to see if we're compatible. I can tell her later where I am."

"That sounds wise," Naomi said. "I'll prepare the guest room."

CHAPTER 35

*E*very evening after work, on her own in her new room, Esther practiced stories to tell Anna the next day. Then she'd venture out into the living room, tell Naomi the story, and they'd discuss it. Each discussion deepened their relationship, sending down roots that were watered with lashings of love and laughter.

Her visits to Anna were Esther's daily highlight.

"Are you ducking out again at lunch?" Sue asked one morning before Esther had called in her first patient. "Where do you go, anyway?"

"Up to palliative care."

"Oh." Sue's eyes widened. "I would have thought palliative care would be the last place on earth you'd want to visit."

"It is confronting," Esther said. "But I've been visiting one of my chemo acquaintances."

"It's always difficult to know what to talk about in those situations."

Ever since she'd admitted to Joy her struggle to talk with 'nice' people, Esther had been praying for Sue, Michelle and Sister O'Reilly. Could this be the first part of God's answer?

"We mostly talk about things my friend doesn't dare to talk about with others. She's only thirty-six." Esther leaned forward a little so that no one passing could overhear. "We've established a pattern where I tell her a daily story." Was this intriguing enough for Sue to follow up?

"What type of stories?" *Yes.* Esther resisted doing a fist pump. The wrinkle between Sue's eyebrows became prominent. "Fairy stories?"

"Aussies might call them fairy stories, but I'm telling her historical stories from the Bible. They prepare my friend to face the future."

Sue knew Esther was a Christian but the topic had never come up before. "Well, that's different. But if it helps, go for it."

Esther couldn't think how to respond and Sue turned and entered her office. She turned back at the door, "Did you ever use your Hydro Majestic Hotel prize?"

"I'd almost forgotten about it. I must make sure to use it once my treatment has ended."

"It would be a suitable celebration."

Their conversation was enough to make Esther hum as she entered the outpatient treatment area. The first step to tackling her issue about 'nice' people had been to have the nerve to open her mouth. God had answered that prayer and he could be trusted to keep answering.

Meanwhile, she'd redouble her prayers for Sue and all the others. Prayer had become her oxygen, giving her life and strength. *Jesus, help them all to see that you have the answers, both to their conscious questions, and the questions they haven't even thought to ask yet.*

*E*very day Anna's room became more home-like as her daughters brought their school artwork to decorate the walls. Masses of flowers filled a selection of vases, and the windows let in the breeze and the sounds of life outside.

Anna was worse. Much worse. The chill of impending loss skittered daddy-long-legs-like across Esther's heart. Despite Anna's weakness, she'd devoured each Old and New Testament story, savouring every detail before chewing it over and digesting it. Now the threads of the stories needed to be drawn together to make sure Anna was fully prepared to face life's biggest challenge.

"All the stories I've told you lead to the centre point of history, Jesus' death and resurrection." Esther pulled her chair close to the bed. "Jesus kept telling his disciples, 'I came to die and on the third day I'll rise again,' but they either ignored him or tried to tell him he was wrong."

"People never give up trying to run the show. I loved that illustration of us as the branch, determined to be independent from God. Dead, dry and unfruitful described me before I started hearing these stories." Anna bent up her knees under the bed covers. "I need to hear the end of the story to make sure I've understood."

"Are you sure you're not clear already?"

"I guess I am. I need to ask Jesus for mercy, then I can go home to him."

Anna's face was pasty white and she had dark bags under her eyes. They must finish the story today. Esther perched on the end of Anna's bed so they'd be at the same eye level.

"Let me summarise where we're up to," Esther said. "The disciples misunderstood Jesus all along. They misinterpreted his miracles, seeing them not as proof that Jesus was God come among them, but as proof he was about to set up an earthly kingdom. They intended to be chief ministers in that kingdom."

Then Esther told the story from the Last Supper through to Jesus' last breath. Anna's eyes were focused on Esther the whole time.

"Jesus was placed in the tomb and the massive stone rolled across the entrance." Esther wouldn't have been surprised if the hospital room reverberated with the crash of the stone.

"I've heard parts of this story all my life but I never saw it as a whole picture," Anna said. "Don't stop—keep going."

"That's the answer to my fears," Anna said when Esther had finished the story of Jesus' resurrection. "If Jesus rose from the dead, then he'll be with me every step of the way." Her chest rose and fell. Her breathing more laboured than yesterday. "Tell me again what his Kingdom will be like."

How could Esther describe something she'd never seen, and make it real and concrete rather than shadowy and ephemeral?

"Have you ever pictured what the world was like on the day of creation?"

Anna stared out into the garden.

"God's Kingdom will be a million times better. Jesus himself will wipe away every tear. Pain and suffering will vanish. Eternal joy. Eternal peace. Eternity with Jesus."

"Sounds too amazing to be true."

"That's because it's beyond our experience. When I doubt, I concentrate on Jesus. I'd be content to spend eternity with him. Everything else is a bonus."

"That's what I want," Anna said, her longing audible. "You've introduced me to your best friend and he's worth knowing. What do I need to do?"

"Why don't you tell Jesus what's on your heart. It doesn't have to be fancy."

"I'm not used to this."

"Just forget I'm here."

Anna closed her eyes and clasped her hands together. Someone, sometime must have modelled that to her.

"Jesus, I thought I knew you but most of what I knew was wrong." As Anna prayed, she relaxed and spoke from her heart.

"Thank you for bringing Esther to introduce me to the real story. Forgive me, and give me the new life you promised. Help me to use any days I have left for you. Don't let me be afraid anymore."

Anna opened her eyes and leaned back. "There. It's done." Then she grasped Esther's hand and pumped it up and down. "Thank you, thank you, thank you for coming. I can't tell you what it means to me."

"You're not the only one who is excited." Esther said beaming with delight. "You're the first person I've seen accept Jesus." She leaned over and gave Anna a huge hug. They clung to each other for a long moment before Esther stood up ready to leave. Both grabbed a tissue to dab their eyes and smiled at each other, the smile of two sisters united by more than mere DNA.

The next morning, Esther received a call from the palliative care unit.

"Tony Agosto has asked if you're able to come. Anna has slipped into a coma."

Two of Esther's clients had cancelled at the last minute, so she asked permission to go to palliative care. She found Tony standing next to Anna's bed.

"Thanks for coming, Anna would have wanted you here." He turned to the older couple on the other side of the bed. Both had tear streaks down their faces. "Esther, let me introduce Anna's parents, Markus and Nina. Mine are looking after our youngest daughter at home."

He turned to look at his wife lying silent on the bed. "We had such a good visit last night. Anna was in high spirits and I thought she might be getting better."

During Esther's physio training, the lecturers had always said a burst of energy was common before people died. "What did the doctor say?"

"They expect this to be it." His eyes glistened. Esther wasn't sure what she should do so she took one of Anna's hands. "What did Anna say last night?"

"Oh, it was mostly the girls laughing and telling her what they'd been up to. We all sang her a funny song. As we were leaving, I leaned over to kiss her goodbye and she said, 'Thank you for being my knight in shining armour.' Then she said, 'I'm not afraid any longer. I know where I'm going.' I didn't know what she meant. Did it have something to do with the stories you've been telling her?"

Talking in front of three strangers made her nervous. But there was nothing to fear, because the Holy Spirit was with her.

"Yes, Anna entrusted her life into Jesus' hands. He promises to take away fear and take us home, and now he's doing it."

"What do you think we should do?"

"Medical research suggests that the sense of hearing is the last thing people lose. Why don't each of us say something? A goodbye. If the rest of us went and got a drink, then it might be easier for the one talking."

Esther went back to her desk and did paperwork. Thirty minutes later she returned to Anna's room. It was obvious everyone had cried but they looked at peace.

"Could you read something from the Bible?" Tony asked Esther.

"Why don't I read Psalm 23. Anna mentioned she liked it." She took her Bible out of her bag and ignored the others. Anna's breaths rasped in and out. Esther took Anna's hand as though Anna was made of porcelain.

"Thank you, Anna. We've only been friends a short time but your friendship has been precious. This isn't goodbye. I'm going to see you again. It might be next week or decades in the future but it will feel like tomorrow for you." Esther lent over and kissed Anna's forehead. "Here's your Shepherd Psalm."

She found the page and read.

"The Lord is my shepherd, I will not want. He makes me lie down in green pastures and leads me beside quiet waters." Esther paraphrased as she went, personalising it for Anna. "Even though I walk through the valley of the shadow of death, I will fear no evil, for Jesus is with me. Jesus has prepared a feast for me." Anna's breath rasped and skipped an occasional beat, but the rhythms of this timeless poetry enveloped her like an eiderdown quilt. "Surely goodness and mercy will follow me all the way to the end. All the days of your new life you will dwell in the house of Jesus forever."

Esther laid her hand on Anna's arm. "Go with God, my sister. There'll be a new morning in that most beautiful of places, and I'll see you there."

Five minutes later, there was a rattle in Anna's throat, one last tiny puff of air, and then nothing more.

CHAPTER 36

$\mathcal{E}$sther completed her final chemotherapy session on the twenty-first of December. She had almost two weeks of holiday ahead as the physiotherapy department was closed for the traditional break between Christmas and New Year. Any holiday, even unpaid, was welcome. The timing was perfect to prepare her for the next battle, radiotherapy.

She had spent Christmas Day at home, her first visit since her father had asked her to leave. She hadn't neglected her mum, however, as they met once a week at a cafe near the hospital. Maybe one day Blanche would visit her at Naomi's.

Every day, Esther slept late and napped in the afternoons. The evenings, she and Naomi reserved for craft and chatting. They had years to catch up on.

The summer sunlight lingered until eight in the evening. Tonight, the fragrance of dry grass and lemon-scented eucalyptus trees wafted through the French doors on a cool breeze. Naomi's knitting needles clicked. Summer should be too hot to knit, but Naomi said it was the only kind of craft she could now do without eye strain.

"I still find it difficult to forgive Dad for keeping me away from you all these years," Esther said.

"I also struggled to forgive him during those lonely years." Naomi sneezed. "But one thing I've learned is that holding grudges only destroys the grudge holder." She finished the row and turned her knitting to start another. "Of course, there was continuing regret and sadness, especially when I saw other grandmothers with their grandchildren."

"Gran, what went wrong?"

"Are you sure you've got enough energy for a longish story?"

"I'll let you know if I can't cope. But would it be okay if I lie down?" Esther picked up a cushion and put it under her head in a way that allowed her to still see her grandmother's face.

Naomi waited until she was properly settled. "To be fair to your Dad, he has never known me like I am now. We become what we are by a series of choices, and he wasn't around for all of mine." She finished her row and laid her knitting to one side. "My father was a gifted businessman. My parent's views about education were progressive, and so my sister and I were given the same educational chances as my two brothers."

It had been obvious to Esther from the first day she met her grandmother that she was well-educated in comparison to other women of her generation.

"At sixteen, I became a teacher and married your grandfather a year later. Although we married during the Great Depression, we were sheltered from the worst because our family's wealth was in land, and not in banks and shares."

"Were you Christians then?"

"Back then almost everyone attended church, but we didn't understand what 'Christian' meant beyond a vague definition of being nice and not hurting others. In fact, Norman and I assumed our financial stability proved God was on our side, and we'd somehow pleased him." Esther curled her legs up as the heat drained out of the day.

"Soon, we had two sons. Ian, my eldest, and your father a year later."

More revelations. "Dad's never mentioned a brother."

"Give me a chance and I'll explain why. If we believed anything in those days, we believed we deserved to be blessed. We had the money to indulge our sons. Looking back, I can see we over-indulged them." Naomi frowned. "They had piles of clothes and toys. We had a nanny, a maid, and a gardener to ensure they never had to lift a finger. They were enrolled in The King's School." Naomi grimaced. "Nothing but the best for my husband."

"Overnight, everything changed." She took a deep breath. "Ian went out with friends and drowned."

Esther inhaled too quickly and coughed. How come she'd never heard any of this family history?

"When the policeman arrived on our doorstep with the news, I fainted." Naomi looked at her lap. "I opted out of life for the next year or more. Norman's response was no healthier. Instead of choosing avoidance, he became angry. He railed at anyone and everyone, especially God. We stopped going to church, and he refused to visit friends and family."

"I'm sorry, Gran." Esther reached across and placed her hand on her grandmother's knee.

"What with my avoidance and Norman's anger, neither of us was in a fit state to care for William. We put him into the school dormitory and only saw him on formal occasions and during holidays. It built a barrier between us." She took a sip of water. "A barrier we didn't have the emotional energy to demolish. All of us struggled to answer the unanswerable. Why? Why Ian? Why our family?"

Naomi dabbed away some tears with a lace handkerchief. "William poured his grief into hard work and soon topped his class.

He learned to debate and honed his leadership skills. He cut out of his life anyone not likely to help him go in the direction he wanted."

Naomi's story conjured up such a clear picture of her father. "Poor Dad. Poor, lonely, empty boy."

"Yes, there are always reasons for the way people turn out. Norman never recovered from Ian's death, and his anger corroded our marriage." Again Naomi dabbed her eyes. "I'd thought my life couldn't get worse, but I was wrong. Norman died of a heart attack. He was gone in less than a minute."

Esther's father had lost both his brother and his father while he was still in high school. "So much pain. How did you become a follower of Jesus?"

"After Norman's death, I spiralled down into depression. Society had no idea how to handle mental illness. I ended up lying in the dark, wanting to end everything but too scared to do so."

Esther clenched her hands. How could her parents have kept her away from Naomi? This woman who had been through such grief and anguish. Esther sat up and shifted across to a seat closer to her grandmother.

"I felt abandoned by life, and if there was a God, by him too. Nothing in my over-pampered childhood had prepared me for tough times."

Now her grandmother exuded peace and joy. How had God changed her?

"Depression was God's sandpaper. It stripped away my selfishness and pride. Sometimes God's grace wears a strange disguise. At my lowest and darkest point, God sent someone to bring me hope."

"God never abandons us, even if it feels like he has. What happened?"

"Norman's secretary was a real Christian. One Saturday morning, she knocked on my door, unannounced. The maid was so surprised to see someone, and probably so fed up with the situation, she let her in. Somehow Louisa convinced me to get dressed and go out into the garden. Much later she told me she had no idea how to help me. She only knew to pray fervently."

"She did the most important thing."

"Yes, but she didn't tell me about the prayer. All I saw was the love and care revealed by her daily visits."

"Wise woman."

"She did occasionally mention her prayers and the difference Jesus made in her life but her comments irritated me, at least at first. It took three months before I said, 'The way you talk about Jesus is different than the way anyone else talks about him. He sounds like he's your best friend. I wish I had a friend like that.'"

Esther hugged her grandmother. "I'm so glad you had someone to point you to Jesus."

"My life changed radically after that. When God's Spirit gets to work, he's the master craftsman. I simplified my life and even learned to cook and clean." Naomi's cheeks drooped and she looked old and tired. "But my life change came too late for William. He went to university, determined to become a success. I tried to warn him, told him he was pursuing the wrong things, but he scoffed at me and seldom came home."

At least one family member had the courage the rest of them lacked. Well done, Gran.

"When I heard William had gone back to church, I praised God. I rushed to the church but returned home deeply troubled. They only taught what people's itching ears wanted to hear."

"Yes, and Victory is the same."

"That's why I don't buy William's books or listen to his radio programmes. His teachings break my heart."

"Have you ever met Mum?"

"Only a few times. I didn't know of her existence until after their engagement. Your father brought her to meet me, but I never managed a private word with her. William dominated the conversation. It seemed unlikely she was the kind of woman to stand up to him."

"You're right, she never has. But it's not easy to do—as I now know from personal experience."

"Do you think your mother was deliberately chosen for those very qualities?

"I've never thought of it like that. Bit scary." Esther whistled.

"I'm not saying it was a conscious thought," Naomi said. "But your mother's dress sense, looks, and hospitality skills have enhanced his image."

She'd shelve this comment to think about later. "So how did the final break come?"

"I did receive an invitation to the wedding. Your father cares too much about his reputation not to ask me. A year later, your parents started at Victory Church. Of course, it wasn't called Victory then. It was a dying church of fifty people. Your father chose the new name and the church took off. Most of the congregation loved Jesus and were thrilled to have a young, dynamic couple come to pastor them." Naomi's lips stretched in a tight line. "The godly ones didn't last long. Any time they disagreed with your father, he had ways to get rid of them."

"I've met a lady who left, and heard about others."

"When I saw how William dealt with conflict, I knew I must try to warn him one more time. I invited him over for a meal and tried to tackle the issue in a roundabout way. I shared some of my own mistakes and regrets. He didn't pay any attention. So I raised my concerns more directly."

Esther grunted. "I bet he didn't appreciate that."

"I've replayed our encounter over and over in my head. Could I have done things differently? Maybe. But I don't think it would have mattered what anyone said. He wouldn't have listened." Naomi blew her nose in a ladylike manner. "He exploded and vowed he'd never have anything more to do with me—a promise he has kept."

"Our family is a mess. It looks perfect, but it's a veneer. Have you seen my parents since Dad left that day?"

"Your Mum came to visit one time, about three years after they married. She'd had trouble getting pregnant. She felt your father blamed her, and implied she'd sinned or had weak faith."

Esther shuddered. "I know exactly how she felt."

"I didn't do much, just listened and prayed. She became pregnant soon after."

Her grandmother had always seemed sharp for someone in her eighties, but now she'd got her dates confused. Or had there been a miscarriage? "She must have lost the baby, because I wasn't born for another ten years."

"Yes. The baby was lost to her."

So at least one miscarriage. Mum had never mentioned it. Perhaps the pain went too deep. "Poor Mum. Life hasn't been easy for her. What happened next?"

"I never saw her again. Either your father found out where she'd gone or she was too frightened to defy his wishes."

"I'm so glad I found you." Esther hugged Naomi again.

"You are a gift I never expected. I've prayed year after year. In my low moments I've sometimes doubted God's power, or his interest in my request. Your arrival has inspired me to trust God that one day our whole family will be reunited."

Esther shifted to the floor and put her head in her grandmother's lap. Tears had welled in her eyes many times during Naomi's story. In her imagination, Norman and William resembled flies struggling in a sticky spider's web, unable to free themselves because they didn't know the bondage breaker.

Esther studied her grandmother's face. This elderly woman had become so precious to her, it almost hurt. Having been reunited, how many more years would they have left?

Naomi smoothed the worry lines on Esther's forehead. "Honey, my story is a sad one but my life hasn't been a disaster. Louisa was God's gift to me for thirty years until she went home to be with Jesus. Through her, I met my church family. Every week I'm blessed to be able to introduce new immigrants to Jesus." She patted Esther's shoulder. "Jesus never ever leaves us alone. He's made life worth living."

CHAPTER 37

*E*sther lay on the narrow plinth underneath the radiation machine. The week before she'd come in to have the meticulous measurements done. Millimetres counted. That day, the doctor had made indelible marks on her skin so that future treatments could home in on the target area.

"Now please keep still," the technician said. "If you have a problem, raise your hand and I'll see you through the cameras. This should only take a few minutes."

The machine overshadowed her. Invisible rays worked their magic without any sensation. The hard edges of the plinth dug into her bottom. Not a place you'd want to spend the night.

The technician returned. "That's all it is, five days a week. Have you read the instruction booklet?"

"Yes. You don't want me to shave under my arm. And avoid powders, creams, and deodorant." Esther ticked them off on her fingers.

"You've got it."

On her way out, Esther dropped in on Michelle, the chemo receptionist. She regularly prayed for her but so far there had

247

never been an opportunity for a worthwhile conversation. Perhaps coming five days a week for six weeks might make a difference.

"Easier than chemo."

"That's what everyone says," Michelle said. "See you next time."

Radiotherapy soon settled into a routine and Esther continued to meet Joy once a week. Nowadays, they mostly shared encouragements and prayed together for their friends who didn't yet know Jesus.

By the end of the fourth week, a radiation-induced burn plagued her.

"*How's* one of our favourite clients?" Dr Webster said. Esther nearly fell over with surprise. "Do you say that to everyone?"

Dr Webster inspected his fingernails. "Definitely not to everyone. Is the burn troubling you?"

"Yes, and it's worse every day. I'm trying to only wear loose clothing but the problem is my work uniform is too stiff." She tugged on the sleeve of her shirt.

"Sister O'Reilly will give you some cream for it. The discomfort should only last a few weeks."

Esther covered her mouth with her hand. "You're telling me to grin and bear it?"

"Basically." He chuckled. "Any other problems?"

"Only tiredness." This whole process seemed to drag on forever. "My grandmother's house is only five kilometres from work so I'm managing to cycle."

"I don't recall you mentioning you lived with your grandmother."

"My father asked me to leave home after my fifth round of

chemo." Her shoulders tensed and she ducked her eyes. *Please Lord, help me to say something that helps him know you more.*

"That's fairly drastic. Are you so difficult to live with?"

Esther gave him a lopsided grin. "I hope not. It's a bit of a long story. I think the main reason was that I was a reminder of failure."

Dr Webster scratched his ear. "I don't understand."

"My father is the pastor of Victory Church."

Dr Webster's eyes widened. "Now that is one church I have heard of."

"My father preaches that if we have enough faith, we'll be healed. I wasn't healed despite everything they did and I'm the pastor's daughter. My presence was a constant irritant."

"Reminds me why I don't like Christians."

Ha ha. She was going to have an opportunity to say something. "Dr Webster, if I meet an incompetent or rude doctor or two, should I write off the whole profession?"

He flushed. "No, I guess not."

Was the door still open? "Jesus once said trees can be recognised by their fruit. If a tree has bad fruit, it's a bad tree. If someone claims to be a Christian but isn't like Jesus, we can doubt his claim. Please, don't write off Jesus because of some of those who claim to follow him." She concentrated on keeping her voice relaxed, as though she had no interest whatsoever in the result. "Check him out for yourself."

Dr Webster's tone mirrored hers. "Problem is, he's not around for me to do so."

"There are some good biographies to introduce him to us."

"You're talking about the Bible."

"Yes," Esther said. "Four of his followers wrote biographies—Matthew, Mark, Luke and John."

"Weren't they rather biased?"

Lord, don't let me scare the fish. "In one sense, yes. All of us have biases, but one of the things I love about the Bible is it includes what his enemies thought." Would Dr Webster ever be willing to examine his assumptions in the same way he tested provisional diagnoses? "It won't kill you to read Luke, and it'll only take a few hours."

"I'd have to give up some of my TV time."

Why did Aussie men always retreat behind humour? She could match him. "If it's true, it might be the best investment of time you ever make."

"Sister O'Reilly will be growling if I get further behind with my appointments."

An obvious change of topic. Esther played along and went next door to pick up the burn cream. There was hope for Dr Webster.

"**S**orry to hear the burn is giving you trouble," Sister O'Reilly said. "Burns are the most common side effects of radiotherapy."

"As Dr Webster so kindly said, I just have to grin and bear it."

"Did he really say that? I apologise."

"Don't worry," Esther said. "You don't have to apologise for him. He's turned out to be a blessing." She wanted to bite her tongue. The religious jargon slipped out before she could stop herself.

Sister O'Reilly raised one plucked eyebrow. "I doubt he's been called a blessing before."

"Bit of a funny term, I know, but I consider you all to have been blessings in my life."

Did Sister O'Reilly think she had a crackpot in her office? What was there about this woman that made Esther want to cringe and be quiet? Why did she curry her favour like she'd done with her father—and everyone she met—for far too many years?

Was it because she wanted their approval more than she'd wanted Jesus' approval? Jesus hadn't allowed Nicodemus to return home under the illusion God was pleased with his good deeds. And neither could she let Sister O'Reilly know her all these months without introducing her to Jesus. Even one sentence was better than nothing.

"I know calling you all blessings sounds a bit odd," Esther said. "You're probably used to people wanting to get out of here as fast as possible."

"Yes, being here is hardly people's idea of a fun day out."

"My grandmother said something to me recently. She looked back at all the hard times she'd been through in her eighty something years and said it was 'grace in strange disguise'."

Sister O'Reilly's brows knitted together.

"Gran meant that although her hardships looked like she was under God's curse, in fact, they were God's love and undeserved favour to her."

"Your grandmother sounds like an unusual woman." Did Sister O'Reilly mean that as a compliment? Esther would respond as if she had.

"She's a special person and I feel blessed to know her." Bother, why did she keep saying 'blessed'? Stupid word to use in ordinary conversation.

"There's your favourite word again."

"It certainly seems to be today. Maybe it's on my mind because ever since my Gran said that phrase, 'grace in strange disguise', it's gripped my imagination. It's taken months of wrestling, but now I can say cancer has become God's grace to me."

"You Christians certainly see the world differently. But gratitude, however strange, is better than griping. I get tired of being viewed as the enemy." Sister O'Reilly looked at the tube of cream in her hand. "I shouldn't be prattling on. Most people aren't too bad, but even one difficult person a day leaves a nasty taste."

"You don't deserve one a year. You've been nothing but helpful." Sister O'Reilly flashed a smile and handed over the cream.

Thank you Lord for helping me get through the 'she's too nice' block. Please don't forget Sue and Michelle need you too.

Esther stood. "Do please give me a kick if I ever gripe."

Staid Sister O'Reilly actually chortled. "With pleasure."

---

*I*n her final week of radiotherapy, Esther saw Rob Boyle come in for his first post chemotherapy check-up. She waved, and he walked across the waiting room to her.

"Isn't your radiotherapy nearly finished?" he asked.

"Yes, it's my last week. I'm looking forward to not having to come in every day for treatment." Esther looked around the room. "Although I'll miss some of the people."

Rob's face lit up with the mischievous twinkle. "I've heard some people become depressed at the end of treatment because they're so dependent on the medical team."

"Like losing your umbilical cord?"

"Good analogy. It's not something I suffered from. I want to forget the whole experience."

"I used to want the same, but I've changed. I don't want to forget any more. Going through cancer should change us."

Rob watched the passers-by in the waiting room for a few seconds. "You're right. One thing I've learned is to take pleasure in simple things. Like being able to taste food again, and spend time with my family."

Should she stick her neck out and say more? Why not? The worst that could happen was that he'd hide behind another joke. "I'd hoped you might remember some of our discussions."

"People are more likely to think about preparing for death when they stare it in the eyes."

The door was still open a crack. She cared too much for Rob not to give it a go. "Jesus isn't just for when you're in a crisis. How would you feel if your children only came to you when they wanted something?"

Rob held up a hand. "Yes, yes. It all seems to work for you, but it's not for me. I'm simply getting on with life."

Esther winked. "Well, you know what I'll be praying for you?"

"I hate to think of you wasting your prayers on me."

"Oh, I won't be wasting them." Esther held back a chuckle. "Your humour will make you an excellent follower of Jesus. After all, he created the sense of humour."

Rob raised his eyebrows. Was this a new thought for him? She must make sure to match her follow-up appointments to Rob's. He wouldn't mind. Like her, he preferred to see someone familiar.

"You still haven't told me what you'll be praying for," Rob said.

Aha. The fish hadn't fled yet. "I'll be praying that you change your mind. That your life will seem empty."

He laughed. "Some friend you are. Pray away. I doubt I'll change."

CHAPTER 38

"Good morning, Esther," Dr Webster said from behind his office desk. "How does it feel to be finished all your treatment?"

"Such a huge relief." Esther hadn't realised how much she'd missed normal life until the end of treatment. "I'm tired, but some of that is because the burn made sleep a challenge."

"It's normal for tiredness to hang around for twelve months or more."

"Hopefully I don't miss any more days at work. I managed not to miss any during radiotherapy."

Last week she'd had another round of blood tests and scans and today she'd come to hear the results. She'd known Dr Webster eight months, and had learned to read him fairly well. He was relaxed and cheerful, a good sign. But her stomach still had knots and a band of tightness stretched across her lower back.

"You're due some good news." Dr Webster smiled and gave her a thumbs up. "So far, so good. The tests are clear."

"Phew." The knots unravelled so fast she almost melted onto the floor. How many months since she'd been truly relaxed? The release of tension revealed the depths of her exhaustion. It would have to be early to bed and slow weekends. Living with Naomi was perfect, as she headed for bed at nine.

"Will my follow-up appointments be here?"

"Yes, and every three months this year. You can't get rid of us that easily."

Little did he know she didn't want to. Not when conversations with potential to impact eternity were on the agenda. Her conversation with Sister O'Reilly had strengthened her belief that God would answer her prayers for Michelle, and Sue too.

Esther reached down into her bag and pulled out a bag of gifts for various people. Dr Webster's gift had slid to the bottom. "I wanted to say thank you for all your support."

"Thank you, but gifts aren't necessary, you know."

"I'm hoping you won't throw them back in my face."

"I might be a bit rough around the edges, but even I don't reject gifts."

Esther handed the wrapped present across the desk. Dr Webster turned it over in his hands. "Feels like books. Would it be related to the topics we've talked about?"

"Good guess." What could she say to intrigue him enough to open the covers? "We talked about the Bible in January, so I thought you'd appreciate a book tackling the question of whether the Bible is history. The author is a Sydneysider who lectures in ancient history at Macquarie University. As he says, 'The Bible claims to be history. If it's not, then there's no point in reading it and following Jesus would be a waste of time.'"

"And the second?"

"Is an oldie but a goodie written by a British author, Frank Morison. The name is a pseudonym. I think his real name was Albert or something. The book is called, *Who Moved the Stone?* Frank writes from the point of view of a skeptic. He knew if he could disprove that Jesus rose from the dead then all the biblical claims would come crashing down."

"Sounds like my kind of guy."

Esther laughed. It would be fun to see this man come to know Jesus one day like Morison was forced to do. "Morison digs into the evidence like a modern investigative journalist. I do warn you though that some of the language is dated. It can be a bit heavy."

Dr Webster grunted. "Sounds like someone else should write a modern version. Maybe I could do it in my spare time."

"You're welcome to do so—if you want to put in the hard work and not just skim the surface."

"Would make a good movie."

"Maybe someone will make a film like that someday."

---

*I*t was almost impossible for Esther to concentrate on eating. This was a pity because food like this deserved to be chewed with appreciation, every bite savoured. She was dining with her parents and Gina in the revolving restaurant on the top of Centrepoint Tower, Sydney's tallest building.

Her father had invited them to celebrate the completion of Esther's radiation treatment and her 'all clear' from cancer. He'd also invited her to bring a friend. Had he hoped she'd invite Nick and try to rekindle their relationship? If so, he was doomed to disappointment.

It had been a toss-up who she'd invite. Sue, because she'd been the best of bosses throughout eight months of treatment. Or Gina, because she'd proved herself a sterling quality friend. Gina had won out because Esther wasn't sure she could trust her father not to say something outrageous, and nothing would shock Gina.

The food was delicious, but the view was a distraction. The restaurant lights were dim, to draw attention to the view of Sydney harbour, hundreds of metres below. Lines of light criss-crossed the inky water as boats chugged from one side of the harbour to the other. The white sails of the Opera House gleamed as though made of pearl. It looked like at any moment it might follow the wind and cast off on a magical musical journey. Every building sparkled. A pirate's hoard of jewels.

The restaurant had one major failing from Esther's point of view. It was full of couples celebrating—special events or impending proposals, judging from the nervous gestures of many of the men. Too many couples staring into each other's eyes and looking soppy.

Esther concentrated on the scenery outside rather than inside. Inside only reminded her of what she'd lost. She should have been married six months by now. Not that she wanted to be married to Nick any more, but she'd love to have been married to someone instead of being twenty-nine and recovering from cancer. At least her hair was growing back. It was wavier than before. Weird.

The waiter gave a discreet cough. He must be used to people staring outside at the harbour, as no one wanted to miss the most spectacular section of the view. Esther doubted anyone ever complained if the food service was too slow. Each of them leaned back as their main course was delivered with smooth service. Gina and Esther had ordered the fish-of-the-day, barramundi, and her parents had kangaroo. Esther had a mouthful of her mother's. Yum. She'd order it next time, if she ever had the chance to come here again.

The chink of high quality crystal and restrained chatter filled the room. What must the three-course meal have cost? What did it matter? It was the happiest time they'd had as a family since her diagnosis. Dad turned on the charm. He related jokes during entrée, spun stories during main course, and recited poems during dessert.

She and Gina giggled so much they had to cover their mouths

with their serviettes to keep the noise down. Esther got the hiccups. The only thing to make tonight perfect, would have been Naomi's presence. But her father still didn't know about Naomi, and now wasn't the time to mention it. Why wreck a delightful evening?

Her father reached over and poured them each a full glass of sparkling apple cider. He raised his glass.

"We're here tonight to celebrate Esther's good health." He beamed at all of them. "Let's drink to Esther and new beginnings."

Esther drank and avoided looking at Gina. She couldn't trust herself not to explode with laughter. The day before they'd speculated about who her father would credit for her healing. Esther had guessed he'd somehow credit the medical system but Gina said, 'No, that would make him feel too much of a pagan. He'll have to rework his theology to still credit God with a miracle even if it was a much delayed one.'

But he'd outfoxed them both. Ever the politician, he'd avoided the issue altogether.

New beginnings. That was something she could drink to. New beginnings for herself and her parents and somehow, a new beginning for their family and Naomi. Her grandmother had been praying for a miracle for too long. Didn't she deserve to see the answer to her faithful prayers?

Esther looked out the windows again. The restaurant had rotated away from the harbour. At several sports fields the spotlights made the grass glow and formed jade-green pools of light. Tiny ruby-red tail lights zipped along the gold arteries of major roads. Hypnotic.

Her father's voice broke into her hypnotised state.

"So when are you coming back to Victory? I know you've always wanted to lead a young worker's group. It's yours whenever you want, and you can take your pick of leaders."

Esther blinked and her stomach turned sour. Her mother laid a hand on Dad's arm but it was too late. The words were out. Why couldn't her father have given them one perfect evening? He loved to play happy families. But the time for play-acting to bolster his reputation was long gone. A facade of harmony brought no real peace.

One day—soon, she prayed—there might be unity. But first there'd have to be deep repentance leading to transformed lives. Meanwhile, what could she say without provoking him too far?

She should have known her father would strive to smooth over their conflicts. He'd had a lifetime's practice in getting his way, and he couldn't imagine any situation where charm wouldn't win the day. His offer would have been a serious temptation before her diagnosis. Maybe it didn't sound like much to others, but the chance to influence a group of young workers would be a dream come true.

But she was a different person than she'd been eight months before. In the apostle Paul's words, she was a new creation. Her life no longer revolved around herself, or her own ambitions and dreams. Once she truly accepted Jesus' death for her, she belonged to him. He was her King. Like Abraham, her feet were set on a journey and she'd follow her Saviour's footsteps wherever they led.

Her father cleared his throat. She'd have to say something. *Lord give me wisdom.*

"Dad, thank you for your offer and warm welcome. There's a part of me that would love to accept, but the new church I go to is small, with fewer resources than Victory. They need me."

Their family had more than one politician.

He shrugged. "You can always change your mind."

She was sure he had plenty he wanted to say, but he loved his reputation too much to argue in this dim place where murmuring voices were the norm. An angry voice here, would be frontline news tomorrow. Australians loved to tear down the tall poppy, and his books and radio appearances made him a very tall poppy indeed. And many Australians were anti-church. They'd be delighted to humiliate a bigwig pastor.

When and if Dad raised the issue in the future, God was more than able to give her the strength and wisdom to respond to anything he threw at her.

Esther looked out the window at the glimmering lights. Each one nothing special on its own but together a glittering necklace. If her life could be a minuscule part of God's universal work of art, she would be content.

Right now she was looking forward to new beginnings. No going back.

Called onward and upward by grace.

STORYTELLER FRIENDS

• Do you want to receive book updates, latest news and offers? Sign up to become a 'storyteller friend' at http://subscribe.storyteller-christine.com/

Once you're signed up, check your junk mail or the 'promotions' folder (gmail addresses) for the confirmation email. This two-stage process ensures only true 'storyteller friends' can join.

• **Facebook:** As well as a public author page, I also have a VIP group you need to ask permission to join.

ENJOYED GRACE IN STRANGE DISGUISE?

In the modern world of publishing, many readers check the reviews before they buy a book. As this book is independently published, the only way it will be 'discovered' by readers, is if you get excited about it. Online reviews are one way to do so.

How to write a review – easy as 1-2-3

1. A few sentences about why you liked the book
2. What kinds of people might like the book?
3. Upload your review - the same review can be used on each site. Possible places are Amazon, Goodreads, Bookbub, Kobo and Koorong (for Australians).
4. If you loved the book please also share your review on your personal social media, or feel free to tell others.

ALSO BY CHRISTINE DILLON

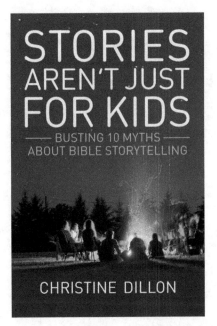

Stories Aren't Just For Kids: Busting 10 Myths about Bible
Storytelling (2017). Free to subscribers and packed with testimonies
to get you excited about the potential of Bible storytelling.

1-2-1 Discipleship: Helping One Another Grow Spiritually
(Christian Focus, Ross-shire, Scotland, 2009).

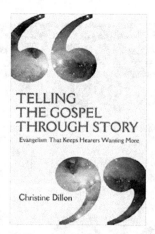

Telling The Gospel Through Story: Evangelism That Keeps Hearers
Wanting More (IVP, Downer's Grove, Illinois, 2012).

ACKNOWLEDGMENTS

I was never one of those people who dreamed of writing fiction.

About ten years ago, I was praying about my work when the ideas for two novels dropped into my head.

"Surely that couldn't be you, Lord," I said.

Silence.

"Lord, if this is your idea, you'll have to push me to do so and give me the ability."

Over the next five or six years the internal pressure slowly increased. One day in 2012, I was reading a biblical novel and thought, 'You're a Bible storyteller, so write a biblical novel to practice'. So I did. Those two practice novels gave me the feel for dialogue and description.

It wasn't until 2013, that I started planning and writing the draft of *Grace in Strange Disguise*. The first three years were tough. I often had to cry out to my heavenly Father for help.

Much of the help came to me via other people.

So a huge thank you to my team. Even if I miss someone out, please know that the One who matters has seen you. You have been one of the best parts of this, 'no longer reluctant' journey.

First, to those who helped me with research. My next door neighbour back in 2013, Phillippa Crossan. You should recognise a few comments from your interview scattered throughout the book. John Boyages, was my medical consultant and coped well with strange cancer-related questions, including treatments back in 1995. All mistakes remain mine, as there were places I changed medical details, for the sake of the story.

In the midst of writing, I really struggled to work out how writing fiction could fit in with being a missionary. Thank you to Marilyn Schlitt for showing me, "It is all related to discipleship." As a result of her comment, the tagline for my website became, 'Multiplying disciples one story at a time'.

There were several rounds of beta readers who read early drafts and made, 'big picture' suggestions on how to improve it. Thank you to Kathy Smail, Alan and Sue Boddy, Claire Urbach and Debbie Farr. Special mention to Lesley Hicks whose comments led to the creation of 'Gina'. Bethany Higgerson who kept saying, "An Australian wouldn't say that or that medical detail is wrong." Kate Blackwell who was both a beta reader and a proofreader and noticed some incongruities of small details. And to Lizzie Reid who joined the team as a seventeen-year-old and has read the entire book three times at both beta and proofreading stage. I have come to rely both on your eyes and your instinct for what is right for a character. I wouldn't be surprised, if I become a member of your cheer squad in years to come.

Much of the first three years of this process was a lonely, hard slog. Then in late 2015, I discovered various Christian writer's groups on Facebook. Australasian Christian Writers and Christian Writers Downunder quickly became my writing community. Thank you for the articles and resources. Thank you to the many authors who have been generous with their time and advice. As publication date has drawn near, they've coped with a myriad of questions about small details.

The Facebook groups helped me find my editors, Cecily Paterson and Iola Goulton. I don't have enough words to thank them. They were both women of courage whose chief concern was that the resultant book glorified God. It was a pleasure to work with you both. You were not only competent, but gracious and gentle as you edited to make the story shine. Thank you for not only telling me what needed to change, but teaching me why. Both of your names deserve to be on the cover of this book. Iola is the reason this standalone book is now at least a trilogy. So, we have more work in front of us.

Laura Tharion and Kristen Young are rapidly becoming friends as we support each other in writing fiction. They're working on novels themselves and you're in for a treat when their books are released.

Joy Lankshear is the queen of design. Even in primary school, it was obvious that art would be your career. This is our fifth official collaboration (three books of poetry and an early Chinese book on leading Bible studies), but you've given your opinions on all my book covers. Thank you for the gorgeous cover for, *Grace in Strange Disguise* and your patience with many of the 'storyteller friends' commenting on it. Without you, I'd probably have had a stroke, because computers and formatting are not my thing.

Kath Henderson, you're another major partner in my ministry. You've designed and managed the Bible storytelling website since 2011. Then you did a marathon effort to get www.storytellerchristine.com up and running. Your student seems to be managing it okay but it's great to know you're there, just in case. Thanks for helping this technology dunce learn to stagger along.

Then right at the end, I had thirty people volunteer to be my, 'advance reader team'. They have worked together to proofread the entire book and write a review. Thank you for your eagle-eyes, helpful suggestions and working to a tight timetable.

I've had several people ask me if William is based on my father?

Thankfully not. Thank you Mum and Dad for your unending support and prayers as your daughter goes off in unexpected directions.

Many others have prayed. Your prayers have prevented me giving up when the task felt beyond me. Particular thanks to Anne Bruning (who listened to many chapters being read to her), my brother and sister-in-law, Molly Whitelaw and Betty Hindley. And lastly, to all of you who are 'storyteller friends' and receive my updates. Thank you. You've been a huge encouragement.

Thanks in advance for your prayers for the next one.

Discussion Guide

There is a discussion guide for *Grace in Strange Disguise* available to download from **storytellerchristine.com**

BIBLE STORYTELLING

This book models Bible storytelling with adults. Is this method something I made up? No, definitely not.

In 2004, I was introduced to this method of communicating the good news about Jesus. At first, I had a lot of prejudices about it. Once I started using storying, I thought it was only to introduce people to Jesus. Later, I discovered it works equally well to teach and train people of any age. Now, it is rare for a day to go by without me telling a Bible story.

• For more resources (in an increasing number of languages)

www.storyingthescriptures.com
Facebook at 'storyingthescriptures'

ABOUT THE AUTHOR

Christine has worked in Taiwan, with OMF International, since 1999.

It's best not to ask Christine, "Where are you from?" She's a missionary kid who isn't sure if she should say her passport country (Australia) or her Dad's country (New Zealand) or where she's spent most of her life (Asia - Taiwan, Malaysia and the Philippines).

Christine used to be a physiotherapist, but now writes 'story-teller' on airport forms. She spends most of her time either telling Bible stories or training others to do so.

In her spare time, Christine loves all things active – hiking, cycling, swimming, snorkelling. But she also likes reading and genealogical research.

Connect with Christine

PROLOGUE

Late 1960s
Sydney, Australia

It was love at first sight.

And second. And third.

Each memory was a lustrous pink pearl from a necklace she now kept locked away. Out of sight but not entirely out of mind.

The first pearl was their first meeting. She pressed so close to the glass that it fogged, blurring the outline of the pink-wrapped bundle beyond. Years of pestering her mother and now the day had come. She had a baby sister.

Finally.

She hopped on the spot. As though her sister read her mind, the tiny eyes snapped open and the little rosebud mouth opened in a yawn. She liked to think that, even then, her sister was seeking her out through the glass separating them.

The second pearl was the memory of her mother as she cradled the baby close and enclosed her in love. Had Mum held her the same way? Like she was the most precious baby in the whole world? Her sister latched on and sucked. She could almost see her growing.

She hugged her arms around her waist. Did her mum remember she had an almost eleven-year-old daughter, or was she too cocooned with the baby?

She leaned forward. "Do you think I'll ever have a baby?"

Her mother smiled. "Probably—most girls do. But don't grow up too quickly. I want my daughters with me as long as possible."

It was special to be wanted. Like being wrapped in her favourite mohair blanket on a winter's evening.

The third pearl was the first time she'd held her sister. The responsibility lay heavier than the child. Like she held a delicate china figurine.

She gazed down. Oh, the little cutie-pie. Solemn dark blue eyes stared back at her. What did they see? An older sister who already adored her? No kid would ever bully her sister. She'd be a hovering presence. A wall of protection. A hero.

The subsequent years had added more pearls. Creamy, dreamy memories. Times that became her only joys in the struggle wearing her down.

One pearl she remembered far too often. It had been a blazing beauty of an autumn. Bright blue skies, crisp mornings, and breezes which blew the leaves in languid eddies.

Her little sister swished through the fallen leaves, giggling as they crackled underfoot. She stooped down and threw armfuls of leaves into the air. They swirled around her in whirls of red, yellow, and faded brown.

Oh, how she loved this little sister of hers. How could she think of leaving her?

She swooped down and tickled.

"Don't, don't," her sister squealed.

They chased each other around the trees until they were both worn out. A sunbeam sliced through the leafless branches and illuminated the toddler in a warm glow.

"Look, look. The sun is shining right on me." Her sister raised her arms above her head, tilted her face to the sun, and laughed as she twirled.

Pure joy.

Another pearl. Another memory to lock away.

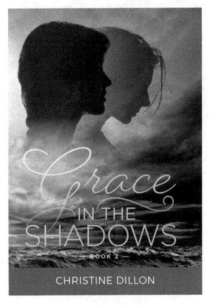

Book 2 in the Grace series

CPSIA information can be obtained
at www.ICGtesting.com
Printed in the USA
LVHW010445211221
706819LV00010B/804